NORTH RUN

L. M. Jones

To Jennifer
Best Wishes
Linda Jones

First published in December 2022

This novel and the characters portrayed within the story are entirely a work of fiction. Certain long-standing institutions, agencies and public offices are mentioned but the characters involved are
entirely imaginary.
The facts relating to Missing Children are true and were drawn from UK data
https://fullfact.org/online/missing-trafficked-children/

Author – L. M. Jones
Book Cover – Photograph - P J Jones
Design & Editing - Paul Smith

Linda Jones Bavoom Publishing

Website:
https://lindajonesukauthor.com
https://www.facebook.com/LindaJonesukAuthor

North Run

Chapter One

Monday

IT WAS ONLY SEVEN AM and she'd already had enough. Slamming her briefcase next to the chair, DI Sarah Allerton surveyed the devastation. Saturday lunchtime her desk had been mostly cleared – now a mountain of files and paperwork covered the space. Clicking on her computer, the screen immediately flashed with the dozens of messages Mike Lawson was supposed to have dealt with. Anger slowly building, Sarah dialled the desk sergeant's number.

'Andy give me an idea when Mike was in over the weekend would you?'

'I'll get back to you, Sarah. The *card reader* was down again. It means trawling through the signing-in log.'

With a mug of coffee steaming beside her, Sarah metaphorically rolled up her sleeves and began. All of Hepsford force was under pressure. In the serious crime division alone there were two senior staff on sick leave and one DI post unfilled. DI Mike Lawson not pulling his weight bloody mattered. Two minutes before nine, her computer pinged with a new message.

"*Mike Lawson.* Sat – 17.15 hrs to 18.50 hrs. Sun – 15.10 hrs to 16.40 hrs. His work log states he was interviewing witnesses at various sites over the two days. No specific details given."

Disgusted, Sarah clicked off the message and sipped her stone cold coffee. She'd put money on it that those 'witnesses' were mates and any interviewing would have taken place in a local pub.

Around her, the serious incident room buzzed with the usual morning activity, officers and admin staff busy at desks or on phones. Overhead, the squeak of the ventilation fans struggled on. Why the hell did she stay? At forty-four she had twenty-two years of service, enough for a decent pension… Or she could ask for a transfer? Except there was Freya. Her partner of six years was finally happy – safe and settled in her teaching job, so why the hell should they pack up and move? And it wasn't about the police work. She thrived on the enigmas investigations threw up. No – when push came to shove – her leaving would give Lawson exactly what he wanted.

As if merely thinking his name had summoned up the man, Lawson strode in, letting the heavy double doors slap closed behind him. Sarah buried the groan as he made a beeline for her desk.

'You're in then, Allerton.'

'These are yours Mike.' Before he could object, Sarah planted a pile of manilla files into his arms. On top, she laid a crisp sheet of paper. 'Messages *you* need to answer.'

He perched his tall frame on the edge of the desk opposite. 'Is it all too much then, need to offload? Perhaps your pretty-boy sergeant could take on a bit more?'

Refusing to bite Sarah repeated. '*Your* cases, Mike. If you have a problem, speak to Finchley.'

'Talking of which, he wants the six monthly report. Pass it here and I'll check it through – finish it off if it needs it…'

Mike was mad if he thought she'd let him take the credit for her work. 'Too late I'm afraid. I handed the report over on Saturday Mike, before I left. Should I ask him to send you a copy?' It was a lie. The report sat in her briefcase out of harm's way.

Mike eased off the desk dumping the armful of files where he'd been sitting. He pulled a yellow log sheet from his inside pocket, flapped it in her direction. 'Before I forget, this was phoned in a few minutes ago. It's all yours. Child protection are having staffing issues apparently. Some kid has gone AWOL from a local children's home. I'm in and out all day, a couple of loose ends to tie up…' He was already striding towards the doors.

'Mike – when the hell am I supposed to find the time to…'

He flicked a vague hand in her direction. 'Speak to Finchley if you have a problem, Allerton, I'm up to my eyes in high-end jewellery thefts. Enjoy…'

Tight lipped, Sarah picked up the pile of folders Mike had abandoned and dumped them unceremoniously back onto his desk. Neil Harper, the unfortunate sergeant assigned to DI Mike Lawson glanced up, groaning at the fresh pile. 'Another day in paradise, Inspector.'

'You and me both, Neil. If I'm wanted, I'll be at a children's home called Lakeside. Hopefully, this will be a quick in and out.'

***

Parking near the doors of the large imposing Victorian house that was Lakeside, Sarah glanced across at her sergeant. Ben Peterson's expression was as bleak as the rain clouds overhead. 'Okay, spit it out, what is the problem. You're like a bear with a sore head this morning?'

The sigh was deep. 'Why the hell are we taking on a missing minor case? We're already up to our ears…'

It was a fair question. Sarah watched the first drops of rain slide lazily down the windscreen. 'Child protection has one on maternity leave and another off sick…'

'And what's wrong with Mike bloody Lawson's team? Let him pick up an extra case for a change.'

'Apparently, Mike wasn't available,' Sarah held up a hand when he began to protest. 'And be honest Ben, would you want him handling a missing child investigation?'

Ben stretched out long legs, his frustration obvious but he didn't reply.

'Exactly, so let's make a start. Hopefully this will be a quick one.'

***

Outside the large bay window of Lakeside's office, the rain was falling in a never ending sheet. Sarah gratefully sipped the coffee that someone had thoughtfully provided, wondering why she had tempted fate. Any hope of an 'easy fix' had disappeared within minutes of arriving. Beside her, Ben Peterson's notebook was filling, rapidly.

'Let me clarify, Mr De-Silva,' Ben said. 'Lee Wiggins left the building at 07.25, accompanied by two other residents, Kate and Dan. Lee should have arrived at his work placement by 08.00. The theft of Sarish Patel's jewellery was discovered at 07.40 by Sarish herself?'

The manager, Rahul De-Silva nodded his agreement. 'Yes, the jewellery is normally kept in the safe but Sarish was at a cousin's wedding on Friday. She was supposed to be out for a couple of days, only she came back later that evening with a sickness bug that's been doing the rounds. She'd put the valuables in her drawer. Sarish has spent most of the weekend being sick, so I'm not surprised she didn't discover the theft until this morning.'

'You believe the jewellery was snatched at some point over the weekend?'

'Sergeant, Lee would not have taken Sarish's things. The lad would have no reason to. Apart from the weekly allowance he receives, Lee has a trust fund he can draw on. There's been no hint of drugs or gambling and he and Sarish are good friends.' De-Silva twisted his hands together, his anxiety obvious. 'I know you think I'm panicking for nothing, Sergeant, but Lee was settled. There is no reason he would have runaway, no reason at all. He was so looking forward to the engineering placement. He's talked of nothing else and then there's his skateboarding…'

Sarah gently interrupted. 'And Lee hasn't absconded previously?'

'Not once, Inspector. He'd been placed with his uncle following his parent's death, but that had broken down. The uncle is struggling to deal with the loss of his brother...'

The brief rap on the door was quickly followed by two wet teenagers. Kate and Dan, Sarah surmised.

Kate pushed back the hood of her coat, her dark brown ponytail danced as she breathlessly demanded. 'Any news Rahul?'

'Nothing so far, Kate. I'm sorry to drag you back on your first day.'

Water dripping into his eyes, Dan slid past Kate to march to the manager's side. 'Lee wouldn't steal anything, you know that.'

'And I'm sure the officers will be happy to talk to you, Dan.' Rahul De-Silva nodded to the chairs near the door where Sarah and Ben waited.

As one, the teenagers turned to face them. Sarah stood, straightening neat brown trousers, dark blue eyes smiling – assessing. 'I'm Detective Inspector Sarah Allerton. This is DS Ben Peterson…'

Kate moved closer to Dan's side. 'Lee was fine when we split up. He wouldn't have stolen anything!'

'Yeah, it's like Kate said, Lee was happy, no reason for him to piss off. He had money, going to work at that engineering place, he'd been going on about it forever.'

'So Mr De-Silva and everyone here has been telling us.' Sarah tucked a strand of short fair hair behind one ear. 'I'm not jumping to conclusions but I do need to ask the questions. It's as important to rule things out… Can you tell me which of you saw Lee last?'

‘That’s easy,’ Kate answered. ‘It was me, Lee didn’t have to be at his work placement until eight, so he went into Mill Hill shop. I saw him come out while I was waiting for my bus.’

‘What time was that, Kate?’

‘Just before seven forty-five because the bus was late and I kept checking my phone. I got on the bus but by the time I’d sat down, a van had parked on the hill blocking my view.’ Kate frowned down at her feet. ‘The van looked a bit like the one his uncle drives.’

Dan nodded. ‘Yeah, he’s always on at Lee about being here, trying to get him to leave so he can work in his garage. Cheap labour, that’s what his uncle thinks Lee is.’

‘I thought perhaps Lee had gone back into the shop, Inspector – I don’t know what happened.’

Sergeant Peterson reached for the door. ‘Once we finish with Mr De-Silva, we’ll come and take your statements.’ The sergeant’s voice was calm-friendly but Sarah caught the tightening of Dan’s muscles.

The manager rose and patiently walked the teenagers to the door. ‘Megan or Lisa are around. Dry off, have a drink, something to eat. I’ll come and find you when we’re done.’

‘We’ll be in one of the sitting rooms when you need us, won’t we Dan…’

‘Suppose,’ Dan’s head turned, dark eyes flickering towards Sarah with something akin to fear. ‘Lee hasn’t done a runner has he Inspector? Something bad has gone down, I can feel it.’

Chapter Two

FINALLY, BACK AT HEPSFORD STATION, Sarah found a harassed DC Jackie Simmons bending over the main computer in the serious crime division, an IT technician at her side. 'It's crazy, Inspector. The whole system is playing up. The computers in Home Invasion and Street Crime units are down too. I've only managed to find a few details on a couple of the staff at Lakeside. It could be hours before I can find any decent information.'

Sarah simply wanted to grab her work and disappear before Mike Lawson put in one of his infrequent appearances. 'Do your best, Jackie. I'll be in Bill Porter's office for the rest of the afternoon. He's still off sick so I may as well use it. Ben is co-ordinating the searches with uniform and traffic and he's filing an article for the *Express* at some point. Keep me updated with details as soon as the computers are back up.'

Jackie's dark brown eyes flickered with amusement. 'Should I tell everyone where you are Inspector?'

'Tell them I'm in archives Jackie, unless it's urgent. Mike Lawson hates the place.'

Sanctuary was a room with windows that opened, a door that she could close and, a big enough table to spread out her work. Quickly engrossed, the tower of files at her elbow dwindled to under half. When the knock on the door came, Sarah glanced irritably at her watch. Almost ten past five, three hours plus without an interruption, a record.

Jackie Simmons looked apologetic. 'Sorry, Inspector, only I need to run something by you?'

'In and shut the door, Jackie. The fewer people who know where I am the better.'

'There's some weirdly interesting background on a Megan Shaw, she's a student social worker on placement at Lakeside – or rather it's about her previous place of work, at a children's home in Hull. It's like déjà vu. Megan had worked in Hull as a youth care assistant for thirteen months. Ten weeks before she resigned, jewellery and money was stolen from a resident's room. During the investigation, an agency staff member said she'd seen Megan acting suspiciously outside the girl's bedroom door, however, the subsequent enquiry proved that Megan was out of the building at the time of the incident.'

'Did they discover who was responsible?'

'Well, that's the déjà vu bit. They suspected a resident, 13-year-old Tanya Daley who went missing at the same time. They couldn't prove it was her because the girl's never been found.'

'And the agency staff member who accused Megan?'

'A Shauna Richardson. The woman admitted that she must have muddled up the days. I've got a name and address, trying to chase her down, but it seems Shauna left the Hull area a while ago. I've tried to reach Megan Shaw to clarify a few points, but her mobile must be switched off.'

Sarah frowned at the pen in her hand. The incident in Hull was well over a year ago. 'I hate coincidences. Tomorrow I want you and Ben back in Lakeside to re-interview everyone. I especially want to know Megan's reaction when you mention Hull. Is there any word yet from uniform on their door to door enquiries?'

'Nothing so far. A CP officer has been in contact to say they're well into the usual trawl of local sex offenders. Traffic are viewing CCTV from the area, hoping to pick up a suspect vehicle. Uniform are doing a door to door in the surrounding streets and Ben said the article won't be in the paper until tomorrow, but has managed to have a piece included on the local radio tonight.'

‘But radio doesn’t show Lee’s photograph does it?’ Sarah sighed at the inadequacies of the system. ‘Never mind, not your fault. Let’s hope tomorrow brings us better news.’

Sarah’s fingers hardly had time to touch her keypad when her alert vibrated. With a sigh, she answered the desk sergeant. ‘Andrew what’s the problem?’

‘Inspector, I’ve a Mr Thomas here, the co-owner of *Hepsford Auto Repairs*. He says he’s worried about a Paul Wiggins, the uncle of the missing lad, Lee. I thought you’d want to know.’

‘I’ll be up – give me two minutes.’

The stocky figure of Steve Thomas was pacing anxiously in front of the reception desk when Sarah and Ben Peterson pushed through the electronic doors. ‘Inspector, I know you’re busy, but I can’t find Paul anywhere. He’s not at his house, pub hasn’t seen him, no one has. Paul’s not taken his wallet and he’s not answering his phone; there’s nothing…’

Sarah nodded to the desk sergeant to let them through to an interview room. ‘We should talk somewhere more private, Mr Thomas. I’m sure the Sergeant could rustle us up a coffee?’

It was several minutes before the man settled. ‘I think he might hurt himself, Inspector. He’s talked about it enough when he’s really down. Losing his twin brother Ian like that tore him up. They were identical you know, couldn’t tell them apart. Now with our Lee taking off… As soon as that manager from the children’s home phoned to tell us Lee was missing, Paul started knocking back the booze again. He’d had a skin-full the night before.’

Jackie’s report from her interview with Paul Wiggins at eleven am, had said the man had stunk of alcohol and was barely coherent. It hadn’t mentioned that Lee’s father was Paul’s identical twin – not that losing any sibling was easy. ‘Is there a chance Paul knows where Lee might be, Mr Thomas?’

‘No, I swear, Inspector. If Paul had an inkling of where the lad was he would’ve told me. We’re close him and me, mates. I’ve known Paul and his twin brother since junior school.’ The desk sergeant came through with the cartons of coffee. Steve Thomas took his, nodding gratefully.

Sarah turned to Ben. 'We'll issue an all-points alert and pull up ID from DVLA.'

'He's not driving; I hid the van keys.' Steve Thomas pulled out a wallet. 'I've a photo if that helps?'

The door had clicked closed behind the worried man but Sarah stayed where she was, drumming fingers on the plastic coated table.

'So much for our quick in and out!' Ben pushed his chair to lean back against a wall. 'There is no way this case can be a simple *nick and run.* I couldn't find a single trigger that gives the lad a reason to take off. Unlike some of the other youngsters at Lakeside, Lee has never absconded. He might have had access to Sarish's missing jewellery, but so did everyone else in the building. He had almost two hundred pounds in his savings account book – his trust account can only be accessed from his place of residence. Then there's his skateboard – his specialist trainers. He paid a hundred and fifty for those less than a fortnight ago. He wouldn't leave those things behind. Either something kicked off on the way to his work placement which scared him enough to make him run or he's been snatched.'

A vivid image of her son snapped into Sarah's head. Ryan might be twenty-two, but hell – a missing child had to rate among the worst of a parent's nightmares. Sarah cut off the drama building inside her brain and concentrated on reality. 'Jackie said you'd spoken to the publicity department about an article in the *Express*?'

'I ended up writing it myself, I'm waiting for an approval email. If I'd left it up to them, it would have been bloody Thursday!'

'And feedback from CCTV?'

'Nothing earth-shattering. A couple of sightings of a van or two confirming Kate's story. Traffic are following those up. The door to door enquiries have given us nothing.'

Sarah rose to her feet. ‘You’ve done everything you can for now, go home – or at least eat something Ben. Ring as soon as anything crops up.’

Chapter Three

THE BEGINNING OF ANY CASE WAS always frustrating and, missing children had to be the worst. At that moment, the puzzle of Lee's disappearance consisted of little more than a couple of photographs showing a grinning red-headed fifteen-year-old. In both pictures Lee was clutching a skateboard. Underneath, were a few paltry lines with the bare information. She might as well take her own advice. Pack up and go home.

It was an automatic response to ring Freya and let her know she was on her way home. Her partner's phone clicked over to voice mail and Sarah had to bury the flutter of anxiety before she left a voice message.

'Hi, it's five-forty and I've just left work, should be home in fifteen. I'll probably be in the gym.' Sarah clicked *off* and tried to concentrate on the dark wet road. Freya would be caught up in a meeting or a disciplinary she told herself; the endless responsibilities of being a senior teacher at the local comprehensive, nothing more sinister.

She could count on one hand, the number of her colleagues' relationships that had survived the stress of the job for more than a couple of years. Stupid hours, the often horrendous task of unravelling the worst of human depravity. Perhaps it was Freya's own heavy workload at the school or the desperate horror from six years ago that kept the relationship strong; whatever it was she was grateful it worked.

With a push of a button, the high gates of their driveway swept open. They'd cost a small fortune to install along with a top of the range security system. The gates had also instigated one of the few serious arguments they'd had. *Paranoid and obsessed* was one of the nicer terms Freya had used – but Freya wasn't home to protect, the double garage was empty. Sarah made her way through the kitchen and into the wide hallway of their nineteen-thirties semi. On the hall side-table, the answering machine flashed green. Pressing *play,* she tapped a foot, unaware of her fingernails digging into the palms of her hand.

'*Hi love – yet another senior staff meeting. Be home by six thirty-seven. See you soon.*'

Stress, relief and hunger were a potent mix. Relieving the first was easy and food could wait. Finding a house with a suitable basement had taken her and Freya weeks of searching but the extra effort had paid off. Sarah stepped down into the airy room, clicking on the overhead lights as she went. Figure-hugging sportswear replaced her work clothes and soon she was stretching out limbs in front of the long mirror. Cycle first – fifteen minutes paced, ten minutes flat out. As the burn began, she dug down, pushing faster, harder. The ten-minute warm-down was intensely satisfying and the temptation to repeat it was hard to resist – but the room had more to offer. Sarah straightened, eyeing the punch-bag with grim determination. It was Freya's least favourite piece of equipment – when she used the gym at all. Hand straps firmly in place, she began: years of worry, frustration and fear had left their toll on the swinging bag. Punch after kick built up the momentum, allowing her ragged emotions to pulse through muscles and surge through her fists. Dealing with the stress of Mike *bloody* Lawson was easy… compared to the constant fear that had dogged her footsteps every day for the last six years. Crazy, she knew. The horror had happened miles away, in Cheltenham – Freya had been the victim of the serial killer – not her. How could Freya have left her fear behind – moved on with her life? If they'd only caught the bastard!

The punches grew harder, faster as memories resurfaced. The hours, days spent scouring cellars, buildings, outhouses, hunting for a faceless murderer who methodically – drip by acid drop – tortured his victims. After weeks of hunting, Sarah and the Cheltenham team found nothing. Apart from being women there were no patterns, nothing to indicate where the killer would strike next. The monster had taunted the police, sent messages, graphic pictures – before snatching a fourth woman. What felt like an impossible task turned into a nightmare. Sarah had fallen hard for the gorgeous woman in their profile photograph – her sensuous eyes, rich black hair curving gently around soft, dark skin. She'd been spellbound the moment that picture had been pinned to the incident board. Every hour they couldn't find her had been agony – until the day the killer made his first mistake. One of the notes he'd sent carried a suggestion of glass particles that could have come from only one place – a long-abandoned Victorian bottle factory.

They'd found his lair; three dead women plus Angela Oxley – burnt but very much alive. Angela not only survived but took on a new identity to become Freya Simpson.

Except – that sadistic bastard was still out there – somewhere.

A final kick sent the bag spinning away. Perspiring heavily, Sarah dropped her head back, every muscle in her body throbbing in defiance – it felt wonderful. Back upstairs showered and changed, Sarah opened the pantry door and breathed in the familiar spicy aroma. She was the main cook, the one who prepped and baked but tonight it would be the freezer and one of the dishes she'd prepared for such an occasion. Pulling out a fish pie, Sarah set it to defrost. The problem was it would take ages. Cutting a slab of wholemeal bread, she slathered on butter and raspberry jam so thick it dribbled off the edges.

With a copy of that day's *Hepsford Express* open on the table, Sarah nibbled and read. The headlines still proclaimed the wonders of *new city* life. Jumping out from the page were photos of babies draped in banners and a school proudly showing their new uniform – a vivid purple to match the city's new official colour. Disgusted, Sarah bit off a chunk of bread. Did anyone with half a brain seriously believe the *new city* hype? Hepsford, for all the council's spiel was always going to live in the shadow of its wealthier northern neighbours.

'Hi, I'm home, had to stay for a senior staff meeting,' her partner's sing-song voice echoed from the hallway.

Sarah swallowed the last of the bread, licking off the worst of the offending sweetness from her fingers. Quickly, she brushed the crumbs into a pocket before Freya walked in. Her partner's hands were full of books, a heavy bag clutched to her side.

'Those aren't all for tonight?' Sarah said as the books landed next to an equally large pile on the table.

'Next Tuesday.' Freya dropped her jacket onto the back of a chair and kissed Sarah lightly. 'Do you want a hot drink or did you have one with that hunk of bread you've just gorged on?'

'Guilty as charged. How about I do the drinks as punishment?'

Freya followed her into the kitchen. 'So how was your day at the office?'

'I didn't see much of Lawson, so on the whole better than usual. Yours?'

'The head of English decided year eights need more emphasis on nineteenth or early twentieth-century literature. I've enough trouble persuading them to read anything, without dumping a load more tongue twisters on them.'

'What's he suggesting, Dickens?'

'Maybe, or I suppose they could read *Kidnapped*.' Freya stared into the distance, the milk carton hovering.

Sarah poured water into the cafetière, enjoying the explosion of aromas as the hot liquid circled the ground coffee. 'They made some decent films of *Kidnapped*. You should be able to find some scripts floating about.' Out in the hallway, their phone rang. Sarah sighed. 'It's going to be for me. You finish off the coffee. Hopefully, I'll only be a few minutes.'

'Sorry Inspector, but there's been an incident I thought you should know about.'

Resigned, Sarah flipped open the pad on the pine table, automatically writing down the time: 19.25. Her sergeant knew better than to interrupt her precious off-duty with trivia. 'Why are you still in the office, Ben?'

'I'd hung around to catch up on paperwork. I was in the central room when Neil Harper came back from a call out, an assault at 16.45 approximately. It happened at the back of the *Cock & Crown* off Hepsford city centre. The victim's young Dan Bridges from Lakeside. He's in a bad way, someone's taken a metal bar to him.'

Sarah frowned down at her notebook and tried to persuade her tired brain to make the connections. 'What the hell was a fifteen-year-old doing in the *Cock & Crown*?'

'He was outside near the bins at the back. One of the bar staff pretty much fell over his body. They thought they'd heard kids messing about and went to chase them off. Dan's lucky they did. It wouldn't have taken much to finish the lad off.'

'So it's bad?'

'Nasty head wound, spoken to the hospital and they've sent him to theatre. He's a fractured clavicle, but it's the head injury they're worried about.'

'You think the attack is related to our missing lad?'

'No idea, but something's going on. I've had a word with Matt Cox, the senior social worker at Lakeside. He told me that Dan skedaddled around 14.00 hrs. Matt's been trying to track him down ever since.'

Sarah never dismissed her sergeant's hunches; she expected him to follow hers often enough. 'Okay, tell Neil – or Lawson if you must – that we'll take the assault case. Any problems let me know, though I'm sure they'll be happy to off-load.'

'Lawson was bitching about being snowed under with those jewellery thefts.'

She heard the bitterness in her sergeant's voice but let it go – no love lost between the two men. 'I'll meet you at the hospital in what, fifteen minutes?'

'I'd make it nearer nine, Inspector. Dan's going to be in the theatre for a while. I'm sorry to ruin what's left of your night.'

'You're supposed to have a social life too, Ben.'

'I have a holiday coming up. It'll keep till then.'

Freya was holding out a consoling mug of coffee when she walked into the kitchen.

'I've put yesterday's chilli into the microwave to warm. You can at least eat and digest something before you leave. We can have the fish tomorrow.'

'I'm sorry, love. I've no idea how late I'm going to be.'

Carelessly, Freya pulled her hair from its binding. It fell to her shoulders in a shining mass, framing her face in a familiar way. Six years fell away in an instant. Sarah hadn't realised how long Freya's hair had grown and she'd reverted to a natural glossy black from dyed red. An intense wave of foreboding consumed Sarah. Turning quickly, she tried to mask the fear. It had been months since she'd experienced anything as intense.

Oblivious, Freya opened the microwave. 'It means I can crack on with that marking with a clear conscience.'

'There is that,' said Sarah. Her voice sounded hollow, echoing inside her head. If *she'd* recognised the familiar profile so might someone else. Fighting to mask an internal struggle, Sarah forced a smile. She'd find the time, phone Amos. Ask him to double-check that no one had discovered that Freya Simpson was really Angela Oxley and still very much alive.

***

Sarah found her sergeant perched on one of the cold metal chairs outside the Intensive Care Unit. Long legs stretched out, he was absorbed with something on his mobile phone. 'I'm checking over the newspaper proof for the Wiggins' case.'

'Have they managed to put the correct details in this time?'

'Pretty much, they only mention his name not where he was living. The picture is rubbish.'

'Did the search of Lee's room at his uncle's house add anything useful, Ben?'

'Nothing; we did discover there's a van missing from *Hepsford Auto Repairs*. We have the registration, but the paperwork shows the vehicle as being on the garage premises for repairs. Steve Thomas and the rest of the mechanics clammed up. All we could get out of them was that Paul Wiggins would know, which doesn't help a jot as he's still AWOL. I've put out an APB on the van. Jackie returned to the garage to re-interview Steve Thomas. It turns out that there's an ex-employee – an Adam Farnes – who Paul Wiggins sacked a couple of weeks ago. Steve Thomas swears he doesn't know why he was let go, although Jackie reckons the man is holding back. Adam Farnes has a record. Two years ago he spent six months inside for drug dealing. He'd worked for Wiggins for nine months before he was given the boot. He's not at his registered address so I've put out another APB for him.'

'Dan Bridges?'

'Still in theatre. The CT scan showed a limited bleed but it's impossible to say whether there'll be long-term effects. His clavicle should heal on its own. Bloody painful though.'

'That's something at least. Have they given us a clue about when he might come around?'

Ben stretched out his arms. 'How long is a piece of string? The doctor's analogy, not mine. Oh, and Matt Cox, one of the social workers from Lakeside is here. He's insisting on waiting for Dan to return from theatre. I've also had a message from the city centre patrol desk. I'd asked them to do a CCTV search to try and spot Dan earlier in the afternoon and they've found something.'

Sarah pushed to her feet. 'We can have a brief chat with Matt Cox but find someone to babysit for us Ben. I'm not happy about leaving Dan without protection.'

An exhausted Matt Cox was seated in the small waiting room to the side of the ICU. Sarah eased down onto a chair, Ben following her cue.

'Dan's still in theatre, Inspector. Everyone in Lakeside is devastated. Rahul De-Silva looks like a ghost. He's taken this and Lee's disappearance hard. Is there any news?'

'Nothing yet I'm afraid. My sergeant tells me Dan ran off this afternoon. Did something happen after we left?'

'It's my bloody fault, – sorry. It's been a lousy day and I'm finding it hard to keep focussed. It was over such a stupid thing. I found Dan near the office just after two. He asked me if he should stay home tomorrow in case you lot needed to talk to him again.'

'I take it you don't think that was the real reason he was there?'

'No idea but when I suggested I'd take him and Kate to their workplaces tomorrow he blew up. Told me *he wasn't f*ing scared* and stormed off. I should've told him to stay put – take some time. I'm an idiot.'

'We'd interviewed him an hour or so prior and my sergeant noted that Dan was edgy. I'm not sure it would have mattered what you said Mr Cox. Sometimes a fuse has to blow.' Sarah was pleased to see the tension ease from his shoulders.

'Do you have children, Inspector?'

Sarah smiled. 'I do. Teenage years are the most challenging. Is there anything else you can tell us before we leave that might help?' He had an easy presence and Sarah imagined that he'd be good with teenagers – although he was only late twenties himself.

'Just before I went chasing after Dan, Megan Shaw, one of the social work students told me something odd. Dan had gone into the kitchen to ask if Kelly, one of the agency staff, was working. Dan told her that Kelly had offered to lend him a computer game. Megan had to tell him that Kelly had gone off sick.'

'Why is that strange?'

'Well, Kelly is agency staff for a start and rarely works in the place...'

'And?' Sarah encouraged, noting the darkening expression and folded arms across his chest.

'Dan hasn't been out of his room earlier than eleven over the weekend and Kelly's worked only a few hours on Springvale, that's the other house at the back that we use for the younger children. He'd have had no contact with her.'

'Unless they'd met up outside the centre?'

Matt's tired eyes blinked into hers. 'Kelly worked on Lakeside once and that was two or three weeks ago. After that shift, I've made sure that whatever hours she's booked in for are worked on Springvale.'

'It sounds like you had concerns?'

'The truth is she came on to me and it was awkward, to say the least.'

'I'm assuming personal involvement between staff on duty is discouraged?'

'Definitely – although relationships do happen, but strictly outside of office hours. It was more that she hardly knew me. There's flirting and flirting Inspector – it felt wrong.'

'Did Megan tell you that Dan was upset when he discovered Kelly had gone home?'

'Megan didn't say. She tried ringing me about four fifteen this afternoon, left a message explaining that she'd bumped into Dan in the city centre and needed to speak to me. I've been trying to return the call but her phone seems to be switched off.'

‘Thank you,’ Sarah stood, there was nothing to be gained by staying. ‘I know it’s hard but I’d advise you to go home. Do you live on your own?’

‘There’s a lodger – helps pay the mortgage, Inspector.’

‘An officer will stay with Dan until we can find out what motivated the attack, but it’s unlikely Dan will be conscious for hours yet.’

‘Do you really think someone might try again?’

‘I’d rather be over-cautious, Mr Cox. Please, if you remember anything else don’t hesitate to ring. You have our numbers.’

Chapter Four

TEN MINUTES LATER THEY WERE WALKING into Hepsford's city central control room. Sarah blinked, adjusting her eyes to the dim lighting. An array of monitors ran in two aisles across the large room.

'Detective Inspector Allerton?' A young officer indicated a small booth set apart from the general run of screens. 'I've put you over here. We found your young man on the corner of High Street and Shafton Lane at 16.29. I've downloaded CCTV from 14.00hrs.'

Ben began scrolling through the images, picking up the main route into the city centre from Lakeside. The timer showed 15.54 when he stopped the video. 'There he is again, Inspector, coming out of the café on the corner of Witchet Street, *Barney's* I think. I'll zoom in.'

Despite the rain, the definition was crisp. Sarah peered at the teenager's features: sullen expression, clenched fists. 'He doesn't look happy, Ben.'

They lost him twice, tracing him again by chance near the post office at 16.19. Dan was animated, talking to someone hunched inside a hooded raincoat against the driving rain. The figure turned and began to walk towards the camera.

'Pause, then zoom in,' Sarah said, sure she recognised the woman.

'That's Megan Shaw, talking into a mobile. I'll make a note to check the time with Matt's missed call.'

'Keep following the lad for now Ben.'

The city centre was criss-crossed with security cameras making it easy to follow Dan's progress. He stopped at the corner of High Street and Shafton Lane and began to pace. 'I'd say he's waiting for someone.' A moment later, Dan pulled out a mobile and dialled, talking rapidly. Even through a lens distorted by rain, the teenager's frustration was obvious. Dan thrust the phone back into his pocket, turned and kicked the wall. The digital display clicked on three minutes before he snatched up the mobile again. Dan was still talking as he turned into Shafton Lane.

'How far is the *Cock & Crown* from there, Ben?'

'The main entrance is on the High Street – fifty metres away I'd say. The alley where he was found is at the rear. You can access it from Shafton Lane.'

Dan disappeared from view as the lower half of the monitor went blank. 'Damn it, aren't there cameras on that section Ben?'

'Out of action. We might be able to pick him up from the other end of the lane.'

It took long seconds before the monitor showed the area they needed. The view of the lane and the entrance to the pub alleyway was empty. Sarah ground her teeth in frustration. 'How can he simply disappear?'

'He must've turned into the pub's yard.'

'How much time's lapsed since we saw him on the corner of High Street, Ben?'

'Less than ninety seconds. He used his mobile at 16.36.'

'His attacker will be there – keep watching. With luck, he'll put in an appearance – assuming it's a *he* of course.'

Ben allowed the video to speed up. At 16.47 a hunched figure raced out into the lane and bolted around the far corner. From the viewing angle it was impossible to work out their gender. 'I'll ask the sergeant here to follow but I'm not holding my breath for a positive ID Inspector.'

'Could that be Lee Wiggins; our missing lad do you think?'

'I'd doubt it. I know the picture isn't great but Lee isn't tall.'

Sarah checked the oversized street map that covered half of one wall. 'Whoever attacked Dan could have gone through the bar of the pub and waited for him near the rear exit.'

'If it is Lee he looks his age. Someone in the pub would've noticed if it was him. I'll trawl through the pub recordings tomorrow and check. Neil Harper's team found the mobile Dan was using but, the sim had been removed.'

'Wind back to where we saw Megan Shaw. We'd better check she didn't head towards the *Cock & Crown* with a metal bar.'

At 17.17 hrs, behind *Fieldings*, the local supermarket, Megan piled several bags of shopping into the boot of her car. Clambering into the driving seat of a small blue Peugeot, she turned right, heading out of the city towards the suburbs. 'She's going home, Inspector. Her flat is in Wetherby Edge, one of the new estates.'

Sarah checked the time: 21.50 hrs. It was late to be making house calls. Still... 'I'm loath to leave this until tomorrow. Follow me to her address and we can head off home from there.'

Fifteen minutes later, Sarah parked outside the three-storey block of newly built flats and waited for her sergeant to pull up behind her. At the glass entrance, Ben checked the security pad, pressing the button for Megan Shaw's flat. Thirty seconds later he tried again. 'Maybe she's a heavy sleeper?'

A neat line of eight garages ran down one side of the residents' car park, a few more vehicles sat outside, braving the elements. Megan's Peugeot wasn't among them. 'Does the place have a supervisor Ben?'

'There's nothing listed. I'll see if I can't raise someone. There are a few lights on.'

The young man who answered took time studying their ID over the monitor. 'Suppose it'll be okay if I buzz you in, only you have to sign the book in the hallway. It's fire reg's.'

‘Before you go,’ Ben asked, ‘Do all the residents have to use a swipe card to enter the building?’

‘Yes – and it’s fingerprint connected.’

‘And do you happen to know which residents use the garages?’

‘Not a clue, sorry...’ The buzzer sang out and the door gently clicked open.

On the second floor, they stepped from the spotlessly clean lift into a well-lit corridor. Sarah took in the pale grey walls and subtle artwork. It screamed high-end – expensive.

‘This reminds me of my dad’s flat in Kent, only the artwork is nicer. It can’t be cheap, especially for a student social worker.’ Ben raised a hand to knock on number five’s door only to stop before his knuckles touched wood. ‘The door’s been forced – lock’s broken.’

Sarah raised a warning finger. ‘Go carefully.’

The place was in darkness and unnaturally silent. It took seconds to check that the one-bedroomed flat was empty. ‘Inspector,’ Ben pointed to the half-opened cabinet drawer and the several papers scattered across the top. Twisting the dimmer light to full, Sarah bent to take a closer look: a couple of paid bills and a copy of a service agreement for the Peugeot. ‘Check the food cupboards and fridge for me, Ben.’ The flat was well soundproofed. They weren’t far from a busy main road but the only noise Sarah could hear were the clicks as drawers and doors opened.

‘Considering we saw her with at least three bags of shopping, they’re pretty bare.’

‘Any milk Ben?’

‘Enough for a cup of coffee; nothing fresh.’

‘So, she didn’t come home. What do you make of the furniture in here?’

‘There’s not a lot of it.’ Ben caught Sarah’s sideways glance and tried again. ‘Things have recently been shifted. You can see dust marks on the floor where that cabinet stood and the impression where the sofa's been moved.'

'I'll check the bedroom. You carry on in here.'

The bedroom was wide enough for a double bed with fitted wardrobes lining one wall. All the doors and drawers were open, clothing scattered. It was impossible to tell if anything had been taken. Back in the sitting room, Sarah found Ben knelt in front of the television studying a large notepad.

'Her college notes. Megan is in her first year of social work studies.'

'There's nothing conclusive in the bedroom. Either Megan is excessively untidy or more likely, someone's searched the place.' Sarah's mobile buzzed at her hip. Tugging off a plastic glove she answered the night sergeant's call.' Chris what's up?'

'Sarah, you put out an alert for a Paul Wiggins? A foot patrol found him a few minutes ago lying at the bottom of Canal Bridge. Paramedics are with him now.'

'Have they said what his condition is?'

'Alive but not great. They'll take him straight to the trauma unit. Is there anyone I should notify?'

Sarah read off the contact number for Steve Thomas and swiftly redialled for city central control. 'Sergeant, we're missing a potential witness – a Megan Shaw.' Sarah read off the registration number, the time and place the vehicle was last seen. 'As a matter of urgency, see how far you can track the vehicle for me.'

'You're in luck, Inspector, we've hit our quiet time. I'll get straight onto it.'

Stifling the yawn, Sarah pushed her weary brain into action. What they needed were more hands on the pump – preferably experienced ones but she'd take what she could. 'Ben they've found the uncle Paul Wiggins, at the bottom of Canal Bridge, barely alive.'

'Attempted suicide?'

‘We wait for the report. First thing in the morning, I want you to pull young DC Aryan Khan back from Mike Lawson’s team. They’ve misused him for long enough. I’m sure he knows how to file and work the coffee machine by now. And before you go off, see if you can’t borrow a few fresh officers. We need someone who can follow up with neighbours. I need the security footage from this place and at least a start made on the background for Paul Wiggins case – we need to treat it as suspicious until told otherwise. Check with traffic and see if that van from Wiggins garage has turned up yet. God – this case is becoming messier by the second.’

***

Monday Night.

It had to have been at least a whole day since he’d been taken Lee decided, though he had no idea where he was. Nothing – no sound, no daylight to give him a clue. It could’ve been midnight for all he knew. A stark light bulb hung high above his head in the box prison of four bare walls with metal door – all as grey as the concrete floor. Lee had woken, shivering, wondering why he’d slept in his clothes but it hadn’t taken long for the gut-wrenching reality to flood back. The narrow mattress was pushed tight against the wall and a couple of blankets had been thrown over him. When he’d lunged for the door, the chain from his wrist had caught around his foot and sent him reeling. Whatever that bloke from the van had shoved into his neck had left him feeling as sick as a dog, but at least the chain reached the toilet and the sink in the corner even if they did stink of vomit.

The gnawing hunger he could deal with – it was the silence that freaked him out. Huddled in the corner of the bed, Lee dozed fitfully, terrified. They’d taken his shoes, emptied his pockets of everything and, most of the time, he sat hunched, a blanket draped around his head trying not to notice the crabby walls. Questions ran through his brain like a juggernaut, none good. His uncle wouldn't do this to him – no way. He was sick, mad that his brother had died – but this? A rattle of metal had Lee gasping with fear. At floor level, a shutter opened revealing a plastic container which clattered into the room along with a single word, '*Food…*'

'Bastard! – they'll be searching. Do you hear me? You can't do this!'

No reply, just the box, a light-bulb and silence.

Chapter Five

Tuesday am

DS NEIL HARPER AND A FEW tech and admin workers were at their computers, concentrating on whatever puzzle they were trying to solve. Their voices were loud enough to be irritating, especially at eight in the morning. Sarah packed up her files and headed to reception and the desk sergeant. 'Andy, is there any chance I could use Bill Porter's room again?'

'I should hang on to the key if I was you, Sarah. No one else has asked for it since Bill went off sick.'

'You are a lifesaver. Is there any news on when he's back?' The DCI hadn't exactly set the place alight but he'd been a steady pair of hands and, after less than five hours sleep, anything would be better than nothing.

'Not that I've heard. Perhaps Amos will be back shortly?'

'I damn well hope so, I'm exhausted. Things aren't showing any signs of slowing down either. Will you let me know as soon as the Chief Super is in? I need to see him as a matter of urgency. Heads up – I had to wake him last night so he's probably not going to be in the best of moods.'

The sergeant's chuckle held no sympathy. 'It'll do the bugger good. I'll make sure there's fresh coffee brewed in his office, usually helps. I'll make extra. You look like you could do with some Sarah.'

Sat at Porter's desk, Sarah surveyed that day's log sheet. It read more like a synopsis for a disaster movie than a police report – Fifteen-year-old Lee Wiggins missing, his uncle Paul fighting for his life, Dan Bridges seriously injured and now, Megan Shaw had disappeared. The report on Megan's car was proving as frustrating as the rest of the scant evidence they had. At 17.29, somewhere along the semi-rural Chantry road, Megan and her blue Peugeot had seemingly vanished into thin air. From the corridor outside, Mike Lawson's unmistakable argumentative drawl broke her concentration. Sarah glanced up, willing the door to remain closed. The last thing she needed was a face to face with Lawson, but his footsteps faded and she gratefully dropped her gaze back to the file and the report from the children's home in Hull. The facts were undeniable: jewellery and teenagers missing from both centres, but – and it was a big but – Megan hadn't been in the building when Sarish's jewellery had disappeared. In Hull, she'd had a cast-iron alibi – and how to explain the young woman's disappearance? Her flat broken into?

'Yes?' she called at the abrupt knock at the door.

Ben Peterson walked in, looking far too awake. 'I thought you'd want to catch up, Inspector?'

'I do but I'm waiting for the Chief Super to arrive.'

Ben Peterson folded his long body into the spare chair. 'I should probably warn you that Mike Lawson is on one. He's not happy that Aryan Khan has been reassigned to us.'

'That's a shame. Where did you send Aryan?'

'He's well out of harm's way, checking out the CCTV footage at the *Cock and Crown.*' Ben shifted in the chair, any trace of humour receding. 'I'm afraid there's no positive news on Lee Wiggins. Officers are still checking out known offenders in the area and the house to house searches have drawn a blank. No one saw or heard a damned thing. Traffic did home in on two vehicles, a dark green van and a blue Vauxhall Vectra, both spotted by a resident as they drove up and down Mill Hill. The van ties in with Kate Declan's statement but the witness who reported the sightings, told us that it's not uncommon. People frequently get lost around those streets. The van is a close fit to the missing vehicle from Wiggins' garage although we don't have a registration for the one seen on the hill.'

'Was there any signage on the vehicle that the witness noted?'

'Nothing, the witness describes it as plain dark green. The ones owned by the garage are a similar colour but have *Wiggins* stencilled on the rear doors. Stencilling is faded, easy to miss. There is unexpected news about Paul Wiggins – a suicide attempt is looking doubtful. He received a heavy blow to the back of his head before he went off the bridge. I've sent a special constable over to the trauma unit to keep watch until we know more.'

'Attempted murder?' Sarah shook her head in disbelief. 'What the hell is going on? Did they retrieve a mobile, any evidence at all?'

'Carl Moyles offered to do the background work for us. I'll ask him to report. I hope that's okay?'

'Absolutely, Ben. Ask him to make it a priority and feed him into the Lee Wiggins investigation while you're at it.'

'Will do. I've spoken to the hospital. Dan Bridges remains unconscious but is making a good recovery. Traffic reported they found a recently burnt-out car near farm buildings off the Chantry Road. I'm waiting for confirmation it's Megan Shaw's.'

'Please tell me there wasn't a body in it?'

'No, the car was empty. Jackie is finishing the interviews at Megan's flats but so far, no one heard or saw a thing. The general search of the building found nothing other than the rear door was on a latch and a side gate unlocked when they were checked.'

'Which tells us that anyone could have entered if they were minded to do so. Is there anything at all to indicate who might want to hurt her?'

There's an ex-boyfriend, Richard Mason. Megan dumped him pretty recently.'

'I'm assuming you're checking him out, Ben?'

'We're trying. Mason works as a driver for the council. His manager informed us he reported in sick yesterday morning. I sent a constable around to his flat first thing but he's not there.'

'Stick him on the board as a possible lead. It's a start at least.' Sarah ran a finger down her page of notes. 'None of this makes sense.'

'Maybe this is about Dan and Kelly the agency worker. When Dan sees Megan in town he confesses he's got a thing for Kelly. Perhaps Lee fancied her as well and couldn't deal with the Kelly-Dan thing? Megan decides to confront the woman and they get into a fight – things got out of hand?'

'It's a theory of sorts, I suppose. Let's hope the lad wakes up soon and with his memory intact, or forensics finds some evidence. We need something solid to work with. Have someone phone the care agency that Kelly White works from. We need to talk to her.'

Ben made a note then reluctantly handed over a printout. 'This was waiting when I checked the inbox this morning. It's from Moira Robins, re *Lamp-light*. She thinks there's a big shipment going out.'

'Oh for goodness sake. Does Moira say when?' A distraction was not what they needed.

'It could be as early as Saturday evening?'

'Why now? We've been sitting on this for bloody weeks.'

'You know what they say about buses, Inspector.'

Sarah checked her watch – ten past nine. 'Let's have everyone who's working on the Lee Wiggins case in for 12.30, including uniform. See if we can't shake something loose.'

Sarah followed her sergeant through to the main incident room. Leaving him at his desk, she headed for the back wall and the two huge interactive boards that filled the space. *Electric Storm,* the innocuous name they'd christened the recent run of thefts of electrical goods from superstores and delivery vans, covered one board. The investigation was currently on hold, awaiting the return of their main player, Tony Ingles. A well know local thug, Ingles had used a mixture of blackmail and extortion to move from small-time thievery into the big league. They could prove Ingles had been in contact with men suspected of stealing lorry loads of electrical goods. They could even link him to a security guard inside one of the superstores. It wasn't perfect of course and, knowing Ingles, he'd probably walk away with a fine but, even if she'd wanted to arrest the lot of them, Ingles had promptly disappeared to Spain, purportedly on holiday. If she pulled in the rest of the crew, Ingles would know within minutes and not bother returning.

With a click, Sarah tapped in the password to open the second board. Another set of digital photographs, lists and diagrams sprang into focus. Boot-leg spirits this time: case name '*Lamp-light*'. The illegal spirits, made in a back-street distillery, were being sold in pubs and clubs all over Yorkshire. It should have been a Revenue Customs & Excise issue but the Leeds-based revenue officers appeared to have a blind spot when it came to Hepsford, a new city or not. After a cursory glance at the case, the Revenue officers had decided that, whoever was doing the organising had to be based in Sheffield or Bradford. Sarah wasn't buying it. Hepsford might have a reputation as a quiet backwater but where better to have a distillery and organise distribution? Illegal booty could be delivered to unsuspecting venues without hassle, a lucrative trade with tens of thousands to be made for the canny entrepreneur.

After weeks of tedious observation, her team had pinned down what appeared to be the core of the operation, a back street pub named the *Blue Beacon*. Closing the place down without identifying the main players was pointless. As soon as the dust settled they'd start afresh somewhere else. It had taken hours of talking at CS Finchley to persuade him that an undercover op was the only way. What helped was DC Moira

Robins' perfectly timed transfer from Paisley to join Amos Brantley's team. Outside of Ben, Jackie, Finchley and of course Amos, no one had a clue that the new barmaid at the *Beacon* was a plant. It seemed that their efforts were about to pay off. Checking dates, Sarah unlocked the secure drawer in her desk and picked up a mobile phone. The text she sent was brief.

'Are *you working Saturday night*?'

The reply was back in seconds. '*Yep.*' There was little else she could do other than hope that Finchley came up with the extra officers she'd need for the weekend. Saturdays were always a nightmare. Returning the mobile to the drawer, Sarah checked through the pages of the diary. A court session was booked for that afternoon at 14.00 hrs. She would message Amos, let him know to meet her afterwards - hopefully he'd have good news.

'Inspector, you wanted an update on Paul Wiggins?' A cheerful DS Carl Moyles was holding out a briefing sheet.

Sarah ran her eye down the note. 'Do we know who the last person was to see him yesterday, Carl?'

'A Steve Thomas spoke to him at 15.20 hrs approximately. Apparently, Paul had finally agreed to come into the station after work to give a statement. I'm driving over to the garage shortly to interview the rest of the staff. We haven't found Paul Wiggins' mobile but, I've applied for phone records. Mr Thomas insists that Paul always carried his mobile with him.'

'Chase up an Adam Farnes as well, Carl. The man was fired from the garage a couple of weeks ago. We need more info on him and that missing van, use extra hands if necessary. We need to find out if Farnes or the van are linked to the Lee Wiggins disappearance.'

Sarah's alert buzzed at her hip – the Chief Superintendent was finally in the building. Armed with the six-monthly review and the recent case file, Sarah knocked firmly on his door.

CS Finchley's rich tenor sounded a little strained as she entered but if he was tired, he was hiding it well. Maybe it was the desk sergeant's coffee? If hers was anything to go by it could easily have doubled up as rocket fuel. 'The DCI's review,' she said without preamble and placed the file onto the pristine desk.

Finchley ran a broad finger over the front cover. 'I must say the new city logo looks good.'

Sarah kept her mouth clamped shut. The cost of changing the logos on signs and headed paper from town to city had already run into millions. Sarah could have listed a hundred better ways for the council to spend what they didn't have. Finchley glanced through the file and ran an appreciative eye over the neatly finished pages. 'Any input from Mike Lawson?'

If it had been anyone else she would have covered. 'No, Sir.'

'And I take it there's been little in the way of support on the ground from him?'

Surprised at his sharp tone, Sarah shook her head. 'Not a great deal.'

He carried on thumbing through the report. For the most part, his expression remained fixed. 'Now these are interesting.' Finchley pointed to the graphs at the end with a satisfied smile.

'I suppose so, at least in relation to the previous set of figures. Those financial cuts they made have begun to show in the stats. Though what I find far more interesting Sir is the increase in street crime since we cut the numbers on the beat?'

Finchley closed the file with a snap. 'Yes, well I'm not sure this is the time for politics.'

No rocking the boat, Allerton. The words danced through her head but the smirk was harder to hide. 'Is there any news on Bill Porter? I was under the impression he was due back any day?' *Please say yes,* she pleaded silently.

'Bill is officially back next Monday.'

'However?' she asked hearing the hesitation.

'I'm afraid it's only for a few days to tie up loose ends. Bill's decided to take early retirement. His heart condition is going to need long-term treatment. A real shame, he was a good officer.' *Past tense,* Sarah thought, *yes, he had been until the pressure of the job had shattered him into tiny pieces*.

The Chief Superintendent pulled a slim manilla file from the top drawer of his desk and continued, 'I am delighted to announce Sarah that, with immediate effect you've been appointed to acting Detective Chief Inspector. Congratulations are in order.'

Her first thought was for Freya – a higher profile would mean frequent media coverage. The second was Lawson's furious reaction when he found out he'd been passed over. Pleasing as that was, she wasn't sure it was worth the worry. 'Me – you want to stick me with a desk job – Sir.'

'You're more than ready for this Sarah and it's long overdue.' Finchley sounded impatient. 'You know as well as I that the inspector and chief's role differ very little, at least here in Hepsford. Goodness sake, you've proven you're more than capable. You've been doing both jobs anyway and, let's be frank, far better than Bill had for months.' He sat back, smugness lifting his usually dower expression. 'And do remember that the title is *acting* – there's still the formal board to agree the promotion.'

Freya would never forgive her if she refused. Sarah forced a grudging smile. 'At least I'll get paid for all the extra work.'

'There is always that silver lining. Now, your current cases. Let's begin with the missing Wiggins lad?'

'There's little to report.' Sarah handed him a summary sheet anyway. 'There have been those other developments which I made you aware of some hours ago.'

'Ah yes, the attack on the missing teenager's friend and the uncle. I believe one of the staff members is missing?'

There was some compensation in walking away from Finchley's door knowing she'd left him in a state of complete meltdown. He seemed to forget she could recite all of her cases backwards, forwards and upside down if necessary. His nice clean notepad was scarred forever.

***

Deciding a large Danish pastry and coffee was in order, Sarah headed for the canteen. Tuesday mornings Freya usually had a free period after ten – a good time to break the news. Freya answered on the second ring. 'Hi, it's nice to hear from you. I've been drowned out all morning by a class of rioting year eights.'

'Sounds like fun, want to swap?'

'For?'

'A desk full of enigmas and a pompous Chief Superintendent who can't decide whether to pat my head or kick me out?'

'I'll stick with what I know, thank you and you're more than woman enough to sort the lot of them.'

'I'm very glad you're on my side.'

'Do I hear a whisper of self-pity?' Freya was laughing at her. 'Just to let you know, I've bought in strong white, wholemeal and brown flour. There should be enough yeast to keep you going for the next century.'

'Things aren't that bad yet, Freya.'

'*Yet* being the operative word! Thanks for the rolls and croissants by the way. I had the whole of the staffroom drooling this morning.'

'Sorry to leave you with the baking.' There had been two trays with a note stuck on the top. Their freezer was packed with half-baked rolls and loaves of bread. The only benefit of waking up at stupid o'clock most mornings. Maybe she should go to that sleep clinic after all – or retire.

‘Switching on an oven and sticking in trays I can manage. All I ask is *you* remember to use that timer I bought the next time you start making? That last batch you baked during the canal murders tasted like bullets.’

Baking was therapy. Kneading soft dough into a pliable mass kept the hands busy, allowing the pieces of whatever she was working on to sift through her head. If the bread and freezer suffered occasionally it was usually worth the price. ‘I’ll try and remember,’ Sarah promised. ‘How did *Kidnapped* go down?’

‘Well, as it happens… Are you just ringing to touch base or...’?

‘What would you say if I told you I’ve been made up to acting DCI?’ Freya’s happy exclamation made her grimace. ‘I take it you’re pleased?’

‘Honestly, Sarah, you make it sound like a punishment. You deserve this. Well done!’

‘Thanks, I’m just tired I suppose. Silly workload as usual.’

‘I’ll buy us a bottle of something special to celebrate. – Oh sorry, Sarah, I’m being summoned, I’ve got to go. Love you.’ The line went silent.

Sarah smiled down at the mobile before tucking it away. Freya was the anchor she could drop whenever the world turned into a bloody mess. She knew she wouldn’t relax until she’d heard from Amos – just to be sure.

***

A fresh-faced DC Jake Forbes handed Sarah a briefing note as soon as she entered the main incident room. ‘You asked about Kelly White, Inspector. She isn’t at her flat. She hasn’t been there since late yesterday afternoon.’

‘That was quick work, Jake.’

He shrugged shyly. ‘I know the special constable on the beat around there. One of the neighbours she interviewed saw Kelly leaving by taxi at around 15.50 yesterday. I have the number for the care agency that employed her. Do you want me to ring them for more details?'

'Track down that taxi first and …'

'I already have.' Jake indicated a telephone number on the sheet. 'The driver dropped Kelly at the Metro station in Hepsford. That's the driver's registration and telephone number if you need to talk to him. Ben also asked me to chase up details for a Richard Mason. It's bad news though, Mason's car was involved in a serious incident.'

Sarah glanced across to where Ben had a phone to his ear, rapidly scribbling a note with the other hand. The grim expression was explained when he twisted the notepad around to show her.

Tuesday 07.34, *Mason's car found at the bottom of a gulley near Wetherby. White male found in driving seat – deceased.*

'Have they confirmed it is Richard Mason?'

'I'm afraid so. They've pulled up a photo ID. They said it's going to take a while to haul him and the car up. Where do you want his body sent?'

Sarah scrubbed at her forehead trying to make sense of this latest incident. 'Make sure they do the forensic and autopsy here in Hepsford. We'll be waiting until Christmas if we send him to Leeds or York. Do traffic think we're looking at an accident?'

'It's too soon to say. Do we hand this over to the other team?'

With the workload steadily mounting it was tempting. From across the room, Mike Lawson's angry retort to some query had her shaking her head. 'For all we know, the whole jumble of events is connected. Let's see how the day pans out.'

'There is more bad news Inspector. We've had confirmation that the burnt-out car on Chantry Road is Megan Shaw's. It was deliberately set on fire, with petrol used as the accelerant.'

'Did we get anywhere tracking down Megan's relatives, Ben?'

‘Nothing so far I’m afraid. Her grandmother, Catherine Stuart is listed as next of kin, but she died months ago in Hull. There are no other relatives that we can trace.’

‘Isn’t there anything straightforward about this damned case?’ The urge to push through the doors, pull on trainers and run was almost too much… Squelching down the frustration, Sarah ran through her mental *to-do list* instead. ‘We’ll need to go back to Megan’s flat, see what we can find. Have Jackie talk to Mason’s workmates, only tell her not to let on that he’s dead. His next of kin will have to be informed first.’

‘What about Mason’s flat?’

With a sigh Sarah checked her watch. There was just enough time. ‘Let’s do that now. We’ve a lot to fit in before the debrief and the court session.’

‘Allerton, I need a word...’ The voice grabbed her attention before the pervading odour of aftershave caught the back of her throat. Sarah saw her sergeant’s eyes roll, his groan barely audible. Mike Lawson stalked towards her, his neat greying hair yellow under the strip light. He was down to shirt sleeves and a tie that had seen better days. The superior expression was one she knew all too well.

Turning her back on the scowling man she spoke quietly to Ben. ‘Ask Jake to chase up that care agency regarding Kelly White. I want to know if the woman is off sick, on holiday or has taken off. If it’s the latter, I want a search warrant for her place of residence.’

‘On what grounds?’

‘She’s a suspect in a theft – that should do the trick.’

‘Allerton, do I need to pull sodding seniority? What’s your fecking game pulling one of my men? I’m right in the middle of a bloody case.’

The six years of his unremitting snide comments and constant undermining had left her battered but far from cowed. The past insults only added to the layers of pleasure as she made the angry man wait. Checking the diary on her sergeant’s desk, Sarah waited until Ben had picked up his notepad and walked over to Jake Forbes. Around the room, no one moved. Turning, Sarah eyed Lawson coldly, noting the creased collar, the flecks of white on the blue of his shirt. He was two years her senior in age and service but might as well have been her grandfather – except the old man had been a likeable old rogue. Lawson was a gold-medal-winning bully who gave misogynists a bad reputation.

'You probably haven't read the email yet, Mike. You'll find that's DCI Sarah Allerton or Ma'am, either will do?' Her words were crisp – clear. A low gasp ran around the room, immediately stifled as they waited for Lawson's reaction. Sarah watched the eyes refocus and sharpen. Give the man his due he hardly missed a beat.

'Is that so? Well, it doesn't give you the bloody right to go dragging off one of my team. Wasting resources as usual and all for a missing teenager. He's probably pissing it up somewhere or shagging his girlfriend more like.'

With an effort, Sarah bit back the retort. Now was not the time for a slanging match. 'If you have a problem with my decision making Mike, I suggest you take it up with the CS, maybe *he'll* have the time to debate the issue – I definitely do not.' Sarah walked the few paces to Jake Forbes' desk aware of the escalating murmurs around her.

'When you're ready, Ben?' The slap of the door reverberated through the room as a furious Lawson stormed out. File under her arm, Sarah walked calmly to the door leaving the whispers to begin in earnest.

Chapter Six

INSIDE MASON'S FLAT it was the smell that hit Sarah first – rotten food, probably curry. On the floor lay a pizza box, crushed in one corner, footprint clearly visible. The sparsely furnished rooms felt empty, uncared for. Behind her, Ben was ushering the inquisitive landlord away from the door with a final, 'Thank you Sir. I'll let you know when we're done.'

'Did the landlord have anything useful to say?'

'Mason paid five months' rent in advance in cash. He moved in around seven weeks ago so was well out of pocket when he ran.'

Methodically, they made their way around the untidy apartment. The bedroom was the worst: clothes, clean and dirty were everywhere. 'He packed in a hurry, Inspector.'

'Check under the bed, Ben. I'll do the chest of drawers.'

Kneeling, Ben flashed his torch. 'Someone's removed a bag or a case from under here. I can see the dusty outline.'

The bedside cabinet was pulled away from the wall, its drawer dumped on the bed. Underneath, part of the sticky tape Mason had used clung to the base, a corner of a brown envelope stuck to one edge. It was impossible to tell what he'd been hiding.

'So, Mason packs in a hurry, grabs his emergency stash and drives off?'

'It looks that way Ben, but why did he run?'

'We know Megan dumped Mason. Perhaps he loses his temper and Dan sees it happen? Mason makes a run for it before his involvement is discovered. Stressed-out, he loses control of the car and wham, straight into a ditch?'

'The timing doesn't work. Dan was already unconscious long before Megan disappeared. Do we know if a bag or case was retrieved with his body?'

'Nothing so far but I'll double-check.'

The rest of the search brought up nothing of interest. Sarah glanced at the time to find it was almost twelve. 'It's late. We should head back to the station.'

As Ben pulled smoothly away from the kerb, Carl Moyles' name flashed up on the car phone. 'Chief Inspector – congrats on the promotion by the way – I'm letting you know that I've found a witness who saw Paul Wiggins at 15.50 hrs yesterday. The witness saw Wiggins leave the garage and shouted across the road to him but he didn't answer, just kept on walking. The witness swears he had a mobile in his hand.'

'Any cameras around to confirm the story, Carl?'

'A local newsagent is helping me out. I'm still waiting for Paul Wiggins' phone provider to come back to me, they're dragging their heels, as usual. I tried to have another word with Steve Thomas about the van, and Farnes, but Thomas had gone up to the hospital.'

'Try leaning on one of the other mechanics, Carl. If both the bosses are out of the picture they might be more forthcoming.'

Back at the station, the central incident room was full of plain-clothed and uniformed bodies. The buzz of conversation faded as Sarah strode to the front of the room. She didn't need to be a mind-reader to know what was the hot topic of conversation. 'Before I start the briefing let me put the rumour mill to rest.' Sarah glanced around at the curious faces; everyone, apart from Lawson and Carl Moyles was there. 'As of this morning, I've taken up the post of Acting DCI – not that it will make any difference to the workload unfortunately.'

An anonymous voice echoed from the back. 'And about bloody time, Ma'am.'

'Thank you for the sentiment. The bad news is things are about to go ballistic...'

'And it's been so quiet, Ma'am.' The officer's dry humour wasn't lost on the room.

Sarah let the bubble of laughter run for a moment. 'Ben, can you outline the key areas of the case so far?'

He started with Lee Wiggins; the litany of events rolled on one after the other, finishing with Richard Mason's body being hauled from the car that morning.

Jake Forbes raised a hesitant hand. 'You should know that we are unable to trace the agency worker, Kelly White. She didn't report in sick and no one can contact her. Her mobile number isn't responding. I've checked with the network and it's a pay as you go.'

'Did you organise a search warrant for her flat?'

'It's at reception.'

Jackie Simmons' report was equally bleak. Inquiries at the flats where Megan lived had turned up nothing new; no one has seen nor heard from her. Sarah pulled up the digital image of the burnt-out Peugeot and clicked it over to the incident board. 'We do know Megan's car was deliberately set alight near the Chantry Road. What we don't know is whether she was taken by force although, given the break-in at her flat, it's looking likely.'

'I followed up with a visit to Mason's workplace.' Jackie continued. 'Mason has only worked there for six weeks and wasn't particularly liked. His colleagues used terms like insufferable, a pain in the arse – and variations of the same. One interesting fact was that he used to drink regularly at the *Cock & Crown*.'

Sarah turned to Aryan Khan. 'Did you have better luck with their CCTV?'

'Their equipment is ancient so I'm running the footage through specialist software to clear up the distortions.'

'Have we had any joy on the green van or that Vauxhall Vectra?'

‘Not yet,’ Ben said. ‘Traffic are continuing to trawl through the traffic data,’

‘We also have an all-points out on the missing van from Wiggins’ garage and for Adam Farnes. Everyone should have details?’ Sarah waited for the nods before continuing. ‘Ben will delegate jobs, making sure warrants are requested. Before we separate, I want to remind everyone that Lee is barely fifteen and he’s been missing for over twenty-four hours. Those golden minutes are fast slipping through our fingers; we cannot afford to lose the momentum. That’s all ladies and gentlemen.’

Expressions were sombre as people drifted from the room. Soon, all that was left was her small team and the aroma of musky scent from too many bodies with little ventilation. Sarah pulled out a chair, allowing herself to roll into the contours of the soft support. Five minutes of rest was all she needed.

From her hip, an alarm beeped. ‘Hell, I’ve got to go.’ With effort, she scooped up her briefcase. ‘Ben, find the time to head back to Lakeside with Jackie. Ask more questions; we need background on Megan and Kelly White in particular. I should be back for four thirty – five at the latest.’

Chapter Seven

LAKESIDE WAS IN MOURNING, or at least that was how it felt to Ben as he settled onto the large sofa. Today, the room was drenched in the November sunlight which did little to dissipate the gloominess. Outside, the long garden was peppered with the russet browns of the last of the fallen leaves. Across from him, Jackie was reading her notes while they waited to re-interview Lisa Albright, a permanent residential youth worker. Ben checked his watch – almost two-thirty and he still hadn't managed to grab lunch. The woman who walked into the room looked older than he remembered, black hair tightly braided, her expression held little of the vibrancy he'd witnessed the day before.

'I'm DS Peterson, this is DC Simmons. I know I spoke with you yesterday, Mrs Albright but, in light of recent events, there are a few more questions.'

'Call me Lisa and please, tell me you've found Megan?'

'I'm sorry, there's no news yet but if you could run through yesterday's events again, that would be helpful?'

Lisa slumped into the seat, her voice dripping with emotion. 'This goes from bad to worse. Rahul – Mr De-Silva – is beside himself with worry, we all are. He's been out for hours, knocking on doors, posting leaflets. I don't think he's eaten since we heard about Lee…' Lisa took a moment to gather her thoughts before she spoke again. 'Everything about yesterday was weird, Sergeant. I keep going over and over it in my head. I couldn't sleep thinking about what it was that rattled me...'

Was it something Megan told you, or someone else?' Ben asked.

'I don't know. I'm not even sure it was about her – that's the problem.'

'Go back to when you first arrived on shift; walk us through it.'

'If you really think it'll help.' Lisa's sigh was heavy. 'Megan was already in the office when I arrived although she should have been off – she'd swapped days because of staff sickness. We chatted about Rees Morgan, an agency worker who was on shift. She mentioned he'd asked her out a couple of weeks back but Megan wasn't interested. I can't say I was surprised. He's too wimpy and anyway she'd been seeing someone called Rick or Richard? Now he was a total waste of space if you ask me. Megan told me she'd dumped him last Friday. Then De-Silva started the usual run through…' Abruptly, Lisa stopped and clicked her fingers. 'Of course! That's what it was! She was late arriving. Something about a notebook...'

'Sorry, Lisa, who was late?'

'The other agency worker, Sergeant, Kelly White. She'd left a notebook in her coat pocket. When the woman walked into the office and apologised, Megan seemed surprised – distracted. I remember nudging Megan to get her attention when De-Silva asked her a question.'

'To be clear, you're talking about Kelly White the agency worker?'

'Yes – it must have been that, Sergeant. The woman only spoke briefly but Megan kept glancing back to where Kelly was sitting.'

'Did Megan talk to Kelly after the meeting?'

'No – although Matt did send Megan to Springvale to pick up the menu sheets, which is when she found out Kelly had gone off sick. She told me later.'

'Do you know if Megan had met Kelly before?'

'I don't think so, Sergeant, and from where we were sitting I couldn't see the woman's face properly. I doubt if Megan could either. I'd worked with Kelly once before, but that was when Megan was off duty.'

Peterson reclined into his chair thinking through the scenario. 'Jackie, do we know what time Kelly White was sent home?'

'07.55 according to my notes. She complained of feeling sick as soon as the meeting broke up.'

'Yesterday evening in your statement Lisa, you mentioned that Dan visited the kitchen before lunch. Can you go over what he said?'

'He wanted to know if Kelly White was working. When Megan asked him why, he told her that she'd promised to lend him a computer game.'

'And you told the officer that you thought it unusual?'

'I mentioned that it felt wrong – didn't sit right. There was no reason Dan would've had any contact with the woman.' Lisa's expression softened. 'Have you heard how he's doing?'

'He's making good progress. The doctors say he should make a full recovery.'

'That's a relief at least…'

'Lee and Dan, were they good friends would you say?'

'Surprisingly yes,' Lisa laughed. 'Lee ignored Dan's swagger. He'd started to take Dan out skateboarding. They even went to football together.'

'No arguments between them recently?'

'No, not at all – and Dan isn't one for hiding his feelings, Sergeant. We'd have known about it if there'd been a problem.'

'Lisa, did Megan ever mention family or close friends, somewhere she might have gone?'

'I know her grandmother died a while back but I've not heard her mention any other family. As for friends, she talked about her fellow university students a fair bit. She was with some of them over the weekend at the *new city* celebrations and there was that boyfriend until she finished with him. He works for the council I believe, driving a minibus which I think is how they met. Megan mentioned he'd kept sending texts – trying to patch things up but she wasn't having any of it.' Lisa's eyes narrowed. 'He hasn't got anything to do with her disappearance has he?'

'We're following several lines of enquiry, Lisa. Did Megan mention him being aggressive or violent towards her?'

'No, nothing like that. The man simply let her down all the time. I've worked with Megan a lot since she started here. She's a wonderful girl: caring, honest everyone here adores her. Her disappearing like this is totally out of character.'

'Thank you for talking to us Lisa. I know this is a difficult time for you all.'

Lisa sank back, relaxing a little. 'Mr De-Silva told me you wanted to interview the youngsters again. There are only a couple here, most are at school.'

'We'll talk to whoever's available – Kate Declan if she's about?'

'Ah, Kate's taken herself off to the hospital, hoping to see Dan. We tried to dissuade her, but she's a stubborn one at times. Sarish is here and Adai?'

'Then Adai. We only had a brief chat with the lad yesterday.'

'One thing, Sergeant. One of our regular night staff told me that Adai had a very disturbed night. The lad just couldn't settle but nothing to do with the sickness bug. I tried to have a word with him this morning but he wouldn't say much, not to me at least.'

'Is that out of character?' Ben asked.

'Adai is usually so laid back that he'd fall off a chair but he's edgy about something.'

To Ben's eyes, the shuffling fourteen-year-old who followed Lisa into the room looked no older than ten. Ben smiled warmly, hoping to ease some of the tension he saw on the lad's face. 'Hi, again. Just to remind you, I'm Sergeant Ben

Peterson, and this is Detective Constable Jackie Simmons. Is it okay to call you Adai?'

The nod was barely perceptible. Ben waited for him to slump onto a chair, Lisa sat off to one side. 'Are you feeling better than yesterday, Adai? You looked a bit rough the last time I saw you.' There was still a hint of grey under his dark skin, but the eyes were brighter.

'I'm okay.'

It was better than a nod Ben decided. 'Adai, we're going to be asking everyone here more questions, about Lee, Dan and about Megan.'

The reaction was immediate. He swung around towards Lisa. 'Why, what's happened to Megan?'

'Megan is missing Adai. That's one of the reasons the police are here again.'

'What's Megan got to do with Lee and Dan? This is stupid...'

Ben cut in. 'It's what we're trying to work out. What I'm asking everyone is: did anything happen over the weekend, anything at all? You might not think it's important, Adai. It could be something small, insignificant, silly perhaps?'

The teenager couldn't keep still. His gaze darted about the room in a frantic attempt to avoid eye contact.

'Adai,' Lisa's quiet word had him twisting in his seat. 'You're not in any trouble. We just need to know whatever it is. Please?'

'I – I don't know. It's nothing...'

'Then tell me,' Ben suggested. 'I promise Adai, if it's not connected, I won't even write it down.'

The teenager's resolve began to waver. 'But you can't tell him – ever. He'll kill us if he finds out.'

'Who are we talking about, Adai?' Ben asked.

'Dan...' the gulp was audible. 'Only I saw them – yesterday morning. It was early, I'd been in the bathroom because I was still feeling crappy. She had him pressed up against the wall – you know, kissing and stuff.'

Ben kept his voice low, neutral. 'Who was with Dan?'

'That blonde one. I don't really know her, she's agency.'

Jackie drew out Kelly White's photograph from a file. 'Is this her?'

'Yeah – Dan didn't want to,' he added quickly. 'She was all over him. Dan kept trying to push her away.'

'And then what happened?' Ben asked. 'Did they go into Dan's room?'

'Nah, I couldn't hear what they were saying or anything. She was only there a few minutes then she left.'

'Is that everything, Adai?'

'Pretty much. I was watching from near the cupboard on the landing. I saw her put this hat on his head, a beanie – West Ham colours I think, then she disappeared downstairs. Dan looked seriously pissed off when she'd gone.'

***

The corridor outside the ICU of Hepsford General echoed under the heels of Kate's boots. She didn't care if De-Silva didn't want her to visit, she needed to see Dan for herself, make sure he was okay. The policeman was a surprise. Sitting to the left of the doors, the constable stood as she approached and eyed her curiously.

'I'm Kate Declan a friend of Dan's. I live at Lakeside?' The constable didn't budge. 'Please,' she pleaded. 'I just want to see him for a couple of minutes. Here's my ID if you don't believe me.' Kate handed him her bus pass, pulled down her mask briefly and mentally crossed her fingers.

'I'll need to check with the staff and my boss first, so wait.' The officer disappeared into the unit. An anxious couple of minutes later he was back. 'The nurse said not to expect much, as they've only recently taken out Dan's breathing tube. He might be a bit restless.'

Dan was propped against a bank of pillows and, in the low light, his skin was a pasty grey. A sling supported one arm and there was a bald patch above the left ear. A clean white dressing disappeared behind his head covering the worst of the injury. Kate swallowed hard and tried not to think of the damage lying underneath.

'It's me – Kate,' she added squeezing the fingers of his good hand. 'Everyone's asking after you, Dan. We all miss you.' She felt his fingers move, or maybe she'd imagined it. 'It's been awful,' she whispered not expecting him to hear her. 'First Lee disappearing then you getting hurt, now Megan is missing...' This time there was no mistaking the clenched fingers. Dan's lips moved, his eyelids straining to open. The lines on the machine beside him began to rise in steep peaks. 'It's okay. Ssh, everything will be fine.' Kate sat in silence, gently smoothing the skin on the back of his hand. Old, painful memories flooded in.

'Are you all right, love?' the blue-uniformed nurse had moved on silent feet to stand beside her.

Kate dried her cheek hoping the nurse hadn't noticed. 'I'm fine – honest. Can I just sit here for a little longer – please?'

'As long as you don't upset yourself. There's no reason why Dan won't make a full recovery, although he's going to have a hell of a headache when he wakes up properly.' The nurse moved to check off numbers from the monitor.

Kate's fingers continued to stroke. This wasn't her dying brother or her parents she reminded herself. Dan *was* going to wake up, *he* wouldn't abandon her like everyone else had. She wasn't sure how long she'd been at the bedside when the nurse tapped her lightly on the shoulder.

'There's a police sergeant outside who'd like a word, a few questions he told me, nothing to worry about.'

Reluctantly, Kate slid her hand from Dan's and walked out into the corridor. The tall officer who'd interviewed her the previous day was leaning against the wall, looking less like a policeman than ever.

'Sorry to drag you away, Kate. Do you remember me? I'm Sergeant Peterson. The staff nurse has agreed to hang around while I ask you a couple of questions if that's okay.'

'Sure, fire away.'

'Can you tell me what Dan's interests and hobbies are?'

The odd question threw her for a moment. 'Well, er, football I suppose. He likes messing about on a skateboard but he's not very good. He's a Hammers supporter. Tries to see them when he can.'

'Does he own the team scarf and the t-shirts?'

'I think he has a West Ham scarf that he wears to matches and someone gave him a beanie with the logo on but he gave that to Lee.'

'That was generous of him.'

'He and Lee are good mates – most of the time.' Kate gulped back her emotions, determined not to cry.

'And was Lee wearing that beanie on the morning he disappeared?'

'Yes – he was chuffed Dan had given it to him – but what's that got to do with anything?'

'Clearing up a few loose ends, Kate. Thanks, I think I've got everything for now.'

Chapter Eight

COURT HAD TO BE THE MOST BORING part of her job, Sarah conceded. Finally, she was free and walking down the steep steps into the chill of the early evening air.

'Sarah, I'm over here...'

Recognising the voice, Sarah turned and smiled. Detective Chief Inspector Amos Brantley, colleague and long-time friend had been away on sickness leave after a hernia op and had been sorely missed. 'I'm sorry you had to hang around, Amos but the court took forever to finish. Thanks for coming.' She stayed two steps up, so she could look the tall Jamaican in the eye for a change. How are you feeling?'

'Fully fit and bored rigid. I'm back in the office from tomorrow, thank goodness. Great news about your promotion by the way, about bloody time.'

'It's only acting up, and I can't say Lawson was as enthusiastic. I thought he was going to have a stroke when he heard the news.'

'It would have done us all a favour.'

Sarah grinned. She and Amos went a long way back. 'It'll be a relief to have a friendly face in the office that's for sure.'

Amos slipped an arm through hers. 'You're looking fit, Sarah. You're still finding time for that gym of yours I take it?'

'I manage to squeeze in a few sessions. Now you've had the all-clear, you could come running with me?'

Sarah had missed that deep rumbling laugh. 'Or learn the piano or take up knitting? Somehow, I don't think so.'

'Well, you might change your mind about coming back to the office when you see what's been cracking off.'

‘I’m meeting up with Carl Moyles for a quick pint after you and I have finished. He’s going to fill me in before the onslaught tomorrow. Shall I walk you to your car and we can talk as we go?’

‘Don’t you go getting the man drunk, he’s still on duty.’

‘So he told me. Promise I’ll make it a shandy.’ Amos glanced over his shoulder, checking they were still alone. ‘I had the *all clear* from Cheltenham this afternoon. Nothing has changed. No enquiries, no new cases. Anyway, why the sudden panic?’

Outside of Freya and herself, Amos was one of only two people in Yorkshire who knew the whole story. He’d worked alongside her in Cheltenham and lived through those horrendous weeks as one woman after another had been brutally murdered. No one on that case had walked away unscathed.

‘Nothing’s happened, which is silly,’ she added quickly. ‘And it wasn’t Freya before you ask. She’s as calm as a millpond.’

‘There’s nothing silly about any of it, Sarah. You ask anytime, but what made you so rattled?’

‘You remember that photograph of her in Cheltenham, the shoulder-length hair...’

‘Fabulous eyes, gorgeous cheekbones, I remember,’ he said softly. ‘It was stuck on our incident board for long enough.’

‘Freya’s let her hair grow again. It’s crazy I know, but there was a moment on Monday when she turned and hell, Amos, no one could mistake her for anyone else. What if...’

‘There have been no enquiries, no hint of anything.’ He stepped in front of her. ‘Talk to her, Sarah. Tell her it’s worrying you. I don’t know, maybe treat her to a new hair-do or something?’

‘Freya hasn’t mentioned any of it for over a year and I have no intention of dumping my crap onto her.’

‘Freya won’t thank you for playing martyr,’ he said softly.

Startled, Sarah took a step back. 'You think I'm exaggerating this?'

'No, I don't.' Deliberately, Amos picked up her hand and rubbed a finger over a bruised knuckle. 'I am wondering why you're sacrificing your own peace of mind? What are you afraid of?'

Objectivity and her finger bloody hurt. 'Now *you're* telling me I'm paranoid?' It was a troubling thought. 'I should be able to deal, I suppose – not act like a skittish mare.' As far as the rest of the world and that psychopath was concerned, Freya – or rather Angela Oxley – had been dead for the past six years. She wasn't about to admit that simply thinking of Freya's old name gave her goose-bumps.

They started to walk again and Amos didn't speak until they'd reached her car. 'If it was me Sarah, six years would mean nothing, especially knowing the circumstances. So no, I don't think you're being paranoid. Tired and over-stretched more like, but I still think you should talk to her. Share the burden.'

Amos left her at the car with a final wave. There was comfort at least in knowing the checks had come back clear. Still, his words had her rattled – martyr indeed! Her mobile rang and, grateful for once for the distraction, she answered. Her head immediately changed gear as she heard Ben Peterson's sigh. 'Ma'am, sorry to rush you, but we finally have some worrying answers.'

'I'm just out of court, Ben. I can be back in twenty, give or take.'

'We could be here a while, so I've asked Jackie to order us in Pizza.'

***

Apart from her small team and the lonely figure of Neil Harper, the main incident room was empty. Neil raised a weary hand in salute, before burying himself in the pile of work Lawson had dumped on him. Right now, there was little Sarah could do to help other than empathise.

'I'll make a start,' Ben said as soon as she was seated. 'Someone went to a great deal of trouble to make Mason's death look like an accident.'

'You're saying it was murder?' Jackie asked.

'Afraid so. The head injury was clever. Forensics state that: *there's no trace of blood on the interior of the door panels or windscreen but there were traces of blood in the boot. A fine spray on the inside edges, consistent with someone being held down and a blow being delivered by a powerful downward swing*. They also found traces of an accelerant. They must have tried to burn out the car to get rid of the evidence.'

'Awkward,' said Aryan. 'How do you manage a good enough swing inside the boot of a car?'

'A heavy ball or balls in a sock the medical examiner reckoned.'

'And there are no doubts about this?' Sarah asked.

'None. The initial sweep of the car found traces of fibres in the boot that appear to match Mason's jacket. They're going to do a second run-through and take a look at the place he usually parked his car. They didn't find any bag or a case, I'm afraid.'

'We can hope they'll pull up something tomorrow. What else?'

Ben's phone buzzed. 'Jackie can tell you what we found out about Kelly and the beanie while I sort this. It's probably the food.'

'And this hat incident happened early on Monday morning?' Sarah asked once Jackie had finished explaining.

'Adai witnessed the encounter at approximately 07.05, not long before Dan left for his work experience. Adai was coming out of the shared bathroom on the male corridor when he saw them. I checked the rota and Kelly was officially on duty from 07.30 until midday. However, Lakeside's CCTV shows a taxi dropping her off at 06.46. The external doors have electronic keypads. All she had to do was use her key fob, enter that week's password and she'd be in.'

'We know for definite that the hat Lee was wearing is the same one Kelly gave to Dan?'

'From the information Adai gave us, it matches the one Kate said Dan gave to Lee. In her statement she said Lee was chuffed Dan had given it to him. Though I don't see why the hat is so important?'

Sarah drummed fingertips on the table, brow furrowed. 'Nor do I, yet.'

'But why risk a liaison at work when they could have met up outside,' Aryan asked.

'Maybe she got off on the adrenaline rush,' Jackie responded.

Disjointed ideas began to bubble, an irritating buzz that refused to be ignored. Rapidly, Sarah thumbed through to the last page of the case file and handed the sheet to Jackie. 'The care agency in Hull will be shut so telephone the children's home where Megan worked. Ask them if they have any photographic ID for a Shauna Richardson, agency care worker. Aryan, check whether Kelly White or Shauna Richardson are on the DVLA register, their addresses are listed on the log.'

The hum of activity built slowly as calls were answered. Sarah kept her eyes on the board refusing to speculate. Aryan was first. 'Sorry, but neither woman has ever held a driving licence of any kind.'

'Don't be sorry. It's what I was expecting. Jackie?'

'The manager doesn't have anything official on file, but says she's pretty sure she has a photograph of Richardson from a staff party. She'll email it to us in half an hour if that would do?'

'Better than nothing. Ask her to send it straight to you. I don't want to get caught up in data protection – need to put a face to the name.'

Aryan sat back, his expression sceptical. 'You're thinking Kelly and Shauna are the same person?'

'Am I, Aryan? I'd rather say I was attempting to exclude the possibility. Ah, Ben at last – food.'

With Neil Harper's help, they devoured the pizzas in record time. Sarah wiped her greasy fingers – Freya would have had apoplexy if she'd been there to witness the food orgy. With a sigh, she brought everyone back on topic. 'Okay, so any results from the *Cock & Crown's* CCTV footage?'

'It's slow going,' Aryan admitted. 'The pub's equipment is from the ark. The program is working but won't be finished for another couple of hours. I could contact IT if you prefer?'

'No, that department is notoriously slow. It'll be next week before we hear a damned thing – stay with it. What's the update from Carl?'

Ben flicked open a page on his laptop. 'Carl is still waiting for the call lists from Paul Wiggins' phone company. Adam Farnes and the van are still missing.'

'Have we any more background on why Farnes was sacked?'

Again Ben studied the screen. 'Carl states that the other mechanics still aren't talking. One minute he was there the next he'd gone, so not much help.'

'Megan Shaw – did she run because she was scared or was she taken?'

'That depends,' Ben began. 'If this Shauna Richardson turns out to be the same person as Kelly White, she might have snatched Megan to keep her quiet about her fraudulent identity. Discovery would be a disaster.'

'Isn't it possible that Lee found out about Kelly stealing Sarish's jewellery?' Aryan suggested.

‘Kelly could have taken the jewellery,’ Jackie said. ‘but she was on duty in the house at the time Lee disappeared, seen by half a dozen witnesses. As for Megan, why would Kelly want to break into her flat or burn out her car? It’s crazy.’

Aryan turned away to answer his ringing phone.

‘Ben, we need to find out where Kelly was heading when she went to the Metro station and whether she was travelling alone…’

‘Chief Inspector,’ Aryan interrupted. ‘That was our Crime scene officer. She’s saying they’ve discovered two sets of fingerprints at Kelly White’s flat. One unknown, the other belonging to Rees Morgan, the other agency social worker at Lakeside.’

Ben’s groan was all frustration. ‘How the hell did he get mixed up in this?’

‘Do we pick him up now?’ Jackie asked.

Sarah combed fingers through her hair as she thought it through. ‘We’ll bring him in first thing in the morning. Make it formal.’

From across the room, Neil Harper’s furious exclamation was not what Sarah wanted to hear. ‘Chief Inspector, you’re not going to bloody believe this. Tony Ingles has been sighted on the Quigley Estate near Liam Carson’s place. Even worse, it looks like he knows you’re on to him!’

Chapter Nine

HOW THE HELL HAD INGLES DODGED into the country without her knowing? Border control was supposed to be all over this. 'Neil, do we know how long he's been back in Yorkshire?'

'It can't be long. According to Jake Forbes, he's looking tanned.'

'How come Jake is involved?'

'*The World's End Pub* is his local. He was about to walk in when he saw Ingles pulling up outside Liam Carson's place. That was less than five minutes ago. He couldn't believe it.'

'Ingles and Carson were at loggerheads last time I heard. What's happening at Carson's right now?'

Seconds ticked by while Neil asked the question. 'Jake has eyeballed a Darren Coulton and Bradley Walters entering Carson's property, Ma'am.'

'But those two are Ingles men. Is there any trouble, Neil?'

'No Ma'am, quite the reverse. Jake is saying there's an animated discussion taking place and two white vans have driven up.'

'What the hell has Carson got to do with Ingles – unless Carson is involved in *Electric Storm* as well as the jewellery thefts?' Sarah caught Neil Harper's panicked glance. 'Are you telling me Mike Lawson *knew* about the connection?' She bit back the fury; she'd save her wrath for the man himself. 'Not your problem Sergeant, we need to concentrate on the mess we have now. Is Ingles still there?'

Again, the wait. 'He's climbing into his car. I've alerted Carl and he's driving towards the estate.'

‘Tell Carl to ring me as soon as he has visual. Is Mike already in the field?’

Neil’s expression was bleak. ‘Can’t reach him. He’s been out all afternoon following up a lead. It’s some betting scam that’s been going down.’

Sarah bit back the sarcasm. ‘Okay, so it looks like we’re on our own again. Neil, tell Jake Forbes he’s back on duty and to stay put. He’s to keep his eyes on Carson’s property and to give you a running commentary. Does he know what Ingles is driving?’

‘I’ve already passed it to traffic, Chief Inspector. They’re doing a remote follow and they’ll keep me updated.’

‘Jackie, find out who’s in charge of uniform tonight. I need Ingles picked up as soon as it’s safe. I want you to work with Neil and sort that between you.’

Sarah picked up her buzzing mobile. ‘Carl, what’s the situation?’

‘Chief Inspector, I’m on the Quigley Estate at the *World’s End* pub with Jake. One van is outside Carson’s house, the other close to that run of garages. A few of Ingles and Carson’s men have started loading boxes from the house into the vehicles. I’ve called for uniformed support but we’ll need warrants for the house and garages?’

‘Be careful Carl. Liam Carson is an old acquaintance and a notoriously difficult sod. I don’t suppose Mike has contacted you yet?’

‘Not so far, Ma’am.’

‘Then I’ll telephone CS Finchley and explain the problem. We’ve got more than enough for search warrants.’ In her head she could picture the estate: rows of brick-built council houses, most sold off. Unfortunately, there were enough cut-through’s to let a whole army escape and she had nowhere near enough officers to provide adequate backup. ‘Carl, keep your officers well away for now. Use your head, don’t try and trap Ingles and Carson’s men in a corner; they’ll turn nasty. Contact traffic division and explain the situation. Tell them, the vans are not to be stopped until they are well away from that estate. That should limit any innocent casualties being caught up. As soon as the vans are clear we'll tidy up the house.'

Carl sounded hesitant. 'I'll do my best with traffic.'

'No Sergeant, you *tell* the buggers! If they try and pull rank, put them straight through to me and tell them I said so.'

'Understood, Ma'am.'

'Good, Ben and I will be there shortly. Keep me informed via radio.' The phone clicked off.

How the hell was she supposed to manage this without adequate senior support? Sarah scanned the dazed expressions around her; she needed them up and fully functioning. 'Here's the bottom line. Ingles is on the run. Carson is off-loading thousands of pounds in stolen goods – we need to act *now*. Does anyone *not* understand what's at stake?'

'We're on it,' Ben called.

'Neil, Ingles is still your priority. Take Aryan and Jackie with you. Liaise with the duty sergeant. There are potentially half a dozen arrests so you'll need additional support. Under no circumstances attempt to collar Ingles on your own. Now get going.'

Less than six minutes later, Sarah was shading her eyes, trying to soften the glare from the wet roads and the late evening traffic. She rubbed at the throbbing pulse in her forehead and dug into her pocket for painkillers. 'How the hell did Ingles – or Carson for that matter – know we were on to them? There's been nothing for weeks.'

'Are you asking?' Ben queried.

'Do you have an answer?'

'Someone must have tipped them off. I'd like to know how Ingles got through customs without us knowing.'

'It's all bloody worrying Ben.' Sarah swallowed the tablets dry, before glancing down at the ringing mobile – Finchley. 'Sir?' He didn't sound any happier than when she'd requested the warrants. She listened to the blast of information, grateful he'd at least managed to sort the admin. 'Thank you, Sir. I'll keep you informed.'

'Damned right you will. One thing before you ring off. Amos is now on duty. It was him or ask for support from Leeds and I couldn't take any more of their snide comments to be frank. I've sent him directly to Neil Harper in case it gets silly. Any news from Lawson?'

'Not that I'm aware of, Sir.'

'Very well and stay in touch.'

'Any good news?' Ben asked.

'We've got the warrants, – and Finchley's called Amos in a day early. He's supporting Neil.'

'Well, that's something.'

Checking the time, Sarah pressed her home number and Freya answered within seconds.

'You're okay?' The mantra never changed.

'I'm fine, but thanks for asking. We're about to put a few more away so you know your taxes are being put to good use.'

'Any chance you'll be home before midnight?'

'Depends which midnight you mean?' Sarah kept it light but could hear the exhaustion in her voice.

'That bad hey? They should pay you treble.'

'I know but the effort will be worth it. How was your day?' Sanity reigned for several minutes as she listened to a wonderfully normal life. 'That school has no idea how lucky they are, Freya.'

'They do, I keep telling them. Stay safe. I'll leave the blankets out for you just in case.'

'Thanks, love. Speak soon.'

She heard her sergeant's sigh and glanced over. 'Are you feeling reflective Ben, or just tired?'

'Tired mainly and that flat of mine is a dreary sort of place.'

'Change something, the flat if you must. It's too damned easy to put up with mediocre.'

'Well, the hours don't exactly help. Finding time to do anything else would be something.'

'Would you consider leaving?'

'Only when I'm feeling sorry for myself, which surprisingly isn't that often. I think I probably need that holiday.'

'We can always dream. How long before we arrive?'

'Less than three. We're coming up to the edge of the estate now.'

They were less than a quarter of a mile from Carson's house when Jackie Simmons rang. Sarah caught the adrenaline edge to the officer's voice as she reported. 'Chief Inspector, Ingles and three further males have been apprehended. Amos is escorting them back to the station with uniformed officers. He said to tell you, he'll book them in and join you when he can. Neil and I are already in the car. ETA five or less.'

'We'll be waiting in Somerton Street. No sirens Jackie, and use radio contact from now on.' With a sigh, Sarah pushed in her earpiece. The low buzz was never comfortable. 'DCI 1 to DS 1 report. Over.'

Carl Moyles came through loud and clear. 'DS 1, all as planned so far. They've finished loading one vehicle and started on the second. They appear to be planning to move off together. Over.'

'They'll split,' Sarah said confidently. 'Tell traffic to stay vigilant. My team will wait for the vans to leave before engaging. Let me know as soon as. Over.'

'I will do, Ma'am. Out.'

Ben pulled smoothly into the side road and stretched out his long legs. 'It sounds like Carl has stepped up to the crease.'

'I take it that's a cricket analogy?'

'Don't know any bread making ones, Chief Inspector.' Sarah ignored the dry chuckle.

From their vantage point, there was little of the action to see other than two white vans speeding out onto the main road. A short while later, the buzzing in her ear changed to heavy breathing. 'DCI 1, are you doing a spot of running, Carl?'

'DS 1, a suspect decided to try and leg it. Caught him though.' Sarah waited patiently for the panting to ease. 'The two vans have been seized, and, as far as we can ascertain, they didn't manage to alert the household. However, I have to report that the driver of the lead van was going for a firearm under the seat. Over.'

'Understood. I'll contact armed response and ask for a presence before we move in. Is there anything else I need to know? Over.'

'I've got one eye on the house. Do you want more?'

'I'll sort that, Carl. Give your team a breather but stay in the vicinity. I'm going to need you again shortly. Out.'

'That's a bit of good fortune them staying off the phones.' Ben clicked open his door. 'I'll dig out our vests.' He nodded to the blue Astra pulling in alongside. 'I'll make sure they're kitted out as well.'

Chief Superintendent Finchley was less than happy when Sarah rang. 'This is turning into a circus, Allerton. Do you really need the armed response unit?'

'We've apprehended two vans full of heaven knows what, Sir, along with six suspects. We need to do this house search *now*, before they realise the vans have been nabbed and start destroying evidence. I'm not going in unprepared knowing there might be guns.'

'Very well, but try and do a decent recon before they arrive. You know what the armed response team is like.'

'I'm on my way to do it now, Sir,' She cut him off.

Taking the vans out of the equation well away from the houses meant the estate was undisturbed. The net curtains didn't twitch and the dark streets played into their hands this time.

'Ben, take Jackie and Neil and cover the front of Carson's place. Aryan and I will cover the rear and use the garden of the empty house that backs onto it. Report our positions to Carl so he can pass it to the armed response team.'

At least it isn't raining, Sarah thought thankfully. They stopped near an old apple tree a couple of metres from Carson's fence.

'Someone's moving in the attic space,' Aryan whispered. 'I can see a shadow on the skylight – might be two.'

Focusing her binoculars, Sarah concentrated on the lower windows. 'There's another moving on the ground floor, Aryan – the kitchen I believe.'

'AR 1 to DCI 1. Over,' the deep tones were instantly recognisable. Inspector Phil Hancock of the armed response team had a grim reputation.

'Go ahead. Over.'

'ETA 20.24 hrs, Details? Over,' Phil never wasted time or words.

'Three suspects, possibly more. Two currently in the loft and one lower ground back kitchen. Over.'

'I hate bloody lofts. We will execute entries via front and rear entrances. Remain under cover until I give the all-clear. Out.' Brief and to the point as usual.

Sarah checked her watch. 20.19 hrs 'Five minutes to kick-off, Aryan. Keep a sharp lookout for runners.'

'That was quick,' Aryan whispered back. 'Don't armed response usually take forever to decide what they're going to do?'

'Oh, they know these houses well. I think their practice base is built around this estate.' Sarah could sense him studying her, trying to work out if she was serious or not.

At 20.23 hrs, grey shadows moved towards the back door. Sarah kept her binoculars trained on the rear windows. In her head she was counting down. Even from that distance, they heard the commands, loud and intimidating meant to disorientate. '*Police, police, we are armed. On the floor, on the floor.*'

A flicker of something caught her eye. Sarah swivelled the glasses to the left, sighting the leg as it appeared over the sill of the kitchen window. A slim figure in bra, jeans and not much else was attempting to make a run for it. 'How's your rugby tackling, Aryan?'

'Don't know, Ma'am, but happy to find out.'

Sarah leapt the low fence, sprinting wide to cut off the woman's only other route. With a yell of defiance, the woman swept up a lethal-looking branch, aiming for Sarah's head. Aryan drove for her legs, toppling the furious woman to the ground.

'Enough!' Sarah wrenched the impromptu weapon from the woman's fingers. 'Cuff the lady and read her rights, Aryan. I'll have an officer bring her some clothing.'

Her earpiece crackled with a message. 'AR 1 to DCI 1, house empty. You are cleared to enter. Two suspects detained and are currently having problems speaking due to the smoke. Over.'

'Good job and my thanks, Phil. My officer detained a third suspect trying to escape via rear kitchen window. Over.'

'A full house then. Out.'

Against her chest, her personal mobile vibrated. Her panic was instant. Only a handful of people had that number and all knew to message first – unless they were desperate.

'Aryan, inform Ben we have another suspect while I sort this.' She took a step away and glanced down at the missed call. Relief left her light-headed: it wasn't Freya or her son. Sarah hit return call.

'Van arrived outside pub two minutes ago. They've closed early. They're taking everything, Ma'am.'

'Moira, why are you whispering?'

'I'm supposed to be cleaning up. I'll try and send you – got to go.'

'Damn them to hell!' Sarah stared in frustration at the blank screen. The deluge of bad news kept right on coming.

Chapter Ten

'ARYAN, GO FIND A FEMALE OFFICER to deal with this lady, now man, run!' Ignoring the swearing woman at her feet, Sarah waited impatiently for Ben to answer her radio call.

'Ma'am we've hit the jackpot. This...'

'We've a major problem. You and Jackie to the car now. I'll explain when I meet you there. Out. Carl, where the hell are you? Over.'

'Chief Inspector, I can't believe what we've...'

The cheerful reply grated. Sarah cut him dead. 'The night isn't over Carl, so don't start celebrating. You and Neil finish this between you, I'm taking Ben Peterson and Jackie Simmons with me. I'll also take two uniformed constables and a plain car. Make sure you detail this place down to the last cat flea, is that understood? Don't take any crap. If anyone wants to argue, you tell them to be in front of my desk first thing tomorrow. Over.'

'Yes, Ma'am, I'll have the constables waiting at the gate.'

She could hear the question hanging but she didn't give him a chance to ask. 'I'll leave Aryan with you, Carl. That was a good job tonight. Out.' She clicked off, not waiting for a reply.

Susan Carson sneered up at her from the damp ground. 'You think you're sodding wonder woman.'

'I'd better be Susan, there's no other idiot around to do the job tonight. Stand up woman or you'll be soaked through.'

'Like you sodding care.'

'It's your backside.'

Aryan came hurrying back, two female officers at his side. 'You're clear to go, Chief Inspector. Ben has driven up by the house.'

Sarah was already moving, shouting orders over her shoulder as she went. 'Work with Carl, Aryan. Remember the chain of evidence – keep things tight.'

Her feet wouldn't move fast enough. Turning the corner of the house, the fumes from the smoke caught at her throat. Uniformed officers were everywhere, huge in their flak jackets. One suspect she didn't recognise sat hunched over, pale and shaken. Another, Liam Carson, stood glowering darkly, handcuffs in place. The rest of the street had woken up. Lights blazed as heads hung out of windows, dogs adding a snarling descant. It took seconds to take it all in. Sarah raced down the path to where Ben and Jackie were waiting. 'How far are we from the *Blue Beacon*?'

They were instantly alert. 'Ten minutes, no seven this time of night.' Ben had already opened her door.

'Jackie, tell the constables in the car behind where we're going and to follow, no siren. They're to keep a decent distance and use the radio. We'll assess the situation when we arrive.' Thirty seconds later they were on the main road. Every part of her body ached, eyelids like lumps of lead. Sarah opened the glove compartment hoping to find something sweet.

'Under the seat, Ma'am, I always keep a couple of glucose drinks stashed.'

'Nice work, Ben.' Sarah popped the tin and drank deeply. The next few minutes were spent explaining to the night sergeant, what was going on.

'I'm running out of space, Sarah. If you could limit your collars to say four or so?'

Sarah managed a laugh. 'Anything to oblige, Chris. Do you have any immediate problems?'

'The usual, a few lawyers doing their song and dance, but nothing I can't manage.'

'Any chance Lawson is contactable yet?'

'No, I've been trying on and off for the last couple of hours.' The criticism was evident even over the phone.

'Is Amos still there?'

'Aye, thank the gods, he's finishing off. I'll pass on the latest info and arrange for him to meet up. You stay safe, Sarah. If you need backup, I have a couple of constables that I could send on? Do you want me to let the CS know what's going off?'

'Yes and yes,' her shoulders relaxed a centimetre or so. 'But tell him I'm incommunicado for the next half an hour.'

Ben interrupted. 'We're almost there.'

She reeled off the address and firm instructions. 'Don't let those officers come thundering in, Chris.'

'No chance. They'll have me to deal with if they get it wrong. I'll tell them to park up and wait until they get word.'

Yet another dark road, she thought, as her sergeant slowed to negotiate the narrowing streets. Walking into the unknown wasn't a new experience – but there'd been a few times down the years that she'd been left with bitter reminders of how much there was to lose. Friends, the colleagues she would never see again – not this time she hoped. They parked at the far end of Albion Street where an open space backed onto a few boarded-up shops with no prying neighbours to give them away. The pub was still a couple of hundred metres further on. At the other end of the row of terraced houses, the vague outline of a vehicle was barely visible. At this end of the city, there was little traffic to bother them.

The radio crackled. 'PC Evans, Chief Inspector. I grew up around here. If you don't mind walking, I can get you opposite the pub and that van. It will mean going through the alleys at the back of the houses.'

Ben expanded the focus of the digital street map. 'Looks feasible.'

Leaving the other uniformed officer on watch, they slipped across the shadowy space and into the relative shelter of the first alley. A corrugated roof rattled as a large tabby leapt away.

'How many bloody cats live around here,' Jackie whispered, as another hissed from an open gate.

'More than enough to keep the local fast-food outlets going.'

'Evans, don't…' Sarah's pocket vibrated again. The phone was to her ear in record time.

'*Trapped in the cellar...*' the line went dead.

'Move it, they must have sussed her.'

They made their way past countless wheelie bins until finally, Evans pointed ahead. 'Next corner, Ma'am.'

Easing in beside a stack of old pallets, Sarah focused on the van now directly opposite, rear doors wide open. Flickering light from the pub's grubby windows cast dancing shadows onto the pavement making it difficult to judge distance. Beside her, Ben crouched like a coiled spring. A shadow loomed onto the pavement as a figure jumped from the back of the van. A muted call rose from the open cellar. '*Stu, give us a hand…*'

'Sod it!' Ben's whispered exclamation echoed her own. Moira Robins' slumped body was being hauled up and out through the cellar doors.

'*Wait*!' Sarah urged sensing the tightening of Ben's muscles. Carelessly, the two men rolled the woman into the back of the van. One turned to disappear back into the cellar while the other clambered into the driving seat.

'Evans, close and secure that cellar access. Jackie, secure those pub doors back and front, buy us some time. Ben, I'll distract the driver while you move around to the passenger side and take him out. As soon as we've taken care of the driver, radio the night sergeant to send backup in immediately – with sirens the lot and get the car down here.'

Grabbing an empty beer can from the several in the alley, Sarah edged onto the street. Pulling her jacket wide open she began to sway. Freya would be impressed she thought, as she danced and sang her way toward the van. 'I've had a lovely time,' she slurred thumping a fist onto the bonnet of the van. 'You wanna drink?'

Startled, the driver swung around in his seat, gesticulating. 'Piss off!'

'Just wanna bit of fun,' Sarah warbled reaching for the door of the van.

Growling threats, he started to roll down his window. 'If you don't piss off I'll...' The air turned blue as Ben Peterson's experienced hands slammed him hard against the door frame.

Sarah ran to the rear of the large van to find Evans already inside, a finger pressed to Moira's neck. 'She's breathing, Chief Inspector, but there's a nasty gash on the side of her head. Do we move her?'

Ben's car pulled to a hurried stop and the uniformed officer jumped out to race back for the other vehicle. In the distance sirens were blaring – it was going to be a close-call.

'More suspects in the cellar,' Jackie warned. 'And someone's hammering on the side window in the bar.'

Moira's groggy but recognisable Scottish brogue carried clearly onto the pavement. 'I'm going nowhere 'till I bloody find it, do you here?'

'Let's move her and fast!' Sarah ordered. It took three of them to persuade the dazed woman to slide into the back of the waiting car. Evans slammed the door shut as a pub window exploded into a thousand shards.

'Ben – get us the hell out of here!'

Moira groaned as she tried to focus. 'Oh Jes' my sodding head. Where's my mobile, did you pick it up?'

Sarah left Jackie to deal with the confused woman while she answered the call from the duty desk sergeant.

'Wanted to tell you that Amos Brantley is less than a minute away.'

‘Tell him we’ve retrieved Robins, but the suspects are about to make a run for it. Vehicle registration is...’ Sarah reeled off the van’s number and make.

‘I’ll inform traffic Sarah. Stay safe.’

From the back seat, Robins’ complaints sounded reassuringly normal. ‘They must’ve grabbed it when the sods knocked me out…’

Jackie was doing her best to keep Moira still. ‘We’ll soon be at A&E.’

‘I’ll be fine. I need a wee sleep is all.’

‘Sounds like she’s had a few,’ Ben said as the car accelerated away.

‘Wish I bloody had. Damn it – did I hit send, Ma’am? – hell, I feel sick…’

‘Moira try and relax. We’ll sort whatever it is back at the station.’

Again, the car phone spluttered into life. ‘It’s Amos, Sarah. I’ve just pulled up outside the *Beacon*. I’ll organise the search and finish off here. How’s Moira?’

‘Grumpy, about to throw up, but very much alive. She’s rambling on about her phone, Amos. I think she must have dropped it during the struggle?’

‘I’ll check it out, don’t worry. I’ve got the rest covered here. The van has disappeared but traffic will pick it up soon enough. The CS unit is on the way ready to do the deed unless you want to come back to supervise?’

‘I owe you one, Amos.’

‘Don’t I know it. I’ve left Carl and Neil ploughing through the Carson end of things.’ There were shouts in the background. ‘I’d better shoot, Sarah, catch you later.’

Chapter Eleven

Wednesday - early morning

The Pit

OUTSIDE, THE NOVEMBER AIR was damp yet mild for late autumn. A few leaves clung on, softening skeletal branches with bursts of ragged amber. Inside, the pit was freezing. The four teenagers exhaled a grey mist with each breath. The heater had packed up a few nights ago so they huddled together as close as the chains allowed, blankets wrapped about their heads and shoulders, the spares draped around their legs and still they shivered. A single bulb shot spears of frigid light through the metal grating, making it impossible to tell when dawn arrived. Simon hoped that food would arrive soon.

Paula coughed, a racking sound that vibrated around the concrete walls. They'd all been ill, sneezing and sniffling, but Paula wasn't improving. Simon's stomach did the familiar queasy dance as the heavy garage doors grated open. Any flicker of hope faded as the familiar voices echoed around the workshop. In the gloomy silence, Simon watched shadows flicker across the grating until the command was again shouted.

'Hoods on!'

Nobody disobeyed.

Inside the hessian sacking, Simon could see nothing. Beside him, he felt Paula's slim frame shudder as she tried to quell her latest coughing fit. He could hear Kayla muttering something trying to soothe her.

A thud – not the usual sack of food landing? Chains rattled – the pulley used to move them in and out of the pit was being lowered. Fear gripped Simon and his stomach heaved, but they hadn't come for him. No – Paula was being dragged to her feet.

'Haul her up. Come on, I wanna have my breakfast.' The man sounded bored.

'No, I don't want to...' The girl's pleas were muffled, already fading.

Simon couldn't stop the words. 'Where are you taking her?' The slap sent him reeling.

'Nowhere you wanna go kid, least not yet. Now shut it.'

Rosa, the youngest started to sob and Simon leant across to feel for her trembling hand. In the garage above they heard Callum, the boss. The bass Scottish accent made the man sound a million times more threatening.

'We'll have to run with five, can't risk someone hearing that racket. And get that heater replaced, it's no wonder they got sick. Just shut that kid up and dump her in the usual spot.'

Rosa's screams covered the worst of the commotion. Simon clung to her, feeling Kayla's hand gripping his. The silence that followed was so much worse.

Callum called down, his voice cold and emotionless. 'Enjoy the extra space. There'll be another joining you soon enough.' The rattle of the grating followed as somewhere nearby a cock crowed.

***

It was the smell of coffee and a lingering sense of urgency that woke Sarah. She hadn't expected to sleep, but exhaustion won out. Something was pressing – important – that she'd meant to follow up and she'd fallen asleep with the worry rattling her subconscious. It had been past one in the morning when she'd left Hepsford station, her colleagues buzzing with euphoria. They'd made more arrests in one night than they'd done in weeks, but it had only taken a glance at the incident board with its unanswered questions about Lee for her to crash back to earth. The Ingles and Carson's of this world were easy but how the hell could they find a missing fifteen-year-old? The puzzle had kept her company as she'd driven home through the dark streets. With a sigh, Sarah threw off the blanket. Sleeping in her clothes was never wise, but what the hell – it didn't happen often. Showered and changed, Sarah searched for her car keys and found them on the kitchen table, next to a bowl of cereal and a carton of fresh orange juice with a note from Freya, large, impossible to miss. *EAT!* It was tempting to pour them straight back into the packet, but Freya had developed a nose for spotting deceit – probably because she'd lived with a DI for six years.

The drive to work gave Sarah space to click her head into another gear, although it took longer than usual to work out what the hold-up was outside the police station. The flash of a camera brought sharp focus. *That's all we need, press on our tail for the next forty-eight hours*, thought Sarah. Hoping there would be room in the underground car park, Sarah drove on, ignoring the flurry of hands and click of cameras. At the barrier, a security guard waved her to a stop.

'Morning, Ma'am. ID please.'

She flashed the slim wallet his way. 'How long have they been camped outside?'

'News must have hit the websites about five, so not long after. We're all looking forward to the headlines.'

Sarah managed a wry smile. 'I can't wait.'

'Morning Detective Chief Inspector Allerton,' Sergeant Andrew Palmer sounded particularly officious as she walked into the rear reception area. He handed over the signing in book. 'I'm afraid the *reader*'s still down.'

A slim man, probably in his forties she guessed, lounged against the counter, a briefcase at his feet. He turned to give her the once over, waves of self-importance oozed from every fibre of his second-rate suit. Sarah didn't need to see his ID to know he was a lawyer.

'Edward Blyth...' a manicured hand thrust a small card onto the page where she was attempting to sign. The edges, she noted, were printed with red and blue stripes. 'I understand you're responsible for arresting my...'

Sarah raised a hand. 'I have only this minute arrived on duty.'

Making a show of glancing at his watch, Blyth swaggered disapproval. 'While Anthony Ingles has been languishing in a cell for almost twelve hours? Not good enough, Chief Inspector.'

'Then he's had seven hours more rest than I have, Mr Blyth.' Sarah continued to write on the form – 08.35. 'Sergeant, please inform Chief Superintendent Finchley I've arrived.'

'Ma'am, DS Moyles needs a word when you have a moment. It's about the assault at Canal Bridge.' Sarah caught the sergeant's wink as she sidled away. The lawyers could go and boil their heads – she wasn't in the mood.

Pushing through the doors into serious crime's incident room, Sarah immediately detected the heightened tension. The source was easy to identify. Mike Lawson sat on the edge of a table glowering at two young officers.

Ben hastily waved her over. 'Morning, Chief Inspector.'

Dumping her bag on a chair, Sarah ignored the undercurrent of hostility. 'What time did you finally get away, Ben?'

'About ten minutes after you, Ma'am. I've been in about fifteen minutes. The manager from the children's home in Hull emailed over that photograph and you are right: Kelly and Shauna are one and the same. The manager also mentioned that the woman was reprimanded for having an inappropriate relationship on the premises with a Richard Gatley, a council gardener. I've got Jackie and Aryan chasing up the Hull care agency that hired her.'

Across the room, Lawson's tirade grew louder. 'What the hell has got up Mike Lawson's nose this time?'

'Discovering that Carson played a big part in *Electric Storm* as well as the jewellery raids. He's not a happy man. It doesn't help that Neil suggested days ago that Ingles and Carson had to be connected. Neil wanted to talk to you about it, but Lawson refused to listen. Told him he was being a wise arse.'

'That would explain his bad mood. How much of the jewellery did they retrieve in the end?'

'At the last count, coming up to seventy-five per cent. Stuffing the goods inside the wall insulation in the loft was a clever ruse. It was lucky armed response made it up there before Carson had finished sealing the place up.'

'Is there a breakdown of what was in the vans yet?'

'Mostly electrical goods from three of the superstores. Even better, Carson isn't prepared to go down alone. He's talking so much that we can't keep up. Ingles is going to have a tough time wriggling his way out of this one.'

'Talking of which – his lawyer is upstairs. We'll need to arrange interviews, though I resent Lee's case losing more time to those idiots.'

'Watch your back, Ma'am…'

Sarah ignored the stalking spectre of Lawson as he strode towards her. 'Ben, before we start on Ingles, ring the CPU and arrange a meeting here for midday. Have we followed up with Rees Morgan yet?'

'Not so far'

'Have someone bring him to the station – this morning. We could also do with another chat with Matt Cox.' Careful to keep her expression neutral, Sarah turned. 'Mike, is there something you need?'

'When were you frigging going to tell me. Did you think it was sodding funny?'

All work in the large room stopped dead, the grating of the overstretched ventilation system filling the vacuum. Sarah eyed the furious man, mentally rolling her shoulders. The days of holding her tongue were long over. 'What the hell is your issue, Mike? Sergeant Hollings and Neil Harper tried raising you half a dozen times last night. Carl Moyles tried. What should we have done? Waited until you decided to put in an appearance? We did what was needed to get the job sorted. Your sergeant did excellent work...'

Spittle lined the corner of his lips as he sneered. 'Bollocks. You've known for sodding weeks about the link with Ingles...'

'Wrong! I did not have prior knowledge of the connection between the two men. If *you* had bothered to share information, that point might have become obvious? *Your* team were given regular updates of the superstore and delivery-van raids, everything needed to make those connections, so why the hell didn't you?'

'Don't you tell me how to do my frigging job. You think you're something, don't you? Nothing's changed, you're still as incompetent ...' He was struggling to stay in control. 'If you were anything like a decent detective I'd...'

She cut across him before he had time to finish the sentence. 'You'd what, Inspector? – I don't have the time or the inclination to waste words on you. Too much to do.'

'And there, I thought you'd nailed all the bastards last night. Lost a few though didn't you?'

He was a tall man towering over her but, if he thought for a second she was intimidated he was wrong. Anger only heightened the redness of his skin, highlighting the broken tracks of purple around his nose and eyes. As Lawson moved a step closer, Sarah caught the whiff of stale alcohol. She'd wondered for a while how much of a drink problem he had. The devil inside her wanted to goad, wanted to push.

'A fifteen-year-old has been missing for over two days, another is in hospital with serious head injuries, a young woman has disappeared. All that happened last night *Mike*, was a load of crap that prevented us from sorting the mess.

You want to feel bad about not being around? Fine, but don't you *dare* dump it on me and my team!' There was a second when she swore she saw guilt.

'Go to hell,' he hissed and stormed out through the double doors without a backward glance.

Around her no one moved a muscle. 'Doesn't anyone in this damned room have work to do?'

The place erupted into life and everyone, apart from Ben Peterson, astutely avoided eye contact. Consciously, Sarah unclenched rigid fists aware her gut was knotted with anger. 'Bastard! I could have done without that this morning.'

'Oh, it needed to be said. He tore into Neil as soon as he'd set foot through the door.'

'Neil didn't...?'

'No, Ma'am. He picked up his paperwork and left. He's a stronger man than I am. If he'd spoken to me like that – well, Lawson would be in A&E and I'd probably be out of a job.' Ben cleared his throat. 'Anyway, onto the morning's update. Moira has a moderate concussion and her memory of the last few days is hazy. They are keeping her in to do a precautionary scan and she'll be off for a couple of weeks. Dan is woozy but coming around.'

Tuning in to her sergeant's report helped the swirling knots of anger unravel. 'Thanks Ben, much appreciated. Last night wasn't easy.'

Ben grinned, his demeanour lightening. 'Fun though, chasing proper villains.'

'I'd enjoy the sensation while it lasts. Give it another year or so and I can promise – it'll wear off.' Sarah ran through her mental list while smoothing out the last ripples of irritation. Lawson would not get inside her head – there was too much to do. 'Give Jackie a ring, ask her to visit Moira after she and Aryan have dealt with the care agency. She could at least take an initial statement...'

The incident room doors swung inward. Half expecting another round with Mike Lawson, it was a relief to see Amos Brantley stroll in. 'Sarah, you can't have had more than four hours?'

'Almost five and a half and you can talk.'

'I'm six months younger than you, remember?' He perched on the edge of the desk, arms folded as he studied her. 'I take it you've had a run-in with Lawson.' It wasn't a question.

'He's a prat, seems to think the world has conspired against him. Is it my fault he wasn't around when the crap hit the fan?'

'Where was he out of interest?' He looked across at Ben who shrugged.

'No idea.' Sarah tried unsuccessfully to ditch the sarcasm. 'Doubtless one of his *special ears* had something to tell him.'

'Well, DCI Allerton,' Amos slid to his feet, all business. 'You'll be pleased to know they've picked up that van from the *Beacon* with the goods still intact. The driver and two passengers are in custody. We've got decent forensics, so we should be able to pick up anyone else involved soon enough. In the meantime, how about I interview Moira? It'll tie in with the effort I put in last night. I'll need the phones you and she used to keep in contact and the log sheet when you can find a moment.'

Unlocking the desk drawer took seconds. Signing the appropriate pages, Sarah handed over the mobile and notebook. 'Apart from the one call Moira made to my personal number last night, all contact we had is registered on there. I haven't seen sight of Moira's mobile, Amos. I assume you didn't find it on one of the suspects or in the pub?'

'No sign so far, they could have thrown it from the van I suppose. Anyway, I'll keep searching. I'll pick up the Paul Wiggins end of things as well. I've just heard that there's a lead on Adam Farnes' whereabouts, so I'll take a couple of uniformed officers to pick him up, see if I can find any link to your young lad. Carl and Neil will stay and finish off the

Carson/Ingles job. Lawson can pick up anything new that comes in. I've already spoken to that stiff-lipped lawyer upstairs, which gives you free rein with the rest of the Lee Wiggins case?'

Already Sarah felt the tension easing from her shoulders. 'It's so good to have you back, Amos.'

'Be grateful for small mercies.'

Her colleague wouldn't quite meet her gaze. She'd known him for far too long to be unaware of the signals. 'What aren't you telling me, Brantley?' The crooked smile was charming – it didn't fool her for a second.

'Sarah, if I knew I'd tell you wouldn't I? Better get on, things to do.' He was gone before she had a chance to dig deeper.

'Ben, what's he up to?'

'No idea – honestly,' he added catching her frown. 'Shall I finish making that call to CPU?'

'Do it and let's have everyone who's been involved in the door to door enquiries in as well. Make it later, 13.30 hrs. Let's see if we can't unscramble a piece of this mess. Now we have some free time, we can fit in a quick visit to Megan's flat. I want to take another look for myself.'

'But the crime scene photos are in the file?'

'I know, which is why I want to go back. There's something out about the place.'

At her hip, an alert buzzed. Picking up the nearest phone she dialled. 'Jackie, you wanted me?'

'Chief Inspector, legal contacted the care agency in Hull so we could access Shauna Richardson's personnel file. We've finished checking and she's definitely a *ghost*.'

It took a moment for the information to register. 'Go on, I'm listening.'

'There's the usual information but we've contacted the numbers for the references she gave and they've each come back as unknown.'

‘What the hell happened with the security checks?’

‘They *were* carried out, Ma’am. There are copies in the file but the addresses must have been bogus, one-time use only.’

‘Have you spoken to the agency manager? Did she interview the woman herself?’

‘Yes and she’s pretty upset about the whole thing.’

‘Do the same checks for her under the name Kelly White for the agency in Hepsford as soon as you can – ask them to send through copies of anything they have on her.’

‘Will do. Is there anything else, Ma’am?’

‘You two have breakfast. Today is going to be a long one.’

Carl Moyles answered her call at the first ring. ‘Chief Inspector, just to inform you, I received a transcript from Paul Wiggins’ mobile provider. Monday morning, he received a text at 08.47 from Adam Farnes. The text reads: *‘You’d better not say a sodding word.’* He also received a call from a different number at 15.39 hrs. The call lasted for twenty-two seconds. It’s from a burn phone, and untraceable.’

‘Have you relayed this to Amos?’

‘I did and he told me he’d be talking to you – only,’ Carl’s voice dropped to a whisper. ‘Mike Lawson collared me first thing. He said something about knowing Farnes of old and taking over the Farnes case. Is that what you want, Ma’am?’

‘No it bloody is not! I’ve already spoken to Amos. This stays with you two. Any problems with Mike, you call me.’

The phone was hardly back on the table when Sarah heard her name being called from the doorway. ‘DCI Allerton, could I have ten minutes of your time – my office?’

She couldn’t exactly refuse the Chief Super. ‘I’ll see you out by your car, Ben.’

Finchley’s office was, as usual, organised to the point of sterility. Apart from the laptop, a single photo frame and a folder, there was nothing to clutter his huge desk. He waved her towards a chair. ‘I’m aware you’re ultra-busy sorting the fallout from last night’s events, Sarah. Of course, I’m thrilled to be able to report to the chief constable the significant success you and the teams achieved. However, we have to acknowledge that it wasn't without problems. Those *knock-on effects*, some of which I alluded to in our previous meetings?'

Finchley cleared his throat. Sarah wished he'd get to the point.

'It's obvious now that the landlord of the *Blue Beacon* was indeed one of the major players. Certainly, the investment of man-hours and undercover work paid off. Who knows, Revenue & Customs officers might listen to us next time? But surely you should have realised that, as a result of arresting Tony Ingles another key player in all this, the landlord of the *Beacon* would be one of the first to find out? As soon as he did, he would want to off-load the spirits? It's an oversight that almost cost DC Robins her life. Furthermore...'

'Sir,' she interrupted, 'Are you implying the *Blue Beacon* was connected to Ingles?'

'Well, obviously it was.'

Where the hell had this come from? Sarah pushed down her frustration, trying to order her thoughts. 'Ingles to Carson yes, which admittedly was a major surprise, but Ingles or Carson to the *Beacon*? No way Sir, categorically not. We've had DC Robins inside for almost a month. There's been feedback from half a dozen sources around the midlands and north east and not one has come back with even the slimmest connection to either of them.'

Finchley blinked rapidly absorbing the news. 'Interesting,' he muttered though she wasn't convinced he was talking to her.

'Sir...?'

'Right, well thank you for your time.' Finchley rose to his feet, the interview over.

Surprised, Sarah stood not quite sure what had happened. 'I will need to talk to you later, Sir. It has to do with the Lee Wiggins case?'

‘Oh absolutely, anything you need. Now, I’m sure you have important things to be getting on with, Chief Inspector?’ He was already hustling her through the door.

‘And thank *you,* Sir,’ but Sarah was talking to the already closed door. *Weird*, she thought, *but he hadn’t had a lot of sleep either.*

Chapter Twelve

MEGAN SHAW'S LOUNGE WAS as sparsely furnished as Sarah remembered. 'Given the young woman has lived here for almost nine months, tell me what strikes you first about the room?'

Ben glanced around, taking in the new sofa, an old but comfortable looking high-backed chair, a cabinet next to the wall with a television perched on top and a small radio resting on a shelf. Apart from a couple of vases, two throws and a soft toy there was little else. 'There aren't many bits and pieces, Ma'am.'

'You're right and only the one photograph, not exactly cosy, is it?' Sarah gave the bedroom a cursory inspection before walking back to study the photograph of an elderly woman, likely the grandmother. Photographed seated in the same old high backed chair, she was laughing, dark eyes glinting with life. 'Well, it's easy to see she's related to Megan.'

Careful not to damage the print, Sarah unclasped the back of the frame and Ben bent to pick up the few pages that fell out onto the floor. The death certificate was a surprise. 'The name on the certificate reads Catherine Marie Jamieson, not Stuart, as listed on the next of kin form and this is a birth certificate for a Louise Marie Jamieson?'

'Interesting – take a look at this.' Sarah held up a photograph that had been slotted behind the one of the old woman. It showed a young couple, just married – obviously in love from the pose. 'Given the likeness, I'd say these must be

Megan's parents. It begs the question why Megan has this hidden away.'

'Family feud perhaps?'

'Could be...'

'DVLA might have an original copy of Megan's birth certificate?'

'You could try Ben, but I doubt it somehow. Why did the grandmother change their names I wonder?'

'Stuart could have been the grandmother's maiden name. I'll see what we can dig up. Do we carry on searching the flat?'

'No, we've enough for now and there's Rees Morgan to interview.' Sarah ran an appreciative hand over the shaped wings and back of the old chair. 'You'd pay a fortune for an original like this.'

'There's a decent house clearance place next to the old market. You might pick one up there?'

'I'll bear that in mind, Ben. Make sure the door locks behind us.'

***

Porter's office was a welcome refuge from the noise and clutter of the incident room. With a short lull before her interview with Rees Morgan, Sarah spread out the snippets of information they'd accrued and tried to make sense of the mess. What the hell was the catalyst for this cascade of disasters? If Adam Farnes turned out to be responsible for Lee's disappearance, it would explain part of the puzzle – disgruntled ex-employee takes his wrath out on the boss and his nearest and dearest? As for the rest – the attack on Dan might make sense if the woman calling herself Kelly White feared Dan was about to report her. Would she really batter the lad over the head with a metal bar and then make Megan Shaw somehow vanish? It was a stretch. And then there was Mason! Sarah underlined his name before scribbling a note to chase up where Kelly White travelled to from the Metro station. Sarah trawled through the witness statements concerning Megan. No one had a bad word to say about her: friends, staff, teenagers, each equally shocked and upset by her disappearance. Having spoken to Megan, it was hard to visualise the woman being involved in Mason's murder. Sarah put the file to one side and picked up the witness statements on Lee. Turning to a clean page, she began to jot down phrases that sprang out at her.

De-Silva's, *'Lee has been settled for weeks now. He's made friends, picked up his skateboarding again – he's happy – it shows in everything he does.'*

Dan's '*There was no reason for him to piss off – He had money. He was going to work at that engineering place. He'd been going on about it forever.'*

Kate's equally insistent – *'He looked so happy. There's no way he'd run away – He had no reason to.'*

Adai's '*Dan didn't want to – She put this hat on his head – When she left, Dan looked really pissed off.'*

Kate's – '*Someone gave Dan a beanie with the hammers' logo on, but he gave it to Lee.'*

The cold shiver had nothing to do with a lack of heating. She'd almost had it last night – before the Ingles/Carson fiasco had pushed every other thought from her head. Sarah plucked out the description of what Lee was wearing that morning – typical teenage clothing: mostly black and dark blue, apart from the maroon beanie with the West Ham logo to the front, the hat Dan was supposed to be wearing? Prickles of doubt crept in. *Guesswork again, Allerton? Bloody second rate copper – you're only here so they can tick bloody boxes.* Sarah picked up the phone, determined not to let Lawson push inside her head.

A short while later, her sergeant looked less than impressed when she explained her theory. 'Lee mistaken for Dan? That's one huge leap, Ma'am, and why target Dan? And what if Kelly was involved, who was she working with? She'd definitely need a partner. No, it doesn't make sense…'

‘It does if you take into account the incident report from the children’s home in Hull. They’re eerily similar, Ben. Theft of jewellery, Tanya Daly missing, everyone at the time assumed the jewellery theft and Tanya running off were linked. We know this Kelly/Shauna woman was in both places so perhaps she’s responsible for both disappearances – maybe part of a trafficking deal? The thefts could be nothing more than a decoy?’

‘How the hell do you go from one missing teenager to that? Sorry Ma’am, but Tanya’s disappearance is fourteen months ago? This is way out...’

‘Is it? The only difference I can see between the two incidents, other than time and geography, is that Tanya had a history of running off. According to the file, Tanya was normally found quickly, usually within a few days or a week at the most. Swap Dan for Lee and what do we have? The same scenario.’

‘This is pure conjecture. The CS will laugh us out of the station.’

’Which is why we keep this quiet – for now. After Tanya’s final disappearance we know there was the usual search, postings on websites...’

‘If Lakeside is anything to go by they really care. They’ve been on the news, radio and there are posters everywhere.’

‘What if a youngster has a reputation for running off, say like Dan? I’m not saying they wouldn’t report it but given Tanya and Dan’s previous history of absconding…?’ Sarah paused, tapping the table as she thought. ‘Tanya reported her mobile stolen twenty-four hours before she absconded, so check with Lakeside, see who’s lost theirs. I’ll put money on it that Dan’s phone has gone missing.’

‘Why would Kelly bother to steal their mobile phones?’

‘GPS tracking and they’d have a useful tool to send decoy messages?’

Ben clicked on his pen. 'So, are you saying we're kicking the Farnes enquiry into touch?'

Sarah could understand his scepticism – she was asking a lot. 'Of course not! However, for the next couple of hours before the briefing, I want you to trawl through missing minors lists, teenagers specifically. Have Aryan help but keep it between the two of you. Concentrate on the ones with a history of running from residential or respite care. If you can, check if money or jewellery went missing at around the same time – maybe a mobile phone as well? I'm hoping I'm wrong and this is no more than my tired brain tripping me up.'

'Isn't this a bit extreme? All for two teenagers and the incidents happening almost fourteen months apart? It has to be Farnes who took the boy – A disgruntled worker out to take his revenge? Or Lee flipped and just legged it.'

Sarah expected – even encouraged – her junior officers to question, it was part of the process and she'd been known to be wrong occasionally. 'Two missing youngsters both in care placements. Two thefts within a tight time-frame of their disappearing. Add to that, Megan and this Kelly/Shauna woman were in the same children's homes when the incidents took place. Kelly leaves Hepsford hours after Lee goes missing and then Megan disappears? The fact that Adam Farnes threatened the uncle…'

'And there's the missing van, Ma'am.'

'Which, according to one of the mechanics, hasn't been seen for a couple of weeks. Farnes and the van do not mean we should ignore other possibilities.' Sarah closed her eyes for a moment. What she wouldn't give for a few hours sleep. 'Adam Farnes would provide us with a simple, straightforward solution and I won't discount the possibility, however...'

'So, this search, do you want it nationwide?' Ben began to write rapidly, covering the page in his neat script.

'Start with the East coast, say from Whitby southward and inland across as far as York.'

‘Any particular time scale?’

‘Two years and keep it to eleven to sixteen year-olds. That should keep the two of you busy for a while?’ Sarah smiled at the groaning sigh. ‘I’ll be interviewing Mr Morgan if you need me. That’s if I can find a free room.’

***

Rees Morgan wasn’t the most prepossessing of men. Admittedly, interview rooms tended to strip away the trappings of glamour but the slim, mousey-haired man seated opposite was anxious. His relentless crossing and un-crossing of legs was infuriating. Sarah swallowed her irritation and tried again. ‘It’s a simple enough question, Mr Morgan. What was your relationship with the woman you know as Kelly White?’

‘I worked with her, we had a couple of drinks together once or twice.’

‘So you were dating?’

Wide-eyed now, Rees licked pale lips. Again, the legs crossed and un-crossed. ‘No – we were just friends.’

He was lying – even her son was a better liar than this man. Sarah was losing patience. ‘I have to remind you that you are under caution. As your solicitor will confirm, there’s a stiff penalty for lying to the police. So, let’s start from the beginning. How did you meet the woman you know as Kelly White?’

Fidgeting nervously, Morgan glanced briefly across at the duty solicitor. ‘About six weeks ago I went to the Care Agency in Hepsford to sort out some shifts and things. When I left, she was hanging about in the doorway. We got chatting that’s all. She told me she was new to Hepsford and that she was signing up with the agency. Kelly had her DBS clearance and references, but it can be hard starting in a new area; you’re usually handed the crappiest jobs. Anyway, we ended up going for a coffee. Basically, she came on to me. She was nice you know, and easy to get on with. A couple of days later she asked me to help her out.'

'Explain, *help her out*?'

'I know the assistant manager at the agency, so I put in a good word for her. What's wrong with that?'

'You telephoned Mr Atkins at the agency and said what, Mr Morgan?' The answer was inside the brown folder on the table.

'I just told you, I put in a good word...'

'For the tape, DC Jackie Simmons is now handing Mr Morgan a copy of a transcript of a telephone conversation, recorded on September the fourteenth at eleven twenty am, at Hepsford Nursing and Care Agency. I'll read out a short section.

'"*I've known Kelly for over two years. I've worked with her on numerous occasions, she's great with teenagers...*" Those statements are lies, Mr Morgan. Kelly was new to this area. Your record shows you have not worked in any youth placements outside of Hepsford. Again, a few lines further on. "*Kelly has masses of experience. Over the years I've known her, she hasn't put a foot wrong...*" Yet at that point, you'd known her for less than a week?'

'It was just a telephone conversation. The agency didn't have to give her any work and they should have checked her references…'

The schoolboy whine set Sarah's teeth on edge. 'The woman you know as Kelly White does not exist – the name she used and her so-called experience are fabrications.'

Rees folded his arms across his chest. 'Rubbish, she'd worked all over. She was always talking about the different places she'd been.'

It was difficult for Sarah to imagine him working with any child. 'This isn't some parking ticket. Providing a reference written or verbal that you know to be untrue for anyone working within the childcare sector is a criminal offence. The consequences of your action left vulnerable young people at the mercy of a woman, who at the very least is guilty of fraud. One of those young people is now missing.'

'Oh, come on. You can't seriously think Kelly had anything to do with that?'

'Do you know where the woman is right now, Mr Morgan?'

'If she's not in her flat or work then she might have moved on again. Kell doesn't like to stay in one place for too long.'

'Well, isn't that convenient?' Sarah smothered her fury – she didn't have the energy to deal with his level of stupidity. 'Officer Simmons will stay and take your full statement. You will give her every detail of the workplaces Kelly White mentioned. Do not think of leaving the city. There may well be more questions.'

'I won't be going to court or anything will I?' The whine was back.

'I'd suggest you have a long conversation with your solicitor, Mr Morgan. Doubtless, he'll provide you with details of likely prosecutions. Officer Simmons, when you're finished here I'll be in the main incident room.'

Sarah checked the door had closed before she released the explosive hiss of frustration. 'What a complete and utter ass of a man!'

'Chief Inspector...?'

Aryan Khan must have been waiting for her to come out. He had the look of a startled puppy, not quite sure whether to run or brazen it out. Sarah grimaced. 'Obviously, that was not aimed at you, Aryan. Did you need me for something?'

'That program I used on the CCTV footage from the *Cock & Crown* has finally worked. There's something you should see. Ben is trawling through the lists you asked us to do, but he said this was urgent.'

The frustration of interviewing Rees Morgan melted away as she watched the footage from Monday afternoon play out. The digital timer showed 16.16 when Aryan stopped the action for the first time.

‘That is Kelly White walking into the bar. In a moment she takes off her jacket and you’ll see her properly. The taxi driver told us he’d dropped her at the Metro station but that’s only a few minutes’ walk away.’ Aryan moved the action on. Kelly White walked to the bar, slipped off the wet coat and bought a drink.

‘She’s waiting for someone,’ Sarah observed as the woman glanced again at the door.

‘Yes and he’s about to arrive.’ The image was blurry but the man was recognisable as Richard Mason.

‘Well, I’ll be damned, not a connection I was expecting.’ The kiss was long and passionate – *gross* her son would’ve called it. ‘They seem to know each other rather well, Aryan?’

‘I’d say so, Chief Inspector. At 16.29 Kelly answers her mobile. That’s the same time as Dan Bridges makes a call from the corner of High Street and Shafton Lane. Whatever they’re talking about she isn’t happy. Watch this.’

The call lasted less than two minutes. As she stuffed the mobile into her pocket, Kelly White’s fury was evident, even without sound from the video. She turned on Mason, jabbing a finger into his chest. The man did his best to calm her down, guiding her into a corner away from curious customers. Sarah called across to one of the uniformed officers. ‘Constable, find out who our best lip reader is and bring them here, fast.’

The footage continued and, whatever Mason was saying, Kelly nodded in agreement. Moments later, she was back on her mobile. lips saying one thing – her expression as cold as the Arctic. Mason turned and walked out of shot. The time showed 16.35.

‘What time was Dan found, Aryan?’

‘The barman’s statement logged it at 16.45 approximately.’

‘Does Mason come back in?’

‘No, Ma’am. The staff member who found Dan told us he heard someone running away.’

‘Well done Aryan, that’s a great piece of work.’

‘There is one more thing.’ Aryan flicked through the digital files. ‘City Central sent me a copy of the CCTV footage covering the immediate vicinity. Ten minutes later, before she re-enters the Metro station, Kelly does this.’ Fascinated, Sarah watched the young woman pull out her mobile and slide off the back, then throw something into the small bin attached to the lamppost. ‘I contacted the Metro station; those bins haven’t been emptied since Saturday. We might be in luck.’

Chapter Thirteen

AROUND THE ROOM, THE EVER-INCREASING buzz from returning officers made it difficult to concentrate. It wasn't surprising; officers involved with the Ingles/Carson cases were still hyped after the mass of arrests of the previous evening.

'Chief Inspector, DCI Brantley telephoned.' Jake Forbes handed over the message.

'Found the missing van from Wiggins garage hidden under a tarpaulin at the back of the house where Farnes has been hiding out. The forensic team are all over it. We should know within the hour whether Lee has been anywhere near it. My best guess is no but I could be wrong. Bringing Farnes in for questioning.'

It seemed the easy option that Farnes had grabbed Lee was fast disappearing. With a sigh, Sarah pulled over a handy stool to catch up with Ben and Aryan. 'Have you dug up anything significant?'

Peterson rolled his neck, groaning at the creak. 'It's like a bowl of spaghetti Ma'am, all the strings twisted together.'

'Would explaining to a third-party help?'

'It's worth a try I suppose, although the information isn't in date order right now.' Ben gulped down a mouthful of what had to be cold coffee. 'Aryan was telling me about some software we could use to help sort out wood from the trees, but we need more data. It's not a program I've used before but he assures me it's legit.'

'How legit are we talking, Aryan?'

Aryan Khan's expression was a hard read. 'I made it freely available to anyone, Chief Inspector. All it does is pull together patterns and highlight inconsistencies. I'll need more data and some time to input…'

Sarah lifted a hand in submission. 'If Ben is okay with this then so am I. Let's hear what you have.'

'So far, we've identified fifteen teenagers who meet the criteria but we've scratched out a few basic details on only seven. Tanya Daly you've heard of – she went missing fourteen months ago. Eight weeks later, Louis James vanished from a children's residential centre in Lincoln and Ainsley Babcock from Northumberland two weeks after Louis. There was nothing else until Whitby four months later, when a Daniel Armson was reported missing from a children's respite centre. Another, Susan Holly, went from short term respite care in Norfolk two months after Armson. However, there was a runner, Joshua Finn, from a children's residential placement in Lincolnshire five days after Daniel. Finally, six months later, Amy Sands disappeared from a placement in Wetherby.'

Aryan took over. 'Six of the seven we've researched had a history of absconding. The odd one out was pregnant. The six, prior to their final disappearance, came back or were picked up easily enough. We've been working our way down the country but it's hard going, Ma'am.'

'You can say that again.' Ben rubbed at his forehead kneading a pressure point.

'Is there any pattern or are we chasing shadows?' Sarah felt her stomach churn as the two men shared a worried glance.

'Probably too early to say for definite, but I think you might be onto something. At five of the six sites, money or jewellery went missing twenty-four to forty-eight hours before the youngsters disappeared. Five sites reported lost mobile phones. As we pull more numbers out and input the data onto Aryan's app we should clarify things.' Ben Peterson's sigh was mournful as he asked. 'What's your gut telling you now, Chief Inspector?'

'The same as yours Ben, that we're about to leap off the edge of a bloody steep cliff.'

***

There was hardly standing room when Sarah walked back into the buzzing incident room – not helped by the numerous uniformed officers, their jackets and radios leaching into the packed space. In her hand she carried the transcript of the conversation between Kelly White and Mason. The guts of the document had torn the case wide open.

Ben shifted his chair to make room. 'Amos said he'll join us in five, Ma'am.'

'I need you to read this before we start, Ben but make it quick.' Sarah watched his expression, muscles knotted in his jaw at the dawning realisation of what they'd uncovered.

'Bloody hell! Not Farnes and his van then? That cliff is more like a mountain.'

'And some – I'll bring everyone up to date but first, let's trawl through the basics.'

Sergeant Roger Chichester from uniform division began the feedback. An easy man to work with, in and out of the office; at six foot three and shoulders built like a prop forward, few would mess with him. He also happened to be one of Sarah's favourite running partners – when they could find the time. 'There haven't been any sightings of Lee anywhere in the city,' he began. 'We've talked at length to his schoolmates. All told us he was happy, the best they've seen him for months. Teachers confirmed the same. There have been no incidents at all, with nothing suspicious regarding grooming or stalkers. I've been liaising with CPU. Between our teams, we've interviewed all in the area on the sex offenders list. There is nothing – not a hint.'

His summary confirmed the information Sarah held in her hand. 'How about Richard Mason's murder. Are we any further forward?'

Roger shook his head. 'Sorry Sarah. We've tracked down known work associates but, so far we've been unable to contact any of his next of kin. Telephone and addresses on references are coming up as unknown. Another *ghost* I'd think. I've also put out a call to DVLA. We'll see if the new software they're using is as good as the hype. Do we still treat Mason's death as a separate incident to the Lee Wiggins case?'

'I'm trying to keep an open mind Roger but, given the news I've just received and now confirmation of his false identity, it appears Mason is almost certainly another piece of the same puzzle.' Sarah scanned the room, trying to evaluate which of the many faces were from traffic. 'Is there news on that green van or the Vectra?'

'The Vectra is out of the running,' an officer confirmed. 'And we've also been notified that the van, found in connection with the arrest of Farnes, has no forensic evidence linked to the Lee Wiggins disappearance. We'll continue to track the last two of the green vans spotted in the area; there's still hope.'

'I appreciate the effort.' Sarah looked around at the attentive faces, before glancing again at the A4 sheet that was about to change everything. 'The news on Dan Bridges, the teenager who was assaulted, is good. He's recovering well although is unable to answer questions until tomorrow at the earliest. The rest of the news is going to be difficult to assimilate. We have confirmation that the woman calling herself Kelly White was using an alias. Previously, in Hull, she'd used another alias – Shauna Richardson. We don't have confirmation of her real name yet but, from a transcribed version of CCTV footage,' Sarah waved the sheet of paper in the air. 'We believe her first name to be *Emily.* From now on that's what we'll be calling our mystery woman. Emily managed to obtain forged DBS clearance documents and is confirmed to have been present at a children's home in Hull where, fourteen months ago, another teenager went missing in similar circumstances.' She had everyone's attention, including Amos who'd slipped into the back of the room to watch events unfold. Sarah licked dry lips, wishing she'd eaten. 'The disappearance of Lee Wiggins has become an A1 priority and not a whisper of this must reach the press. Once I've explained, I'm sure you'll understand why. Less than fifteen minutes ago, I was handed the transcript of a conversation that took place on Monday late afternoon in the *Cock & Crown.* It's between the woman Emily and our murder victim, Richard Mason. It's a brief précis and mostly in Emily's voice, but there's enough of Mason for us to understand the gist. I quote:

Emily – *You stupid dumb idiot. How could you mess it up!?*

Mason – *I didn't – what are you on about?*

Emily – *They took the wrong f*ing boy – that's what. I told you, brown hair and he'd be wearing that hat. The one they nabbed is a sodding red head! Of all the useless...'*

Mason - *I bloody told them – don't blame me...*

Emily – *Crap – this is so messed up. That kid they took was never going to run and now I've got the other one on the sodding phone. How the hell did he get my number?*

Sarah looked up. 'The rest of the conversation is difficult to follow as they changed position but, the footage shows Mason leaving the bar and heading out towards the rear of the pub where shortly after, Dan Bridges was seriously assaulted. There is more I'm afraid.' Taking a deep breath, she plunged into the findings from Ben and Aryan's research. As she drew to a close, the stunned silence lasted for several seconds.

'You're telling us there are at least another six kids missing?' The anonymous words set off a low rumble that rolled on around the room.

Ben stretched to his full height. 'We found fifteen potential youngsters after less than two hours' work and we've hardly scratched the surface. It's – well it's terrifying.'

No one disagreed. Sarah broke into the pregnant silence. 'There aren't words to describe how appalling this is but we have to absorb it – quickly. Lee Wiggins was snatched on Monday, in error it seems. The intention was to take Dan Bridges. The snatches are usually well-planned and coordinated.' She waited until all eyes were focused on her. 'We can't start speculating about the why's or how many, we need hard evidence about what we do know – which means going back in time, finding out how many other children's homes Emily worked at and the aliases she used. We need to do it fast if we're to stand any chance of finding Lee Wiggins alive.

'Jake Forbes has copies of Emily's photograph taken in Hull and another from her ID here in Hepsford. The DBS forms she used are perfectly legit, it's the names, personal information and written references that are excellent forgeries. The managers from the social care agencies in Hepsford and Hull swear that they always phone to check on DBS clearance and references and both remember doing so for Emily. That tells me this group is organised. We know that whoever is behind these kidnappings is prepared to act and clear up after mistakes. On Monday they took the wrong boy – Richard Mason failed in his attempt to kill Dan Bridges and was probably killed because of it. Is Emily's swift departure because she's afraid? She ran quickly once she'd found out what had happened. We need to find her before they do.'

'And Megan Shaw, Ma'am?'

Jackie Simmons' question instantly conjured up an image of the young, petite woman. 'Still an unknown. According to everyone who knows her, it's out of character for Megan to disappear. She was working in Hull when Tanya Daley, another teenager, went missing. We need to keep an open mind about why she vanished, but I fear she may have recognised Emily, guessed some of the truth and then become a victim of the kidnappers.' Sarah looked across to Roger Chichester. How many uniformed officers can I borrow for a few hours?'

'Six, including myself, barring any major alerts of course.'

Sarah turned to the liaison officer from child protection. 'Any thoughts on how we proceed?'

'Hell Ma'am, this is off the scale.' The jeans and loose-fitting top gave the young woman the air of a disillusioned teenager. 'I'll need to ring my boss, get him in on this.'

'How long?'

'Greg Roberts is days off…'

'I'd forgotten that Greg was back. Who's your senior when he's not around?'

'It was Bill Porter. CS Finchley has been stepping in.'

'Excellent, we'll have a chat with him. In the meantime, Ben can organise our extra hands. We'll need to delegate an officer to act as a central information receiver. Jake are you up to the task?'

The young officer nodded reluctantly. 'Of course Ma'am, anything you need.'

'We need to start contacting the children's homes where the missing teenagers were living. I want to know how many places the woman worked at and the aliases she used.

Ben, once you've finished organising the troops are you and Aryan happy to stay with the digging?'

'Of course Ma'am, although I'll take a couple of helpers if I can.'

Jackie Simmons interrupted. 'Given Mason's relationship with Emily, isn't it possible they worked as a team?'

'Good point. Add a photo of Mason when you contact the children's homes and contact the local councils where those fifteen youngsters went missing. Let's see if they know our man.'

The room was coming alive, the hum of conversation building. 'Before everyone disappears – we'll give it three hours of intense information gathering then re-group. I will be with the CS bringing him up to date. After that, you'll find me in the canteen.'

***

Finchley for once didn't hesitate. He took one look at the case sheet Sarah handed him and picked up the phone. The only sign of emotion was a tightening around his mouth.

'DI Roberts, it's Chief Superintendent Finchley here. A major issue has arisen. Return to the station as soon as possible.' Sarah had to admire the way he listened to an obviously angry man, his expression neutral. 'Report to me and I shall be only too happy to give you details. However, it would be inappropriate for me to do so over an open line.' He replaced the receiver. 'So, tell me what you've organised so far, Chief Inspector?'

Fifteen minutes later, Sarah watched the young officer's retreating back, not envying her the meeting with Greg Roberts one little bit. Pulling out her mobile from an inside pocket, Sarah rang her anchor in the storm.

'Hello you, how's it going?' Freya sounded as cheerful as ever.

'Bearing up.'

Freya's laugh was unexpected. 'Are they putting you up for a medal then?'

'Sorry?'

'The news – you must have seen the reports on the web? *Hepsford City – A Force to be reckoned with? Hepsford – Our Gotham of the North? Who needs Batman and Wonder-Woman with officers like ours?* I'm going to buy several copies and frame them when it comes out in print.'

'You are not serious?' Sarah started to laugh.

'Are things likely to calm down for a bit?'

'I'm afraid not, or at least not for a while.' Sarah sighed, hearing an answering one from the far end of the line. 'Sorry love.'

‘Don’t you dare apologise! Just stay safe and make sure you eat. I’ve enough school work to keep me busy for the next month!’

‘I’ve no idea what time tonight, hopefully before midnight, depends.’

‘Stop fretting. Anyway, I’ve good news. The drama club is putting on another performance next year.’

‘What, another musical?’

‘No, we settled on *A Midsummer Night’s Dream*.’

‘Lovely, I’ll be fluent in yet another of Shakespeare’s finest.’

‘You enjoy it, and you’ll get to paint scenery again.’

‘Lucky me! Would you do me a favour and leave the laptop out if I’m late? Thought I’d try and give Ryan a shout tonight, New Zealand time differences being what they are.’

There was a moment’s pause. ‘No problem at all. I’ll text and let him know you’ll be in contact soon. This case, it’s a child isn’t it?’

Sometimes she swore Freya was a witch. ‘Maybe, but I just need to talk to my son?’

‘Of course you do. I miss him very much – and you. Oh, don’t forget we’re at Tom and Jason’s tomorrow. Love you.’

Her sanity in a crazy world. Sarah sighed and pocketed the phone.

Chapter Fourteen

Wednesday 15.20

ROGER CHICHESTER HANDED BEN a sheet of paper. 'Tabitha Adams is another alias for Emily. She used it in Lincoln but in Norwich she went under the alias of Susan Woodruff. We've put her fingerprints through the main criminal database but nothing's come back. I'm about to try juvenile and hope I have more luck there. There are two positive ID's on Richard Mason, real name Andrew Woods. He's worked in the same areas as Emily using two different aliases, so maybe we should be looking at pairs? Anyway, most local councils subcontract their work out, so it's taking a while to track his routes. How far do you want to take this, Ben? It's likely to turn into an impossible maze.'

'That's what I was bloody thinking. Hell, I need a break Roger, can't see straight, let alone think.'

Roger pulled the sheet out from Ben's fingers. 'Go eat man, you look exhausted. You'll be no good to anyone until your blood sugar level is back on the chart. We'll keep on plodding.'

Stomach rolling, Ben walked into the canteen and almost fell over Amos Brantley.

'Perfect, you're just the man I need.'

Ben's eyes lingered hopefully on the hot food counter. 'Sorry Sir, but I need to eat.'

'Not a problem, I'll join you. I can always use another drink.' Once Ben's plate was loaded they found a seat in a corner. 'I'm trying to tie up a few loose ends. Last night – hell it feels like days ago doesn't it – can you take me through events from say, 18.00hrs?'

Frowning, Ben looked up from the forkful of curry he was holding. 'Right, give me one second.' Shovelling in a few mouthfuls, he patted a pocket to find his notebook.

'17.14hrs I called Sarah and we agreed to meet back at the station. I fed back preliminary details from the medical examiner and forensics. We ate pizza.' Ben forked in another mouthful and ate quickly. 'We talked it around for a while…'

Amos listened, jotting notes occasionally. 'At what time before leaving the station did Sarah contact Moira Robins at the *Beacon*?'

'She didn't, and I'm not aware the Sarah contacted Moira at any point. She received a call from Moira whilst we were involved in Liam Carson's arrest. Aryan Khan was with the Chief Inspector when the call came in. There would've been no reason to contact Moira and anyway, we were too busy trying to set up the Ingles/Carson catch. Why are you asking, Sir?'

'As I said, loose ends,' Amos smiled but Ben wasn't fooled.

'There was no reason to contact Moira. Yes, we'd had the heads-up that there was likely to be another shipment out over the weekend, but that was a couple of days away.'

'Talk me through the protocol used for contacting Moira?'

With a sigh, Ben took a quick mouthful before continuing. 'Mobile with a new sim card, a burn phone essentially, which was always kept in the locked drawer. I and the Chief Inspector had the only keys. The telephone number and minimal details of the officer involved were kept in the secure log which stayed with the desk sergeant under lock and key. Moira had memorised the chief inspector's personal number, but strictly for emergency use only.'

'The usual then,' Amos observed.

'We never phoned her. If we needed to make contact, we used a system of texts or emails. The last message sent was that morning – by Sarah. I believe it read, "Are you working Saturday night?" Ben shrugged and scooped up the last of his curry. 'We received a one-word reply: "yes".'

‘The mobile Moira Robins used to contact you, who did she hand it to once she’d been retrieved from the *Beacon?’*

Ben frowned. ‘Sir, I have no idea. I was busy in the front of the van taking out the driver. I think PC Evans was the first to reach her. He and Jackie helped Moira out of the van. I don’t remember seeing a mobile at all and I certainly didn’t book one in. I seem to remember Moira asking where her phone was. I assume it’s still missing?’

The evasion was textbook. A shrug – another question. ‘Who were the other officers who had access or knew the details of the case?’

‘Well the CS of course. You were away and Bill Porter was off sick. I’m assuming Mike Lawson knew the basics, although he wouldn’t have known about Moira – there was no reason to tell him or his team. It made it easy, her being new to our patch.’

‘Cheers for that, Ben. Do me a favour and keep this conversation strictly between you and me for now.’

Ben studied the detective’s serious expression. ‘Is this an official enquiry, Sir?’

‘Finchley and I have an understanding.’ Amos pushed his notebook into a pocket and picked up his drink. ‘So, any plans for that holiday you’re due, Ben?’ The subject it seemed was firmly closed.

Chapter Fifteen

DI GREG ROBERTS, LEAD OFFICER of the child protection unit sat with arms tightly folded, while Sarah patiently outlined the details of the case. He hadn't bothered to change. Tight-fitting climbing trousers and top accentuated his athletic build. From his expression, he wanted to be anywhere but in Finchley's office. 'Show me this data,' he said, holding out a hand for the page.

Sarah managed to keep her expression dispassionate as she passed it over, no point rattling him further. Greg scanned the document with a hint of a scowl. 'You're basing all of your assumptions on what, a few guesses and untried software?'

'No Greg, I'm basing the case on cold, hard fact. All the program did was speed up the process. And before you go off on one, the information has been triple checked.'

'Damn it…'

'Oh, I wanted it to be wrong so much. This is a summary of what we have so far,' Sarah passed over another sheet. 'Officers in Hull confirmed the Emily and Andrew Woods connection. Woods was calling himself Mason here in Hepsford. His body turned up Tuesday morning, another conundrum. Right now, we're trying to identify where the pair worked before Lakeside.'

Greg ran an eye down to the end of the document and sighed. 'Fair enough, you're forgiven for dragging me in, Sarah.' He looked over to the silent figure of the Chief Superintendent. 'How do you want us to play this, Sir?'

Finchley sounded bleak. 'I don't need to remind you both that we are sitting on a ticking bomb. We can't let a whisper of this leak to the press. We do need an official name for the case – offers?'

'*North Run*,' Sarah responded. 'Seems appropriate.'

'As good as any I suppose. I'm consulting with the Chief Constable shortly who may well apply for a news embargo. In the meantime, Sarah, you're appointed lead officer. Greg, use whatever resources you can to profile this. Call in experts, whatever you need. Mike Lawson will deal with any new cases that arise, so leave him clear. Amos and his team will finalise the Ingles/Carson cases and the Paul Wiggins assault. If he has any time left, he'll help out where he can. I've asked the other teams to release officers wherever it's possible, although DI Coleman is stretched to the limit in the home invasion unit. She's working with one acting DS and a handful of uniformed.'

'And the *Blue Beacon*?' Sarah asked.

'In hand,' Finchley said curtly. 'Any other questions?'

Sarah waited for Finchley's door to close before she asked, 'So where were you exactly Greg, when you got the call?'

'Nearly at the top of the crag at Kilnsey. I knew I should've left my sodding phone in the van. He looked mournfully down at his climbing gear. 'I suppose I'd better go and change.'

'If you want anyone to take you seriously, that's probably a good idea.'

'Congrats, by the way. I only found out today about your promo.'

'Thanks,' she smiled up at the youngest inspector in Hepsford force. 'When did you decide to come back? Last I heard, you'd left us for the bright lights of Birmingham?'

'About five hours after arriving. I did my eighteen months and got out, fast. I've achieved more in the two months I've been back than I ever did there.'

'That bad?' she said surprised.

'Too many hands in the cooking pot and talking of which, Sarah, are you still baking?'

‘Occasionally Greg, and I have a distinct feeling this case is likely to be one of those. I’ll catch up with you later, once you’re in something less revealing.’

Walking into the main incident room, everything had changed. The room dividers were pushed up against the rear wall. An officer sat at each of the ten desks, either bent over a phone or peering at a screen. The hum of conversation was intense, satisfying. Centre back, the incident boards gleamed with the patchwork of crossed out aliases, photographs and captions.

‘Kent, Ben,’ a female voice called. ‘It’s the same pattern exactly, only no sign of Andrew Woods or Emily in any disguise.’

‘That’s it then,’ Ben replied. ‘There must be at least two more teams out there.’ He glanced over, obviously relieved when he saw her. ‘Good timing, Chief Inspector. We’ve hit a dilemma. Do we follow the new teams we’ve discovered or stay with Woods and Emily?’

‘It’s coming up to five so I suggest everyone stops for something sweet and sticky. Be back in ten and we’ll review what we have.’ There was an immediate thumping of chairs as the room emptied.

‘I’m fine,’ Ben assured her. ‘My late lunch is still going down.’

‘So, are you going to tell me what Amos was after?’

‘Ma’am?’ Ben blinked trying for innocence.

‘Don’t piss me off, Ben. This place has eyes everywhere.’

‘Amos said he was tying up loose ends with the *Beacon* case.’ Her sergeant didn’t flinch. ‘That’s it, I swear. I tried digging, but he wasn’t having any of it.’

Irritated, Sarah sank onto the edge of the table. ‘I hate bloody games.’

‘I think I could probably manage that sticky bun and a coffee, after all. Would you like something?’

‘Is that your attempt to put me off, Ben?’

'Yep, is it working?'

Sarah heard the door swing closed behind him, grateful for the peace that followed. The air stank. The extractor fans were losing the battle – again. New city finance had yet to sink as far as Hepsford police HQ. Maybe the rumours were true and they were closing Hepsford down to create a mega force based in Leeds? The idea left her cold. Sarah pushed the repulsive notion firmly out of her head. In front of her, the incident boards were a jumble of random information: dates, times, age, gender, ethnicity. The latest number of missing teenagers had shot up to thirty-seven. No one was taking bets on the final tally. The murder of Andrew Woods – alias Richard Mason – was a complete mystery. Did the man have anything to do with Megan's disappearance? And where the hell did they take the youngsters once they had them?

'Sarah?' She flinched and Greg Roberts smiled apologetically. Jeans and jumper had replaced the climbing gear.

'Where are your squeaky shoes, Greg?'

'At home,' he smiled disarmingly. 'What had you looking so intent?'

'There are too many damned questions. Why are they being snatched, where are they taken...'

'The why is probably simple – sex trade or harvesting organs for sale – but you'd need a ready market for either.' Greg ran a tanned finger under the number thirty-seven. 'It's not as easy as people think to off-load human merchandise.'

'You make it sound like some sort of commercial enterprise…'

'With this many involved, that's exactly what this is. One or two youngsters, possibly up to six or seven a year could be for a home grown group, but not on this scale. It has to be organised for a larger market. Social media sites are full of stories about thousands of youngsters going missing every year, but most of those are found speedily, within hours if not days. However, there is a significant number, a thousand, maybe fifteen hundred or so each year, who remain missing long term and there are others who are never reported as missing – slip through the net entirely.'

'A nightmare, Greg.'

'Let me do my thing Sarah, no point speculating until we have more data. Didn't you say that someone here has an App to help identify potential patterns to the snatches?'

'Aryan Khan, on secondment from uniform to CID, why?'

'*The* Khan – as in Meldlife Electronics?'

'All I know is he used to work as a games programmer before joining up. Why are you laughing, Greg?'

'Khan was the brains behind Meldlife. The company pretty much fell apart when he left. What the hell are they doing sticking him here in Hepsford? Unbelievable.'

'Greg,…'

'Sorry, but he's one of the best in his field.'

'Is that right? Well, in my world he's just stepped up to the bottom rung, doing okay, but doesn't need you or anyone else piling on the pressure. Am I making myself clear?'

Undaunted, Greg continued. 'It's good to be back, Sarah. Let me know when he's updated the latest info. Meanwhile, there's no point traipsing back to the other side of town – sorry, *city*. I'll use the admin office next to Porter's and start phoning around.'

Sarah watched him nod at Ben as they passed in the doorway. They were similar in so many ways. Independent thinkers, decisive and both bore the marks of being under her tutelage for better or worse. '*You have to let them fly*,' she murmured, quoting one of Freya's favourite adages. She wasn't so sure her sergeant and past rookie would appreciate the sentiment much.

Ben handed her a steaming carton of coffee. 'Any thoughts, Ma'am?'

'Why take Megan… unless she ran of course?'

'My money would be on something to do with Emily.'

'And the motive?'

'Megan might have recognised Emily that morning and put two and two together?'

'She would have seen her for less than a few seconds, Ben?'

'Even so, it must have been a shock for Emily seeing Megan, she was at Lakeside using an assumed name remember.'

'Keep going…'

'Emily couldn't afford to be associated with Hull and Tanya Daley's disappearance, so she had to make sure Megan was out of the picture.'

'But why risk taking any work at Lakeside at all? That makes no sense.'

'Perhaps Emily didn't realise Megan was based there at first. When she did find out, maybe she got cocky, saw it as a challenge? After all, Mason/Woods was posing as Megan's boyfriend. He could tell Emily when Megan was working. We know the agency worker Rees Morgan was also having some sort of sexual relationship with Emily. It would have been easy enough to squeeze him for dates, times etc. And it worked. Emily's couple of shifts were on completely different days – up until Megan is called in on short notice to cover staff illness.'

'I suppose it fits?' Sarah conceded. 'Did we find anything at Emily's flat hinting at something more than the one-off casual encounter Rees Morgan admits to?'

Peterson flipped through the file. 'There are a couple of bottles of shower gel etc. but nothing specific to a man. I'll have the items checked for fingerprints.' He reached over to answer his ringing phone.

Sarah perused the brief list of contents. It read like the flat of a student or someone constantly on the move – no personal photographs, a few items of clothing left in the wardrobe, stale milk, along with a refrigerator half full of convenience food and no sign of a toothbrush or paste. Sarah turned to the last page. A neighbour saw Emily returning to her flat at 13.20 hrs on Monday. The same neighbour, a Mr Morris, reported seeing her leave by taxi at 15.50 approx.

'Ma'am, that was traffic. They've managed to exclude twenty-eight of the twenty-nine green vans, so with any luck…'

'I doubt they'll appreciate you calling it luck, Ben. How long before we have a definitive answer on the last?'

'Whoever was driving stayed on the back roads and away from the cameras. Unfortunately, Highways are up to their eyes with RTI's.'

'A long shot then.'

'It always was, but they're good and if anyone can track that van…'

Sarah appreciated his optimism. 'You've met Greg Roberts, Ben?'

'Briefly, one of yours I understand?'

'He had that pleasure. He's heading up the CP unit. 'Get to know him, work with him. We're going to need many different angles on this.'

'Will do.' Behind them officers were drifting back. 'If Woods was taken out by the group because he got it wrong, the implications for Emily aren't good are they?'

'All the more reason to find her before it's too late. Did tech pull anything from that sim we retrieved from the Metro bin?'

'Unfortunately not. Someone had thrown in half a carton of cola and that would destroy pretty much anything. I did discover how Dan Bridges got hold of Emily's mobile number. Mr De-Silva called into the station earlier to ask how things are going. He told me the staff numbers are always listed in the back of the office diary, so it would have been easy for Dan to sneak in and copy down her details. De-Silva's looking rough, Ma'am. I swear he's aged twenty years.'

‘A job like his must take its toll – I certainly couldn’t do it. I know it’s a slog Ben, but keep on digging. How long before Aryan thinks we’ll have enough information to be meaningful?’

Ben’s smile was more a grimace. ‘It’s that piece of string again, could be a long night.’

Two hours later and the thought of leaving work had barely crossed Sarah’s mind when her alert beeped at her hip. Wearily, she pressed the night sergeant’s number.

‘Sarah. I need you at interview room two, pronto.’

‘Chris, what the hell’s happened now?’

‘Mike bloody Lawson, and I think you’d better make it quick.’

Chapter Sixteen

LONG BEFORE SARAH TURNED onto the main corridor, she heard Lawson's furious tirade. Ahead, Chris Hollings leant nonchalantly against the door of interview room two, a tense Carl Moyles beside him.

'If I want to interview the sodding witness then I bloody well will. Who the hell do you think you are, Moyles? I don't need some puffed-up arrogant little sod telling me what I can and can't do…'

'Inspector Lawson, enough!' Sarah moved until she was elbow to elbow with the furious man. 'If you have an issue – you talk to me, not harangue an officer in a corridor. Carl is carrying out *my* orders.'

Lip curling, Lawson turned to eye her dismissively. 'What's your problem, Allerton? Adam Farnes has nothing to do with your missing kid. Afraid I'll steal some of your thunder? You always were a control freak...'

Sarah saw the muscles in Chris Hollings' arms tighten – thankfully, he kept his mouth shut. 'As of this moment, *Inspector,* I have no idea who or what is involved any more than you do. The decision isn't up for negotiation. Carl *will* continue to investigate under the supervision of myself and Amos. I suggest you leave and allow us to continue with the interview.'

She thought he'd bite back – saw the intent behind the eyes and almost hoped he would. With a last sneering glare, Lawson flounced out through the double doors.

Carl didn't try and hide the relief. 'Thanks Ma'am, that was bloody awkward.'

‘Awkward!’ Chris shook his head, disgusted. ‘The man is a pain in the bloody backside and I don’t care who hears me. You should’ve heard him laying into Carl.’

‘Thanks for intervening Chris, it’s appreciated.’

‘Any time. It’s a good thing these interview rooms are soundproofed or our friend Farnes would’ve had an interesting time. Fortunately, his solicitor is at the desk taking a call.’

‘Are you happy to persist with the interview, Carl?’

‘Absolutely, Amos will be here shortly so we’re good. Mike Lawson insisted that all he needed was five minutes with Farnes and he’d have the whole thing sorted. I tried to tell him that the Amos was on the way, but he wouldn’t listen…’

‘Where is Amos out of interest?’

‘Face-timing his kids before they go to bed, but I didn’t tell the Inspector that.’

Sarah smiled, enjoying the image. ‘You are wise beyond your years, Carl. Please tell Amos that I’m heading home. If he needs me, I’ll be baking.’

***

Sarah kept it together until she was through the double doors but the latest confrontation with Lawson had left her seething – the man was a bloody liability. Praying she wouldn’t bump into him on the way out, Sarah messaged Chris Hollings asking him to have her car dropped off at her home. Thankfully, when she walked in to the changing rooms they were deserted. Pulling on trainers and running gear, Sarah slapped the digital monitor onto her upper arm and began stretching reluctant muscles. Rain thudded against the small windows, but she didn’t give a damn.

When her mobile rang Sarah almost ignored it. ‘Martha – hi, what’s up?’

Inspector Martha Coleman didn’t mince words. ‘Sarah – it’s that bastard Mike Lawson, are you okay? I heard him sounding off at Carl and rang Chris. Who the hell does he think he is?'

'I'm fine – well sort of and thanks for stepping in. Me, being promoted over Mike's head hasn't helped…'

'If he'd been given the DCI's position, Sarah I'd have walked. Between him and bloody staff shortages, the job's impossible.'

'Oh God, I'd forgotten he's your supervisor as well.'

Martha's laughter was bitter – angry. 'The only time I've seen Lawson is in the sodding corridor. I don't know how you work in the same room as the man. I'd apply for the serious crime vacancy but I'd be inside for his murder in less than a week... Sorry, better go and sort out some of this mess… and congratulations, Sarah you bloody deserve the promotion.'

Pushing Lawson to the back of her mind, Sarah stepped out into a wet night. The seventeen-kilometre circuit she'd picked was all street work. Deliberately, she'd chosen the steepest route, forcing the pace on difficult sections. Lifting her face to the cooling rain, she eased down around the tight corners. Concentrating on staying upright in the slippery conditions, left no room to think of anything else. By the time the security gates came into view, she was soaked through and panting hard, thigh and calf muscles burning with the effort. The only concerns left in her head, were how soon she could be in the shower and the gratifying realisation that Lawson and his bullshit could go to hell!

***

Thursday 07.30 hrs

Sarah climbed behind the wheel of her car, enjoying the comforting aromas of baked sugar and fruit that rose from the bags she'd placed on the back seat. Outside, a thick fog hung low and only metres away, the street lights were barely visible. Lowering her window, Sarah edged forwards stopping at the dropped kerb, hoping her ears would pick up what her eyes couldn't see. The revving of an engine was close – automatically, Sarah threw the car into reverse, a nano-second before vicious sparks lit up the fog as a huge bull-bar smashed against the roundel of the gate. It was impossible to see the driver, the number plate gone in an instant. Pulsing lights flickered against her closed lids as the wave of adrenaline hit. Long seconds passed before Sarah could lift a trembling hand and report the incident.

'Bloody hell Sarah, are you all right?'

'Shaken not bounced, thanks, Tracy. I didn't get a make, but I'm pretty sure it was a Land Rover discovery with a large matt-black bull-bar attached.'

Tracy Bates, that day's desk sergeant, didn't hang about. 'I'll have CCTV straight on to it. Shall I send someone to pick you up?'

'No, I'll take a taxi. The fog is horrendous and Tracy, please don't make this common knowledge. Let's keep it between you and me – for now?'

Sarah heard the hesitation, knew she was asking a lot. 'If you're sure, Sarah. Stay safe.'

Freya had been her usual calm self when Sarah explained and, for once, hadn't argued about travelling to school with a friend. The taxi arrived promptly. The driver glanced curiously at her in the rear-view mirror, but seemed happy to let her sit in silence with her thoughts. Could it have been an accident, someone losing control in the conditions? Who was she kidding? A bull-bar that size had to be illegal. It would have taken out the front of the car and her without any problem. As the cab wound its way through the dark streets, the incident kept replaying in her head.

Tracy Bates smiled her relief when Sarah walked in. 'Morning, glad you've made it in safely. I've several messages for you.' She handed over a pile of notes with the signing in book. The new page was already half full.

‘I see I’m not the first in?’

‘Not by a long way. Young Aryan Khan arrived about five. He gave the night sergeant a right hard time.’

‘About what for heaven’s sake?’

‘Wanted to link up some computers,’ Tracy shrugged. ‘Don’t ask Sarah, I still haven’t got my head around it. Anyway, they came to a compromise, apparently.’

‘You mean Chris Hollings told him to sod off.’

‘Pretty much, but Greg has sorted it, so all’s peace and love again.’

‘Thanks for the heads up.’

‘You’re looking a bit peaky, Sarah. Are you sure you’re okay?’

‘It wasn’t the best start to my day, Tracy. Let me know if traffic has any joy tracing that damned car will you.’

The buzzer on the main door rang loudly and, with a sigh the sergeant checked the small screen. ‘Looks like I’ve got my first punter.’

Sarah pulled out a neatly wrapped package and slid it onto the counter. ‘A couple of cakes for later. With everything going on, I think we’re going to need a sugar hit.’

‘Anytime is good by me Sarah and thanks.’

Ben and Greg looked up together as she walked into the incident room. Aryan Khan sat between them, eyes glued to a screen. Officers were everywhere, phones to ears, scrutinising evidence sheets.

‘Morning Chief Inspector,’ the general chorus rolled around the room.

‘I’ve got it, Ben! You want me to put it on the big screen?’ Aryan glanced up, saw Sarah, and immediately jumped to his feet. ‘Sorry, Ma’am, didn’t see you.’

‘We’ve upped the tech a little.’ Greg pointed to the enormous monitor now hanging on the wall.

‘So I see. Did Chris avoid the heart attack when you manhandled his precious machines up here?’

'Not to worry Sarah, I've taken full responsibility.'

Sarah managed not to smile. 'Very astute of you Greg.' Turning to Aryan she asked. 'In simple terms, tell me what has everyone so excited?'

'I didn't mean to create a fuss, only it came to me about four-thirty, so I thought...'

'Your diligence is commendable Aryan, but perhaps you could explain?'

'It's probably easier to show you, Ma'am.' With a flip of a button the monitor came to life, a large graphic filling the screen. 'This is a map of the UK from the Scottish borders including Wales. It shows the number of missing youngsters we've identified, currently standing at sixty-seven. To keep it simple, I've called them *runners*.' The map was immediately covered with a flurry of black flags. 'Next, I gave each *runner* a colour tag depending on age and gender.' The flurry happened again, the black flags turning into either blue/yellow or blue/white or red/yellow or red/white. 'Blue is male, yellow is eleven to twelve years old, the white indicates thirteen to fifteen. The red indicates females.'

'With you so far,' Sarah said, aware the whole room was watching with her.

'I next asked the program to find patterns using dates, location, gender, etc.' Aryan pressed another key and lines began to appear, each vividly coloured, passing through no more than six flags, some less. 'There is one confirmed pattern – I've called it a *set*, which is currently repeated five times. Each of the five sets you see highlighted consists of six *runners*, all snatched within a four-week time-frame. The *runners* in each of the five sets have been snatched from places a minimum of one hundred miles apart they're all from different counties. If there's a snatch from somewhere in Yorkshire say, then there isn't a repeat from the area for at least another two months.'

‘Can you show me the map with just the confirmed sets,’ Sarah murmured. Again Aryan typed and she watched the screen change. The five sets were highlighted in vivid colours, flashing an ominous deep red.

‘Of the five sets,’ Aryan continued, ‘these three – occur almost immediately after each other, only a five-day break between each.’ Three of the lines began to pulsate. ‘The other two sets are currently random, but I think that’s only because there are large areas of the country we haven’t researched.’

Ben tapped the screen with a slender finger. ‘Given the info we have, you’re saying that every four weeks six are snatched, followed by a five-day break and start again?’

‘That’s what this is showing so far.’

‘And Lee’s set?’ Sarah asked.

‘It’s not complete.’ Aryan typed and a broken line began to flash orange. ‘I’m as sure as I can be that the first of the youngsters was snatched after a five-day break.’

‘Only five youngsters,’ Sarah murmured. ‘Do we have names?’

Photographs appeared down one side of the screen. ‘Lee Wiggins, fifteen, from Hepsford Yorkshire, ‘Rosa Kolinski, eleven, from Chichester Sussex, Paula Hancock, twelve, from Dover Kent, Simon Hitchin, fourteen, Ambleside in Northumberland, and finally, Kayla Morris, thirteen, from Nottingham.’

Ben broke the silence. ‘So have we scared them off or will they try for the last one?’

‘That’s going to depend on how good their news network is,’ Sarah replied. ‘Greg, what’s your take?’

‘If they know we’re onto them they’ll quit, they’ve too much to lose. If they’re still in the dark – well – there’s no reason why they wouldn’t go for the sixth.’

‘We have to assume they know nothing. There’s been no hint in any of the papers about a trafficking ring, only Lee’s disappearance.’ Sarah studied the monitor for a moment.

'Aryan, is there any way we can predict where they are likely to hit next?'

'I'm having a problem with the small amount of data. I don't know if there's enough available for clearer results. I can ask the software to make the best guess, but...'

'Do it, that has to be better than nothing. You've already done a great job.' Sarah turned her back on the embarrassed officer and left him to his work.

'While he's sorting that, the rest of us can talk numbers. Six snatched every four weeks. Even allowing for the five days off that's at least sixty over twelve months. We've only found that number over two years. Even allowing for the odd month off, we're coming up way short – why?'

Apart from the tap of Aryan's keyboard, there was a long silence. Roger Chichester tapped the map. 'We've only covered the eastern side of the country – it has to be happening across the UK. It would be less conspicuous that way.'

'Or, they've another source altogether,' Greg suggested. 'It could be refugees or poorer families from inner cities.'

Jackie looked shocked. 'Families selling their own, here in the UK. Is that likely?'

'The families may not know what they're sending their youngsters into,' Greg responded. 'What if there were promises of training, a better life?'

Sarah cut in. 'If we want to find Lee before he's shipped off to wherever then I'm not sure we have time to work on that angle right now. We should concentrate on checking care placements nationwide. If we still come up short then we investigate other potentials, agreed?'

Greg nodded. 'Happy to, Sarah. I'll work with Ben, collating info from counties nationwide. Two hours should tell us one way or another.'

'So anyone, thoughts on where they might be holding Lee and hopefully the other four?'

‘It has to be the coast or bloody close,’ Ben said. ‘Maybe near a ferry port?’

‘Or an old aircraft hangar or warehousing,’ Roger added. ‘Easy for transporting and no one notices lorries in and out. Unfortunately, there are enough private airfields around to fly out a whole damned school if they wanted.’

‘I’ve contacted agencies in Europe and asked them to dig around,’ Greg said. ‘I’ve explained we need to keep this close to the chest for now.’

‘Have you run across this sort of thing before Greg, or anything like it?’

‘Not me, Sarah, but one of my contacts in Holland had, although that involved someone in India. I’ll double-check.’

Aryan interrupted. ‘Chief Inspector, the software has come up with a few suggestions.’ The screen flickered to show Lee’s pattern with the five known flags. Like ghostly apparitions, six other flags flashed black to grey. ‘We’ve got Norfolk, Hampshire, Berkshire, Leicestershire and Cambridgeshire.’

‘Okay ladies and gents, I want to know how many potential children’s homes and care agencies we have in each of those counties. Don’t speak to anyone yet until we’ve decided on a cover story – yes Aryan?’ he was fidgeting nervously beside her.

‘If it’s going to happen, then the snatch could be as soon as Saturday and no later than Monday?’

‘Understood! You heard the man, let’s go to it!’

Chairs scraped and the hum of activity rose. ‘Aryan, is the program now at a stage where Ben or Greg can input information?’

‘Yes, I’ve already talked them through it.’

‘Good – unless you want to stay with the computing?’

Aryan turned his back to the screen. ‘If they need anything, they can ring. I was always good on the help desk.’

‘Greg, you and Ben are far better at the tech side than I am and there are a couple of things I want to follow up in Hull. I’ll take Aryan with me. Hopefully, we'll only be a couple of hours. In the meantime, keep up the pace and Ben, don't forget to chase up the forensics on Emily's flat.'

Sarah turned to Jackie. 'I want you to concentrate your effort on Emily. Work out how long she worked for each of the agencies using her aliases. It might give us a baseline for the rest. I'm assuming other teams will have a similar set-up. Once you have a list of care agencies and children's homes in those counties, start working on winkling out likely *players*. Don't get hung up on females, there could as easily be male workers. And do me a favour, distribute these cakes.' She handed over the large bag at her feet. Any questions?' Sarah gave it three seconds before picking up her briefcase. 'Good. Aryan you can drive – I'm assuming you've passed the test?'

Chapter Seventeen

AGAIN, SARAH READJUSTED THE passenger side mirror, her sharp eyes focusing on the queue of traffic behind them.

'Is there a problem, Chief Inspector?'

'Not at this moment, Aryan, just checking.'

'Are you worried one of Ingles or Carson's heavies might try to pressure you into dropping the charges?'

There was humour in his words, but he was far too close to the truth for comfort. Sarah kept it light. 'Aryan, have you been watching gangster films or some such rubbish? You keep that clever mind of yours concentrating on the road. I want to do Hull and be back at HQ asap.'

Twenty-minutes later, Aryan drew to a stop outside the children's home. The deputy manager ushered them in with a resigned smile. 'I'm grateful you're not in uniform, Chief Inspector. That's never a good start to our day.'

They were shown into a light, pleasant room, the television, children's artwork and deep sofas softening the starkness of the sixties building with splashes of colour and warmth. 'We'll be out of your hair as soon as we can,' Sarah promised. 'Before we start, I need to ask one question – about a Philip Gatley, a council gardener. Was it Megan Shaw who reported him and Shauna Stevenson for misconduct?'

The deputy manager seemed taken aback but answered readily enough. 'I wasn't involved in the investigation but I believe it was a member of the kitchen staff who filed the report. Unless there's anything else, I'll chase up the staff you wanted to see.'

Alison, a lady in her mid-thirties, remembered Megan well and had liked her. The woman had little to say about Shauna Stevenson (Emily) except that she hadn't been liked by anyone.

Sarah wound up the short interview. 'Thank you, that's been useful.'

'Is that it?' Alison sounded surprised.

'We needed to confirm certain details,' Sarah assured her. 'I'm grateful for your time.'

An older man was next to step warily into the room – West Indian, Sarah surmised by his accent.

'Thank you for talking to us, Mr Houghton. We have a few questions and I promise not to take up too much of your time.'

'Okay, ask away.'

Again Sarah explained but this time as she mentioned the women's names, there was a flicker of something. 'Is Megan all right? You're not here to tell us that she's hurt, are you?'

'Why would you think that?'

His shrug was more anxiety than attitude. 'Well, being police and all, it's usually bad news.'

'Tell me about Shauna Stevenson, Mr Houghton.'

'A nasty piece of work. I tried telling the manager, but she wouldn't hear it at first.'

'Can you be more specific, Mr Houghton?'

'There wasn't a bloke she didn't try sleeping with – serious, even me and I'm almost twice the woman's age. I never trusted her around the older boys either. Mind, most wouldn't give her a second glance, they had more sense.'

'What was her relationship with Megan?'

'She hated her, Chief Inspector, though I don't know why. Megan wouldn't hurt a fly. I'd see Shauna watching her sometimes with this look on her face, as if Megan had crawled out of the swamp or something. Did you know she accused her of stealing? A pack of lies the lot of it...'

Sarah gently cut him off. 'And Shauna never explained why she resented Megan?'

'Not as far as I know, certainly not to me. I did wonder if Shauna knew her from a previous children's home.'

'Are you aware of anyone Shauna or Megan knew outside of the workplace?'

'Not Shauna, no. There was only Megan's grandmother as far as I remember. I'm sure Megan said her gran was from Scotland originally. Other than that, I never saw Megan outside work. She is all right though, Megan?'

Sarah smiled reassurance that she didn't really feel. 'We very much hope so, Mr Houghton.'

Minutes later they were back in the car. Aryan switched on the sat nav. 'Where next, Chief Inspector?'

'Gatley or Emily's old flat, whichever is the closest.'

'Emily's flat then. It's pretty central.'

The engine purred into life. 'I was thinking about how Emily would have been paid, Ma'am. Not for the care work but I can't imagine she was doing the other stuff for free. She must have another bank account; one the tax people wouldn't be able to trace easily. We didn't find cash anywhere in her flat or evidence of her splurging notes to pay for anything. We know she went to Leeds on Monday evening and what time she used a cashpoint. We should be able to identify the account she withdrew from. It might give us a different alias at least?'

He was remarkably astute for a rookie, Sarah thought, but she let it go. 'That's an excellent piece of reasoning, Aryan. Ask one of the techies to follow it up when we get back.'

Aryan drove them into Winston Street, a couple of miles away from the children's home. The road was quiet, houses and flats neat and well maintained. Sarah chose the flats, leaving the adjoining houses for Aryan to visit. The response from neighbours was disappointing. Only one person on the ground floor remembered Emily but knew nothing of any visitors.

Aryan was waiting for Sarah by the car. 'I think we might have something, Ma'am. There are a couple of lads who've lived here for over three years. They recognised Emily's picture, say they have a photograph of one of her visitors and the car he was driving. They've gone to dig it out. They told me the car arrived at night, a couple of times a month.'

'What was so special about the car to make them take a photograph?'

'It's an Audi R8 V10 plus, worth every penny of a hundred and twenty grand. They described the driver as male, average build, in his early thirties. They rarely saw him and, if they did it was usually dark, so the description is pretty vague.'

The taller of the young men handed Sarah a Tablet. The screen was filled with the sleek lines of the Audi they'd photographed. 'Can you imagine cruising around in one those. You could buy our place for what it costs. We thought we'd try and fool our boss at the restaurant, pretend we'd won it.' The young man pointed to the head and shoulders of a figure in the background. 'That's the owner. He appeared as I clicked.'

While the two men teased each other, Sarah leaned in to study the photograph. The registration was clearly visible. The image of the owner was ill defined, but they might be able to enhance it in tech. It took moments to download the images and another couple to explain to a surprised Ben what they'd sent.

'I'll chase it up straight away,' Ben promised. 'Just to say, we've found a total of thirty-two agencies in those counties. I've put three special constables on with Jackie to start digging.'

'We are on the way to chat with Gatley. I'll call when we're on the way back.'

It was a short drive through the city and Gatley didn't look happy to see them. He ushered them into his tiny flat, scooping up magazines and mugs to allow them to sit. 'We need some background information on a woman you know as Shauna Stevenson, Mr Gatley?'

'Her?' His unshaven cheeks tightened into a scowl. 'Bloody pain in the arse. She dropped me like a hot brick not long after we were reported. I could've strangled her to be honest. It was not my idea to make out in the shed. Shauna appeared, you know. Lost me my sodding job. It's taken me forever to find another…'

'I'm sorry, Mr Gatley – did you ever visit Shauna at her flat?'

'A few times but she came here mostly. Her brother wasn't happy about me going to her place.'

Sarah pulled out a photograph of Andrew Woods. 'Do you recognise this man?'

'That's her creep of a brother. I didn't like him much.'

'Did you ever meet anyone else, any friends of hers perhaps?'

'A couple of times when I dropped into her place, a bloke was hanging around. Shauna said it was her landlord, I didn't get a name. He always left as soon as I arrived. Mind, if he was her landlord he was a long way from home.'

'Could you describe him?'

Gatley's brow furrowed as he pondered. 'Scottish by the accent, late twenties, early thirties, dark hair with blonde streaks. Whoever he was, he had an expensive taste in clothes, always wearing top of the range trainers, watches…'

'Is this the same man?' she held out the image of the Audi she'd downloaded.

'Might be. It's not a great picture is it?'

Back in the fresh air, Sarah let the details trickle through her head. The Scottish connection was probably a red herring but hearing it mentioned twice in less than an hour was like a traffic light stuck on amber; she couldn't ignore it. 'Take another look at the grandmother, Aryan. Try a trace via the Scottish registry. If the name on the death certificate we found in the flat is correct, it shouldn't be too hard.'

'And we believe Megan Shaw is really Louise Marie Jamieson?'

'Do we?' Sarah smiled at the young man's flustered expression. 'Never assume. Find a way to confirm although I doubt that will be easy, given her passport is registered in her alias. I'll find out where Matt Cox is this morning. With luck, we can be back at the station by eleven.'

Matt Cox was at home for the day. The tree-lined street Aryan finally parked in was filled with detached Edwardian houses, more suitable for retired professors and executives than a lowly bachelor social worker.

'These places cost a fortune,' Aryan commented while they waited for the door to be opened. 'I didn't think social workers earned that much?'

'They don't – interesting though. Ah, Mr Cox, thank you for seeing us at such short notice…'

The young man stood on his doorstep in ratty slippers, baggy jogging bottoms and a jumper, obviously worn for comfort rather than style. Sarah instantly warmed to the man. 'I am sorry to disturb you on your day off.'

'Please, call me Matt and it's fine, anything I can do to help. I've been so worried about Lee and Megan…' Stepping aside, he showed them into an elegantly tiled hallway. 'Can I offer you a drink?'

'No, we won't take up any more time than we have to. I'd hoped you might be able to tell me more about Megan, her background maybe?'

Matt pushed a hand through his hair as if trying to shake out some thoughts. 'That's hard, Megan rarely talked about herself, not that she's sullen or difficult you understand. We chat for ages, just not about personal stuff – or not hers.'

Sarah frowned at the squeak of a floorboard above their heads. 'Matt, could we use your sitting room or kitchen?'

Freya would have been green with envy, Sarah thought, admiring the high ceiling, all the original features and the dreamy tiled fireplace. 'This is nice. Have you lived here long?'

Matt's smile stripped away ten years. 'My great aunt decided to leave the place to me two years ago, which was fantastic, except it needed a complete renovation. New roof, electrical wiring, plumbing – everything needed replacing. I didn't have the heart to sell the place, too many memories. Sorry, it's not my story you wanted to hear is it.'

'Not at all. I can completely understand why you would want to stay.'

'I managed to persuade the bank to give me a mortgage but I've had to give in and take a lodger.' Matt nodded to the ceiling. 'Warren's money has been a godsend and there's loads of room.'

'Ah – is that who's upstairs?'

'Warren works from home most of the time, or at the local Uni.'

Sarah brought the subject back on topic. 'So, Megan – you're fond of her?'

The slight flush was charming. 'When I found out she'd dumped her boyfriend I'd been planning to ask her out, so yes.'

Maybe the wind had picked up and was rattling the old windows? Casually, Sarah walked to the door, feigning interest in a small lino print. 'Did Megan talk about her family at all?'

'Megan talked about nursing her grandmother. I know she died. She did tell me about the accusation in Hull. That shook her up. I think it was one of the main reasons she left the area after her grandmother's death.'

'Is this print by a local artist?' Deliberately, Sarah rattled the door handle. From the hallway hurried footsteps moved away towards the stairs.

'I've no idea, Chief Inspector. It's one of the things I inherited. I like it though.'

'Thank you, Matt, that's all for now but if you do think of anything else, please don't hesitate to ring me.'

As the front door closed behind them, Sarah cast a curious glance at the window above their heads. 'I don't like eavesdroppers, Aryan. Someone was listening outside that door. They're probably being nosey but let's check them out…'

Aryan didn't try to hide the heavy sigh. 'I'll add it to the list, Ma'am.'

Chapter Eighteen

UNAFFECTED BY SARAH'S APPARENT distance, Aryan drove steadily through the building traffic. His silence was appreciated by Sarah; the pieces of the puzzle were complicated. 'To add to your list Aryan, concentrate on finding out where Megan and her grandmother were living before Hull.'

'And do you still want me to dig into grandma's Scottish background?'

'Definitely.' Sarah caught the sideways glance but didn't respond. They were almost at the turning for the underground car park when Sarah spotted the transit van parked up in the small side road. 'What are they up to? Nothing good I'd imagine.'

'Do you recognise that van from over here?'

'It belongs to one of the local newspapers. You go ahead and start digging. I'll find out what the reporter is after.'

'I didn't even notice the van was there,' Aryan admitted.

'Oh its years of practice, Aryan' *Mixed with a massive dose of paranoia after this morning,* Sarah thought.

At reception, Tracy Bates glanced up from the note she was writing. 'It's been a quiet morning at this end, Sarah, no messages.'

'So, you've no idea why we have an *Express* van hiding over in Denby lane?'

'Really? Give me one sec and I'll check the external monitors for you.' Tracy zoomed in on the vehicle. 'That's Grace Smith by the colour of the hair, although I've no idea why she's still hanging around. It's been as quiet as the grave.'

‘What about Greg or child protection officers – are they in the building?’

The sergeant scanned the log. ‘A liaison officer arrived an hour ago, Greg’s been here all morning. Is there a problem?’

‘Grace Smith can make a mountain out of two grains of rice. She’ll have seen child protection officers arrive and be making up her own story. Do you still have a contact at the paper?’

‘I might do,’ Tracy winked. ‘Leave it with me. I’ll see what he can root out. On that other matter from this morning, there’s been no luck with the street cameras. The weather conditions were horrendous.’ Tracy shifted uncomfortably. ‘Sarah, don’t you think it might be an idea to have a lift into work for the next few days?’

Sarah frowned. The sergeant was an easy read. ‘Who did you tell Tracy, spit it out.’

‘Might have mentioned something to Amos, but he promised to keep it to himself. I’m sorry, but what if something happened to you, I couldn’t live with myself.’

At least she hadn’t told Finchley. Resigned, Sarah gave in gracefully. ‘My fault, Tracy. I shouldn’t have put you in that position.’

‘You’re forgiven and that cake was particularly nice.’

Sarah’s first thought as she stepped into the central incident room was that Ben looked exhausted. The digital board on the back wall was now a maze of lines and data. From a distance, it looked more like a street map.

‘I have a few things to tell you, Chief Inspector.’ Ben pulled over a seat, hardly waiting for her to be settled before he launched into an explanation. ‘Greg has spoken with a few colleagues in London and Europe. The best analysis so far is that the youngsters would be kept until they have captured six or eight then sold on, which fits with the information we have. The latest intel comes from Turkey and the middle-east and Greg is trying to identify likely routes. He also mentioned that

MI5 are twitching like a hive of angry hornets and insisting that we feed them into the investigation.'

'And have the whole thing grind to a halt while they play politics? What did Greg say?'

'He feels the same. He's told them that he'd leave it to his lead officer to update them as appropriate. In the meantime, would they please send any intel they have on recent child trafficking rings?'

'And I bet they loved that – I'll wait for the fallout. What else have we got?'

'Closer to home, Jackie and the others have found another two fake agency staff. A Chris Atkins, real name John Timpson. He moved to Leicester from Suffolk six weeks ago. He's currently employed as kitchen staff at one of the larger units. The other, a Rebecca Short, is proving more elusive but could still be a *player* – she's new to the Cambridge area. We know she worked in Derbyshire recently where there was a *runner*. We're still trying to trace the specifics of her work record. She doesn't drive so we've had no luck with DVLA.'

'What's the hitch, Ben?'

'Bloody red tape. We can't get a straight answer from the agency she's working for in Cambridge.

'But there's no problem with this John Timpson's records? What's the difference?'

'One of the local agencies in Cambridge had its fingers burnt recently. A care worker tried to sue for breach of privacy. Now their legal department is being overly cautious and we're paying the bloody price.'

'Phone Police HQ in Cambridge and speak to our counterparts. Tell them that Rebecca Short is suspected of using a false ID and that it's now part of a serious crime initiative. We need warrants immediately. If we're proved right, they'll be fed into the investigation directly. Emphasise there's to be no contact with the suspect. It's information only at this time.'

‘I’m on it,’ he was already scanning for the numbers. ‘I can’t tell you how frustrating this last hour has been. I’ve had Mike Lawson over here every two minutes. God knows what he wanted.’

‘Was he looking for me, Ben?’

‘No idea, he wouldn’t say. Sorry, Ma’am, it’s ringing...’

Sarah left him to it. There was too much else going on in her head to worry about Mike bloody Lawson and his stupid games. She found sanctuary once again in Bill Porter’s office, away from the mess and clutter of the case. Carl and Neil had left her and Amos a mound of paperwork ready to be signed off, which was fair enough. The Ingles/Carson cases had been reduced to a few files – a success of sorts she supposed. She was a realist at heart; it would only be a matter of time before another pair of hopeful entrepreneurs stepped into their shoes. It didn’t depress her particularly – as long as she stayed roughly ahead, all was well. Sarah wasn’t so sure it was a philosophy the Chief Constable would condone but the CC was so out of touch she might as well be living in Australia. The paperwork kept Sarah busy and off everyone’s back for the next couple of hours. When the knock on her door finally came, her pile had been reduced to almost nothing.

‘Aryan, you look worried?’

‘It’s this search you asked me to do, Ma’am.’ Aryan handed over a sheet with a single row of entries. ‘Megan Shaw. I can trace her work and home addresses via her national insurance number but only for the last four years. She’d had a variety of jobs: waitressing, shop work, but every address prior to Hull is coming back as unknown. The only legitimate addresses I can find for her are the current one and the one in Hull. I tried using the name on the birth certificate you found, but that gave me nothing at all.’

‘Is this second address for the grandmother some kind of care home?’

'The Laurels? Yes, Ma'am. They only take privately funded patients who have a life-threatening or terminal illness. The grandmother was there for just over three months before she died. She had renal cancer. The matron told me there was a granddaughter who had nursed her at home before that.'

'That sort of private care would cost a fortune. How the hell did they pay?'

'Well, it wasn't insurance. When the grandmother first arrived, she made a one-off payment of eighty thousand pounds, which covered her stay.'

'The more I learn the less I know.' Sarah mentally slotted the latest information inside her busy brain. 'Did you have any more luck with tracing grandmother?'

Aryan hesitated. 'There are dozens of Catherine Marie Jamieson's,'

'I'm hearing a 'but', Aryan?'

'There was one Catherine Jamieson, the second wife of an Alastair Jamieson. She was reported missing over twenty-three years ago. According to a police report filed in Glasgow, she disappeared in 1997. The Jamieson family she married into are well known to the Scottish authorities.'

'Impressive, Aryan – have you eaten?'

'No, I...'

Ben Peterson's head followed the rap on the door. 'Sorry, but more information has come through?'

'I'm on the way. Aryan here is going to the canteen. When you've eaten, run what you have on the Jamieson clan through the databases and see what comes up?'

Sarah followed her sergeant into the main incident room. On the large monitor, two photographs stared out at her. The rest of the screen showed the map, now with a terrifying hundred and seven flags.

Ben pointed to the male. 'You're looking at twenty-six-year-old John Timpson and below is twenty-three-year-old Rebecca Short, real name Elena Williams. Cambridge Police took prints off her application form at the agency and found a match. Elena was convicted of shoplifting four years ago in Newport, South Wales. She disappeared immediately after the case was heard, fine unpaid. Elena was brought up on a local estate, and left school at sixteen with three GCSE's. Her family appear clean with no criminal records.'

Sarah studied the young woman's profile. Belligerent eyes gazed out at the camera. There was no hint of worry or fear – simply boredom. 'And Timpson?'

He is twenty-six, born in Worcester and has one younger sister. Father still alive, mother deceased. He left school at sixteen with no qualifications, trained as a van driver when he was twenty-one. Aged twenty-three he was picked up for selling dodgy cameras at a local market and given a formal caution. He was convicted a year later for selling imported tobacco and handed a three month suspended sentence.'

Sarah sighed – a familiar picture; both had chosen to live on the edge of society and made an easy mark for any criminal gang. 'The profile of the woman Emily, is it much the same?'

'Pretty much. We finally tracked down her real name – Emily Cotton. Born in Kings Lynn, she was convicted of shoplifting at the tender age of fourteen. She has a similar stable family background, certainly nothing to indicate she was heading this way.'

'Any idea yet which of the counties is our most likely target for the next *runner*?'

Peterson hesitated. 'A difficult one to call. These two are the only potential *players* we've identified. It's possible we've missed one entirely, however, with the information we have so far, Leicester or Cambridge appear to be our best options. Both the *players* I've mentioned are due on shift Saturday and Sunday at 07.30 hrs.'

'I don't suppose either force want to babysit for us, Ben?'

'Unlikely Cambridge will. They've two music festivals and a political protest taking place in the city centre on Saturday.

They'll do what they can. Leicester can do more and are happy to play ball.' Ben handed her the printed sheet.

'The problem is, if we grab these two now, we're going to alert the rest of the teams; they'll disappear without a trace. What are our chances of tracking down further *players* in other counties – say in the next twenty-four hours?'

'Countrywide – not great.' Ben pushed his chair back to swing on two legs. 'Finding these two took officers three hours of painstaking searches, that and a huge dollop of good old fashioned luck.'

'I take it you don't fancy the odds?'

'I won't be placing any bets but I'm more than happy to rally the troops.'

'Then we do what we can. Speak with Leicester and arrange surveillance. Tell them two bodies inside, plus CCTV on the perimeter. Are they happy to liaise with you?'

'So far, Ma'am. If I need any more clout, I'll let you know.'

'We're going to have to send someone down to Cambridge as well. I'm not prepared to have this side-lined because of some local politics. I hope you and Jackie have your bags packed?'

'As ever. I've details of the children's homes they're working in. Do you want me to contact them and arrange everything?'

'No, I'd better do that, it's dodgy ground. We already know one of their staff is bogus and we're essentially asking them to run with it.' She checked the clock and sighed, it was already 14.50 hrs. It was going to be another long evening. 'Is there any news yet from traffic about the green van or the blue Audi?'

'The Audi was registered to a company called *Euro Collect and Hire* based in Lincoln. The car was sold on five months ago. I've contacted the local force and they're checking their records. I've put in an urgent request to the DVLA for vehicles registered to the company. As for the other trace Ma'am, the sergeant taking the lead on this in traffic is convinced that the last green van is part of the deal.'

'And that isn't wishful thinking?'

'That's what I asked too. I hope he's wrong or it's going to cost me twenty.'

'We give it another couple of hours Ben, then suggest to the sergeant in traffic that he and a few of his team stand down. If there is a snatch, we're going to need them fully functioning. I am not spending the weekend arguing the toss with Central Traffic in some unknown city.'

'Will do, Ma'am.'

'Any luck with the forensics from Emily's flat?' The forensic teams' overtime budget must have gone through the roof.

'Some – Emily Cotton had a male visitor recently and it wasn't Andrew Woods or Rees Morgan. They found hair and bodily fluid on the sheets in a wash basket, as well as fingerprints that don't match either Morgan or Woods. No luck yet on finding a match.'

'Keep up the momentum and, if anyone needs me, I'll be in the canteen for fifteen or so. Leave the numbers for the children's homes in Cambridge and Leicester on my desk. I'll sort those after I bring Finchley up to date.'

Sarah decided to eat first and settled on soup. She and Freya were staying with friends that evening; Tom and Jason were used to Sarah's random workload so, whatever time she turned up, she could pretty much guarantee there would be mountains of food. Something she couldn't resist were the trays of pastries. Her internal debate, deciding between a Danish or custard slice, was almost resolved when Aryan Khan appeared at her side. With a sigh, Sarah dragged her eyes up to his flustered face.

'This had better be good, Aryan.'

'Sorry, I would have waited but...'

'Just spit it out, man.'

'Those names, Catherine Marie Jamieson and her granddaughter, Louise, Interpol have red-flagged them. I received this message saying to contact them immediately. I thought you should know.'

'Interpol,' Sarah frowned at the complication. 'Well, we *have* opened a can of worms. Did you make a response?'

'Yes – I lied. I knew they'd be able to track the request to us, so I umm, I told them it was a query about an old passport that had been found – sorry.'

It was a ruse she'd used several times herself but not one she'd expect a rookie to know. Sarah leaned in and lowered her voice. 'I'm beginning to suspect there's something you're not sharing, Mr Khan. Care to explain?'

'Ma'am?'

'Who's fast-tracking you and please don't lie?' Sarah held his gaze until his shoulders slumped in defeat.

'Homeland Security,' he admitted quietly. 'It's part of their new '*In house learning strategy*.' They want their techies to be field trained from the ground up. I swear, I'm here to work as part of the team.'

'I don't doubt you, Aryan. And I imagine using your tech skills wasn't part of the plan?'

'We've been specifically told not to. I'm in so much trouble when they find out.'

'Did you lie about the program?'

'No, Ma'am! It's mine and freely available.' Aryan sounded genuinely shocked.

'In that case, you've nothing to worry about. Greg or Ben are astute enough to have applied the program. I'll have a word. So now, this problem with Interpol: did they give any details at all?'

'Only a contact number,' Aryan handed her a slip of paper.

'We'll try another angle first I think, before involving this lot. You said the Jamieson family were known to the police – start with old national news reports.'

'How far back do you want me to go?'

Sarah gave it a moment's thought. 'Start at twenty-five years and move to the present day.'

Sarah opted for the Danish pastry. Her teeth sank into the sweet crust as Amos Brantley swung into the chair opposite.

'I hope that's not all you've had?' He helped himself to a chunk off the side. Sarah pushed his fingers away as he tried for more.

'It's none of your damned business if it is, Amos.'

'Finchley is back. Oh, and Tracy told me to tell you she's had a word. Grace Smith at the *Express* is doing a piece on "Rehabilitating sex offenders". Does that make any sense to you?'

'Grace Smith's van is parked in Denby Lane. She has to be tailing Greg Roberts.'

Before she could stop him, Amos tore off another piece of her pastry. 'And, I was also wondering if there was any reason you chose not to share the fact someone attempted to kill you this morning?'

'Oh, for goodness sake, Amos…'

'Don't you make light of this. Tracy was worried sick and so the hell am I. She said you were ashen when you arrived. What the hell were you thinking, not telling me?'

'It could've been a simple loss of control…'

'Bollocks! – don't,' he said as she opened her mouth to argue. 'You are slap bang in the middle of a bloody great storm. God knows whose cage you've rattled.'

'That's a strange mix of metaphors…'

'You know exactly what I mean Sarah. What if the tables were turned and it had been me in that car?'

'Okay, point taken. Hell, you're worse than Freya.'

'The problem Sarah, is that I could run off a list of at least ten who would be thrilled to have you out of the picture – dead, injured, I doubt they'd care that much.'

'Ingles and Carson aren't stupid, Amos, they're going down for theft. They know if they behave themselves they'll be out in five, probably less…'

'Oh, they're way down the bottom of my list.' Amos drummed his fingers in a sharp staccato beat, refusing to drop the steely gaze. 'So, if you don't want me to take this to Finchley, this is the deal. For the next week it's a taxi to and from work or one of us drives you. No running on your own…'

'You may as well slap me under house arrest!'

'If I tell Finchley he'll probably pack you off to Sunderland or worse, Kent.'

She laughed, dusting off a few crumbs from her fingers. 'You must have been so bored while you were off sick?'

'Jen and the kids are away,' he admitted. 'They're visiting her brother in Wales for a week. And don't change the subject – do we have a deal?'

'Okay, I'll play nicely at least for a few days – I promise.' Sarah checked the time. 'I need to sweet talk Finchley into sending a couple of bodies to Cambridge.'

'Why bother sending anyone? I thought it was a watching brief?'

'The traffickers have already picked up five youngsters, I'm not taking any chances. Cambridge force is cold to lukewarm about the whole deal. I'm afraid they'll let this Williams woman slip through the net. It also means that I'll have Ben and Jackie on hand to do an immediate interrogation – covers both bases. I'll give it until midday Monday, if nothing breaks by then we'll pick up the Williams woman anyway. I'll charge her with falsifying ID but hopefully we'll have found a few more *players* by then.'

'It would be more fun if we went down and did it ourselves, Sarah. It would certainly make it harder for any jobbing hit-men.'

Sarah laughed. 'I can't see Finchley agreeing to that one. We're way too expensive for one thing and too damned old.'

'Excuse me, we are not *that* old and I'd love to see Finchley's expression when you suggest it.'

'In your dreams, Brantley.' Sarah checked her watch again. 'I must ring Freya. We're staying at Tom and Jason's tonight and I need to let her know I'm likely to be late.'

'Tell her I'll drop you off at Tom's so she doesn't worry.' Amos watched as she picked up the last of the pastry and began to chew. 'Don't you sometimes wish we could go back: training college, uniform in Cheltenham? Think about what we missed, how much better things would be now we've some experience under our belt?'

'Are you crazy? You're forgetting those long wet roads, sore feet and anyway, I wouldn't change what I have now for anyone.'

'And I was going to accuse you of being an unromantic soul.' Amos was silent for a long moment. 'Half of Talbot House fell in love with Freya you know.'

'Excuse me?' Sarah caught her breath surprised at the sudden intensity.

'It wasn't only me,' he said softly. 'I reckon most of the team had fallen for her. You must have realised? We had to look at the photographs, those gorgeous dreamy eyes, for days on end. Freya was – is – beautiful and when we finally found her, it was like being hit in the chest by something hard, I could barely breathe. Trust me, it wasn't easy knowing the only person she had eyes for was you.'

'Amos – I had no idea.'

'You, being my best buddy, made it that bit easier to swallow. Then I got the inspector's post up here and I found Jen. Thankfully, my world turned the right way up again.'

'Why the confession now?' Sarah was stunned. How could she have misread him so badly?

'Having time to reflect, sorting out old crap, you know, the usual guff.' Amos leant back studying her intently. 'And then you asked me to check up on Freya and it hit me. You've had six years of living with the fear, wondering if the bastard is still searching for her. Me, I'd forgotten, tucked it all neatly away. Not you Sarah, you've had to live with it every single day.' His eyes searched hers until she felt naked.

'It's not like that, Amos.'

'Yes it bloody is. You've built a wall so thick nothing gets through.' Amos reached over and squeezed her hand. 'Throughout your career you've been side-lined, sneered at, constantly passed over for promotion when you were always the best of us. That's bad enough. Then came all that extra worry on top. I don't know how you've survived.'

'You're not ill are you?' Sarah tried to laugh it off but he wasn't having it.

'I'm being serious. I'm looking at a woman living on a knife's edge. How many hours of sleep are you averaging a week? Twenty, twenty-five if you're lucky? Finchley needs a rollicking for not drafting someone in. How the hell did he expect you to manage on your own? Lawson is – well – let's not go there,' he said firmly. 'You've got so much pent up inside you right now, something has to give. Sarah, this morning's incident wasn't some trivial act. I took a look at your gate post. There's a huge chunk missing – that could've been your bloody neck! You're so used to living with the stress, you're not even aware of the risks any more, not when it comes to you.'

The worst of it was he was right. 'Fair enough, I'll bow to your wisdom and take the taxis and, as soon as this case is done, I'll talk to Finchley about some leave.' She toyed with the mug while she studied the man opposite. 'And talking of confessions Amos, why didn't you say something earlier. It must have been hell for you when I transferred here from Cheltenham?'

He shrugged but the smile came easily. 'By then I'd had time to adjust. The distance helped. I knew the woman we rescued was never going to fall into my arms and profess her undying love. That was the fantasy, Jen was the reality. And don't forget, by the time you arrived I had my own team. You ended up with Bill, so it wasn't a problem.'

'And now?'

'I'm lonely with Jen and the kids away,' Amos admitted. 'It's much worse having spent the last three months together. I was only sore for a few weeks. It's been fantastic being off.'

Sarah began to laugh, 'Oh dear, you're not seriously thinking of early retirement are you?'

'It's bloody crossed my mind a few times. Jen won't hear of it until I know what I want to do.'

'She's a bright lady. You'd be a nightmare without a purpose.'

'I need to get back into the swing of things I suppose.'

'Well, as lead officer I'll make sure I keep you busy, DCI Brantley. First off, how do you feel about handling a couple of delicate phone calls for me while I plead for money with our CS – unless you want to swap?'

'How can I refuse?' Amos began to push away from the table.

'Before you go, how is Moira doing? I haven't heard a dicky bird.' Sarah caught the tension, the tightening around his eyes.

'To be honest, things are a little complicated. Moira is fuzzy about what happened, can't remember what the hell went down.' Amos leant across the table, his deep voice barely a whisper. 'She's staying in a safe house for a while, not happy about it, but someone's tried to break into the cellar of the *Blue Beacon* a couple of times since Tuesday. I've had to put a twenty-four-hour watch on the place. Once your investigation is over and I've got the workforce, I'm going in there with a team to pull that place apart.'

'Surely the CS unit went over it?'

'They did a surface forensic sweep of the cellar and distilling equipment, catalogued what they could see, but it'll take days to pull everything out and check it all. The Forensics department is reeling from the work you've been sending their way.'

'What the hell are they after Amos, any idea?'

'My best guess – Moira's phone. One of the last things she remembers is being in the bar, snapping a shot of three men talking with the *Blue Beacon's* owner. She has a vague memory of running down the cellar stairs, which I think is when they hit her. I've searched, Carl's looked, but I'm damned if we can find the bloody thing.'

'Have you tried ringing the mobile?'

Laughter softened his solemn expression. 'Seriously, Allerton?'

'It's always worth checking, Amos. And how about Farnes, did he throw Paul Wiggins over the bridge and more importantly, why?'

'Adam Farnes is refusing to say a damned thing, but it looks like Paul might survive after all. Who knows, maybe he'll give us some answers.'

***

Chief Superintendent Finchley paced his room while Sarah outlined the current situation. It was unsettling when he wouldn't look her in the eye. If she was going to send officers to Cambridge it needed to be the following day at the latest. Finally, he turned to face her. 'I can fully understand Cambridge's problem. Who will you send?'

'Ben Peterson and Jackie Simmons; Cambridge are happy to have them as temporary attachments, with your permission of course. Once on the ground, I'll have one in-house while the other monitors the exits. Cambridge agreed to sort the technical side if we're prepared to man it. They'll give us an extra body if their capacity allows.'

'Decent of them,' he said blandly. 'And Leicester?'

‘Fortunately, they’re in a position to put in two officers and maintain the monitoring for us. Amos is talking to the managers of both centres to explain the issue.’

‘That’s the part I’m having a problem with. We know they have fraudulent workers alongside highly vulnerable youngsters.’

‘Not at this moment, Sir. They won’t be on duty until the weekend. We’ll pick those two up once we’ve pinpointed as many potential *players* in other areas as we can. I’ve alerted all the regions, asked them to keep a watching brief but, without decent intel about the *players* in each of the children’s homes, we’re out on a limb.’

‘And if the plan goes awry and one of the youngsters is taken?’

‘If we pick Williams and Timpson up now, the whole investigation is blown wide open. We’ll have lost any chance of finding Lee and the other four.’

‘It’s all surmise, Sarah. Lee Wiggins was probably moved out of the country within hours of being taken, and as for the others...’

‘Not according to Greg Roberts’ most recent analysis.’ Sarah handed Finchley the briefing note. ‘I’ve five officers spending every moment chasing down other potential *players*. As soon as we make our move on Leicester and Cambridge that chance will be gone.’

‘Very well, but increase the number doing the research. Use as many bodies as you need – whatever it takes. On another issue, Sergeant Bates told me about the *Express* van outside. I’ve spoken to the editor and invited the journalist, Grace Smith in for an informal discussion with the *New City Strategic Team*. She’ll be here at 13.00 hrs on Wednesday. Let’s hope our little problem has resolved itself by then. It could prove embarrassing otherwise?’

Stunned, Sarah could only stare. ‘What City Strategic Team?’

'Why, the one you've just set up Chief Inspector, involving closer liaison with CPU, serious crime and fraud?'

'Clever, Sir,' she admitted admiring the move.

'I have my moments. I also told the editor that, if he or any of his reporters attempt to follow any of my officers without due cause, I'd lock them up so fast the lawyers wouldn't know what hit them. That was much more fun.'

'Thank you – I take it the news embargo wasn't agreed?'

'No, too much red tape and things are moving so fast there's not a lot of point. The Chief Constable has agreed to review the decision on Monday if necessary. She's also concerned about resources, Sarah. *North Run* is becoming a national problem. Leeds central has a greater capacity to deal with issues like this…'

'Sir, with respect, handing this over now is the worst possible solution. We'd lose vital hours – days even. It isn't a case of simply downloading files; the officers working the case understand the complexity. Think of the amount of time we'd waste trying to bring Leeds up to speed. Time which could be far better spent chasing down potential bogus workers. We've a narrow window of opportunity to find Wiggins and can't afford to waste a moment…'

'Like it or not *Acting* Chief Inspector, the spotlight is firmly on you. *I* know you are capable of heading up what is fast becoming a nationwide team. I have no doubts about your abilities but the Chief Constable is rightly concerned about potential outcomes. In her eyes you are new to the post – unproven. You had better be one hundred per cent bloody certain about any actions you set in play. Do I make myself clear?'

'Crystal, Sir.'

'Very well. I'll inform the Chief Constable that activities will be coordinated from Hepsford for now. I expect to receive regular updates, understood.'

'Absolutely, Sir and thank you.'

Chapter Nineteen

Thursday evening

LEE WAS LYING IN THE BACK of the van struggling to view anything through the hessian sack. It was hard enough to breathe. He fought the nausea, determined not to throw up. He'd been asleep when the cell door opened and the first he'd known about what was happening was when a rough bag was thrown over his head.

'One word and you'll regret it,' The male voice was deep - threatening and Lee didn't argue.

A blast of fresh air and dim light seen through the sacking offered a brief relief – until they tied his arms behind his back and rolled him into the van. The journey seemed endless. He heard mumbling somewhere close but with the bag over his head and engine noise, he failed to make out anything. Intermittently, the van stopped in traffic and the voices became clearer.

'She arrived this morning, she's no idea he's dead.' The male voice again, low and gruff.

A female asked, 'What the hell did Callum say to get her to come, Mark?'

'He pretended he was Laurence, got a thing for him hasn't she.'

'And she believed it?' The woman began to laugh.

'Why wouldn't she? Bloody deserves it and all – Jade, pass us a peppermint would you?' The conversation was smothered again as the van moved off again.

Whenever the van cornered, Lee rolled helplessly, landing hard against something solid, hip throbbing from the impact. Stretching tied hands as far as he could, he sought something to cling onto. The bag did muffle a yelp when his searching fingers found the tip of a long, sharp screw. Again the van slowed and Lee braced, determined not to lose his grip.

'They reported it as an accident.' Jade seemed to be reassuring her partner.

'And there's been nothing more in the papers?'

'Not so far, but I'm with you. I wish the boss would give it a break for a bit, just go with the drugs. Trevor's positive he's going for another.'

Lee was desperate for the van to move off again, terrified he'd lose his one chance to work the screw loose.

It felt like hours later when the engine fell silent and, when the doors opened, this time there wasn't any whiff of fresh air. 'Get him out, make sure you do a proper job of cleaning up.' This voice was new, the Scottish accent heightened the threat.

No point fighting, not yet. Rough hands grabbed Lee's legs, dragging him out. Moments later, the rope on his ankles was sliced off – metal cuffs slipped around his wrists.

Mark from the van spoke, close to Lee's head. 'You'll do as you're told. Mess up and I'll beat you senseless, no difference to me.' Something heavy was being dragged, metal on something hard. Without warning, Mark grabbed Lee from behind, hoisting him into the air. 'You kick me and you won't see tomorrow.'

Through the gap at his chin, Lee saw a gaping hole in a concrete floor. Whatever he was standing on moved downwards, jerking awkwardly from side to side. The already dim light faded fast and his body jarred as the base hit solid ground. Booted feet landed with a thud beside him.

Mark's words now echoed. 'No one cares a toss about you so don't go thinking anyone's looking.' Roughly, the man pulled Lee's hands to the front, slotting a rattling metal chain through the bands on his wrists. 'In a few days, you'll be taking a nice little trip. Until then, you keep it quiet, understood. Now sit, and leave that hood on 'til I tell you.' A foot caught him hard on the chin as the man leapt back toward the light.

Chain clanking, Lee reached to tear off the sack. 'Not yet!' The urgent whisper came from beside him. 'They'll be watching. Wait.'

Seconds, minutes – years ticked meaninglessly past before, '*You can take them off!*' echoed down.

Lee's ears vibrated with the thud as metal slammed into place above their heads. He tore at the sack, pulling it away. For long moments he saw nothing but vague shadows.

The figure beside him introduced himself. 'I'm Si, Simon Hitchin. Over there is Kayla and next to her is Rosa. There was another until a couple of days ago but...'

Lee didn't ask, his eyes were still adjusting to the dim light. Opposite, the girls were bunched, silent. 'I'm Lee. How long have you been here, Si?'

'Me – about two weeks I think, hard to say. What's the date?'

'About the tenth of November, I think.'

'Yeah, that'll be about right. Kayla was a few days after.' Again Si clammed up.

'What about Rosa?'

'She thinks she came a couple of weeks before me.' Lee felt the shrug.

Now his eyes had adjusted, Lee scanned around. Above their heads, a square metal grille covered a hole, spears of light piercing the gaps. Six benches filled the space and a stinking toilet occupied one corner. Leaning over, Lee whispered in Simon's ear, 'Is that grate locked?'

There was a shake of a head followed by a long sigh. 'Not that it makes a difference.' He rattled his chain. 'Believe me, we've tried to break them.'

'What do you think they're planning to do with us?'

From the bench opposite Lee heard a low sob. Kayla put a comforting arm around Rosa. 'We don't talk about it, right!'

'Rosa's not even twelve,' Simon muttered. 'She's been much worse since Paula…'

'Have you any idea where we are?'

'Nope, Kayla reckons it's somewhere on the south coast but I'm not so sure; one of the men has a bit of an accent.'

Silence blanketed them again until Lee lifted his hand and the chain rattled. He tugged hard, testing its tension, resisted by the concrete. 'This place looks like the examination pit in my uncle's garage. What's that on the floor?'

'Rubber sheeting,' Simon muttered. 'It gets slippery, be careful. The chains are long enough for us to reach the toilet. We've a bench each and there are a few blankets. We're forced to have a shower once a week and we're fed a couple of times a day. They're supposed to take us up for a walk around the garage each day as well. They call it exercise.'

Across from him, Kayla's bitter laugh was easy to interpret.

'I take it that doesn't happen often?'

'You're a bright one,' Kayla muttered. He guessed her mocking was for show.

'Is the boss the one with the Scottish accent?' Lee asked.

'See, I told you he was Scottish, Ky.'

'Do I look like I care? Sod off, Si.'

Occasional wafts of warmth drifted down through the grating. Lee could smell the fresh air so there had to be a window in the garage above, some way of reaching the world outside. Right at that moment, the pain in his side where the screw dug in felt great.

'What time of day is it Si, do you know?'

'It must be getting late. They usually feed us after dark.'

They talked in whispers, stopping altogether when the grate opened and a bag of food swung down on a rope. Lee ate his ration quickly then began to pace the confines of the pit.

Kayla started to swear. 'Will you bloody well sit down? What do you think you are, some sort of frigging escape artist?'

‘And maybe I am,’ he hissed back but sat anyway. He was going to need to work out when the garage was left empty, if ever.

‘We use the sacks as pillows,’ Simon told him when Lee started to yawn. ‘There’s a blanket underneath. It’s not easy staying warm but they’ve put a new heater in the garage – at least it isn’t freezing any more. That’s what did for Paula I reckon.’

Kayla hissed at him again. ‘Shut up! I don’t want to talk about it.’

Simon sniggered ignoring Kyla’s low growl. ‘Welcome to your first night in hell, mate. ‘Room service isn’t up to much, but at least the air is free.’

Chapter Twenty

Friday

SARAH WASN'T SURE IF IT HAD BEEN the red wine, Tom's excellent food or exhaustion but for once, it was her alarm that woke her from an untroubled sleep – a rare thing. Leaning across the unfamiliar wide bed, she planted a soft kiss on Freya's slim shoulder and felt her stirring in response. The acid scars remained visible – white now, more shadows under her dark skin. In the dim glow of the nightlight they appeared to move, coiled serpents preparing to strike. With an effort, Sarah turned away – no room for fantasy, the real world was traumatic enough.

'Did you sleep at all?' Freya's words were heavy with sleep.

Sarah pulled the duvet up over her partner's shoulder and whispered, 'Like a log. Go back to sleep, you don't need to be up for an hour or so.'

I'm glad you slept. I've been so worried about you.' Freya yawned, blinking sleep from her eyes. 'Don't look at me like that, Sarah. I wanted to say something last night but with Tom and Jason hovering, it didn't seem right. I wish you'd tell me what's wrong?'

'It's nothing – really, pressure at work.'

'For a detective, you are one awful liar.'

'Sorry love, I know the past few months have been hard on you…'

'Sarah!' Freya sat up, all signs of sleep gone. 'Will you stop treating me like I'm still a victim. This isn't six years ago. You don't need to handle me with kid gloves!'

Sarah ran a finger along her partner's slender wrist grateful for their closeness. 'I wish I had your inner strength, Freya.'

‘For goodness sake woman, you must be stressed to hell to come up with crap like that. For pity sake, take a break, it’s been months. You’re going to explode if you don’t stop soon.’

‘Have you been talking to Amos?’ Sarah sank back against the pillows, wishing she could curl up next to the woman she loved and hide away from the world for the next month or preferably twenty.

‘No – why, should I?’

‘It’s nothing. I just need a day off – go for a run.’

‘Sarah, a damned run is not going to fix this. Take back some control, will you? Life is more than your job. You go into work this morning and you *will* book leave. What do they owe you – is it four or five weeks now? You ask for three minimum and I don’t care how bloody busy you are.’

Sarah held up her hands in submission. ‘Okay, it’s a promise! I’ll put in my leave form first thing this morning.’

Freya’s expression softened into a warm smile. ‘I mean it, three weeks minimum, do you hear. Mine starts December the nineteenth – I’ll be ringing to check, so make sure you do just that!’

Closing the door on the sleeping household, Sarah climbed into Amos’s waiting car. It was warm at least as outside, the rain had given way to an icy chill. Apart from a gruff, ‘Morning,’ Amos was unusually silent. Sarah let a mile or so slip past before she asked. ‘Problem?’

‘Paul Wiggins died during the night. He had a massive stroke and, to add to our list of woes, Farnes is still playing silly buggers, refusing to say a word.’

‘How sure are you he’s responsible for clobbering Wiggins?’

‘We’ve enough circumstantial to put forward a decent case but something is out of line, Sarah. Farnes has been acting weird. The on-duty cell officer rang me at two am to say the guy was pacing the cell like a trapped rat, not eating either. I’ve put him on suicide watch just in case.’

'Is this since Paul Wiggins died?'

'He hasn't been told. When Carl and I interviewed him again yesterday, I got the feeling he's scared out of his wits. Something or someone has rattled his cage.'

'You could try talking to Steve Thomas. With Paul dead, he might be a bit more forthcoming? I got the impression he and a few of the other mechanics know a great deal more about Adam Farnes than they were letting on.'

Amos flashed the first smile of the morning. 'It's worth the extra couple of miles to pick your brain, Allerton. I might even buy you your first coffee.'

At Hepsford station the night team were hovering. Mercifully, it had been quiet, the bad weather dampening the high jinks on the city streets overnight. A few weary officers leant against walls, counting down the minutes until they could officially leave. Most were in the central incident room scanning for potential *players* in the identified children's homes. Chris Hollings looked as fresh as if he'd recently arrived on duty.

'What have you been drinking Chris, liquid speed?'

'The coffee machine's struggling to keep up Sarah, but we've made a lot of headway. It's a good thing the central databases don't close or we'd have had a seriously bad time. As it is, we've trawled through dozens of staff from every county on Aryan's list and a few more besides. So far, we've five definite *players* other than Timpson and Williams.'

'Incredible work, Chris. You and your officers deserve a bloody medal.'

'A mention in dispatches will suffice, Sarah.'

Are Ben or any of the team in yet?' Sarah glanced at the large wall clock; it was coming up to seven.

'They're grabbing food while they can. Between you and me Sarah, I might be regretting the decision to let them loose on my computers.' He nodded behind to the array of monitors and sighed.

‘Are there any left down in uniforms’ control room, Chris?’

‘I’m not sure I want to look, but they’d better come back without a bloody scratch.’

The slap of the double doors announced the team’s arrival. Staying partially hidden at the rear of the incident room, Sarah watched with interest as Aryan directed officers to the spare monitors, hooked them onto the wall-plugs, connecting cables as he went. The man was in his element, answering queries without a pause. To her left, the wall was rapidly transformed into what she thought of as a mini multiplex. The CS was going to have apoplexy when he saw it.

‘Which film are you planning to screen first?’ she asked as the fixing and checking finally began to slow.

Everyone jumped. ‘Morning Chief Inspector, I had no idea you were in.’ Ben glanced back over his shoulder at all the tech. ‘Chris told us we could haul this up from uniform’s central office. It means we can widen our search parameters. Officers can input data and view different parts of the country without impacting our current investigation.’

‘Just don’t break anything Ben. How long before this is done?’

‘Five and we’re all yours. Aryan said we just need to plug in the extensions and adaptors.’

As soon as the team had found their seats Sarah dived straight in. ‘Ben and Jackie will leave for Cambridge this afternoon. I want them set up and in position before anything kicks off. Despite the regional spread, this task force will continue to be a Hepsford led operation. All communications will be controlled from here, liaising with Cambridge and Leicester. Aryan Khan will be in charge of inputting information into the software as it arrives, so make sure everything goes through him, please.’ Sarah held up Chris Hollings’ folder. ‘The night team have unearthed five more suspected *players* and officers will continue to search throughout the day.’ She paused to check her list. ‘Did we receive feedback about vehicles registered to *Euro Collect and Hire*?'

Jake Forbes answered. 'Not so far. I'll ring back as soon as we finish here. Forensics left a message re the DNA at Emily Cotton's flat, though. There are no matches on any of our databases.'

'Did forensics find anything further in Woods' car or Megan's flat that might help us narrow things down?'

'Absolutely nothing, Ma'am.' Ben said. 'Whoever ditched the car and turned the flat over did a professional job of cleaning up.'

'Is there any luck with the number plate on the green van yet?'

Ben shook his head. 'Only a partial. Traffic said the plate had been obscured by what looks like mud. They are continuing to track it to see if the van joined the A1 or M62.'

The threads were refusing to be caught and the frustration had Sarah tapping her fingers. 'Aryan, I need that follow up information re-grandma. And, did you find anything on our nosey lodger?'

'Sorry Chief Inspector.' Flustered, he began to flick through his notebook.

'Pass that one on to Jackie. There's still a few hours before they need to leave for Cheltenham.'

Using a desk at the back of the incident room, Sarah hungrily consumed the tidbits as they were seeping through. Neighbours in the flat opposite Emily's had sworn they'd seen a slim man in his thirties visiting her, heard them arguing, though only in muffled voices. Frustratingly, the image of the Audi driver from Hull was yet to be enhanced. Sarah picked up the telephone, determined to speed things along – maybe her seniority would help? Put on hold, as usual, Sarah nodded the waiting Aryan Khan forward.

'There's some information on the grandmother, although the story is bizarre. It reads more like the synopsis to a novel.'

'Read me the outline while I wait for the imaging department to answer.'

Aryan cleared his throat. 'Catherine Bruce, the younger of two daughters, was born in Dumfries in Scotland in 1948. She married Alastair Jamieson, also of Dumfries, in 1971. They had one son, christened Ian Lewis Jamieson. Alastair Jamieson had previously been married to Catherine's older sister, Rosemary who died during the birth of her second child, Callum Jamieson.

'May 1998, in Liverpool, a warrant was issued for Catherine's arrest following the murder of her eldest stepson, Anthony Edward Jamieson also her daughter-in-law, Louisa Jamieson, Nee-Trent. Louisa had married Catherine's son – Ian – two years previously. The report states that it was Anthony, the stepson, who was suspected of the young woman's murder.

'Louisa, the daughter-in-law, had given birth to a baby girl three weeks before her death. According to the report, the baby had been christened Louise Marie Jamieson. The child disappeared at the same time as the fatalities.

'Forty-eight hours after the deaths of Anthony and Louisa, a Lewis William Jamieson, aged seventy-one and the much older half-brother of Alastair, was found dead in a supported housing unit for the elderly in Liverpool. He died from an apparent insulin overdose. The Coroner reported an open verdict on the old man's death.

'Intriguing – Carry on Aryan.'

'This is when things became strange, Ma'am. I tried to do an in-depth search on the Jamieson angle. However, other than the information I've already told you, all I could discover was that Ian Lewis Jamieson, Catherine's only child by the marriage, travelled to England in 1995 aged twenty-three. He met and married Ms Trent shortly after. Ian went missing in December 1997 and is believed dead.

'When I tried to continue the search on-line the programs were cut off – frozen. I've asked a colleague to try but the result was the same. Greg spoke to one of his sources in Glasgow who've also been warned off. All they can tell us is that Alastair Jamieson, now eighty-three, is a company director of an international exporting firm, mainly to India, South Africa and South America. He's been investigated by fraud and serious crime on a few occasions but nothing's stuck. Callum, the surviving son, is expected to take over the family business from the old man when he dies.'

'Well, Megan's grandma did do a good job of staying under the radar.' Sarah's respect for the old woman increased by the second. 'As much as it pains me to say this, I think we'll need a conversation with Interpol at some point. Is there anything else.'

'Jake has had some success with the vehicles registered to *Euro Collect and Hire* at last. They have eight vans and five cars listed in the name of the company director, James Smith. Companies House shows there are a couple of other listings for that name, so...' Aryan stopped as his tablet bleeped at him. 'Sorry Ma'am, I have a hit.' He studied the screen. 'Mr James Smith also trades under the name of Saul James. He's down as a director of another company called *Morecliffs* which trades in auto repairs and parts, a garage presumably.'

'Is there an address for this Morecliffs business, Aryan?'

'It's in Lincoln. I'll search and come back to you.'

Once again the disembodied voice from the imaging department repeated the '*sorry for your wait'* message. Frustrated, Sarah cut the line dead. 'Jackie, where do we find most of our information related to young people in care?'

'ContactPoint – our UK central police database, regional…'

'That's what I thought. Is Greg anywhere close?'

'He's grabbing a coffee. I'll ask him to bring some through.'

Sarah glanced up at the digital wall clock and watched it click over to 10.01 hrs. Over seventy-two hours had ticked past since Lee had been snatched. Any hope of finding Lee – or any of them – was slipping away fast.

'Skinny Latte one sugar and a pastry, Sarah. Jackie said you wanted to talk?' Greg slid the small tray in front of her, pulling a chair forwards for himself.

'I'm wondering how the hell you identify a potential *runner* out of the thousands of youngsters in care, Greg?'

'A nice simple question to start with then?' His dark eyes studied her over the rim of his steaming drink. 'Not easily, unless you have official access or you've breached security on the databases.'

'We're talking social care networks?'

'Social care, criminal justice – anyone with the right level of clearance can access pretty much anything. You'd need to know the systems to target but the broad data, like numbers of absconders in a specific region would be found in monthly updates. Like every other government agency, each council uploads their data, including that for social care. It wouldn't give you specifics on an individual, of course, but you could pick up patterns relating to missing youngsters. It's a whole different ball game if you wanted information on an individual.'

'So, what you're implying, is that the organiser of the trafficking is someone inside the social care network?'

'Wow – that's a huge leap, Sarah.' Greg's eyebrows furrowed in thought. 'It's possible I suppose but it's more likely to be someone with expert cyber-security knowledge. You can hire help to snatch the teenagers but will need technical expertise to identify the youngsters first.'

'You're no help at all, Greg.' Sarah raised her coffee and offered a wry smile. 'One straight answer would be nice.'

'It's interesting though. Whoever it is, they're exceptionally well informed and organised. Each database has inbuilt security – you can't simply dig around searching sensitive information.'

'Isn't that exactly what they've been doing for well over two years? Either that or they've someone in each county, checking every care home?'

'It's a dilemma, Sarah. If we so much as hint at a potential breach of security on the databases, the central Cyber unit will be all over the investigation like a rash – we'd lose control in a heartbeat.'

'Don't, Greg. The Chief Constable has already made rumblings about moving the whole shindig to bloody Leeds – as if that would help. This stays with us until we know we have a fix on those teenagers. Moving the investigation or shutting down the databases does nothing and we'd alert the traffickers. The youngsters would vanish, the gang disappear and we'd be left with nothing but ghosts – which is *not* going to happen!' Sarah was uncomfortably aware that the room had grown quiet.

Greg raised a hand in mock submission. 'I'm not the one disagreeing with you, Sarah. It's the CS and above you need to convince.'

Sarah broke off a piece of pastry. 'Then let's hope the CS comes back in a good mood after he meets with the Chief Constable. And God help us if MI5 get wind of what's up…'

'Sorry to interrupt, but I thought you'd want this.' Jake Forbes passed over a printout. 'It's from the imaging department, they've done the best they can, or so the note says.'

Sarah gave the image of the Audi driver a cursory glance. Pass this on to uniform. Ask someone to show it to the neighbour of Emily Cotton, as soon as possible please.'

'Will do – and traffic asked me to tell you that the green van was sighted on the A158 near Lincoln. Unfortunately, it's disappeared again…'

The name chimed like a bell. 'Lincoln did you say? Aryan mentioned *Euro collect and hire* had links to a garage in Lincoln.'

'Definitely Lincoln, Chief Inspector. Traffic said they were sorry they lost it. The camera coverage isn't great on the outlying areas.'

Greg was up on his feet. 'I'll find Aryan and see what else he found out about that garage. We might finally have ourselves a break.'

Sarah's stomach churned with the rush of adrenaline. 'I need fresh air, Greg to clear my head. I'll make myself useful and take that photograph to the flats.'

***

The area where Emily Cotton had chosen to live was eerily similar to the one in Hull. Decent enough not to have the police calling every few days and sufficiently cheap not to raise any eyebrows. Was that luck or the machinations of an astute woman? Right now Sarah didn't have the answer so, instead, pressed the intercom.

'Mr Morris, it's Detective Chief Inspector Allerton. I'm sorry to bother you again. Could I have a few minutes of your time?'

Inside his flat, Mr Morris's bright hazel eyes looked up from checking her ID to regard her with some surprise. 'It's a bit much sending a Chief Inspector. Is everyone else off sick?'

'Not at all. I was in the area and this is important.' Sarah slid out the print from the envelope. 'It's a little hazy Mr Morris, but take a good look. Do you recognise this man?'

'Need my glasses,' he patted the top of his head before turning to search the table next to a small sofa. Sliding his spectacles on, he studied the image for a few seconds. 'It's not the best photo I've ever seen but I'd say it's him. Every time I saw the bugger he had that same look. Moody like, probably his Scottish heritage.'

‘You recognised his accent?’

‘Well, I would as half my family come from there. Not that I heard much, only mutterings.’

I don’t suppose you saw what he was driving did you, Mr Morris?’

He stroked the image of the Audi with an arthritic finger and laughed. ‘Well, it wasn’t one of those. Something dark red I’d think, although it’s hard to tell at night. It had a big engine, I could hear him revving the bloody thing. I hope that’s been some help, lass?’

‘Very much, Mr Morris, and thank you again for your time.’

Sarah pushed down the pulse of excitement as she relayed the information to Ben Peterson; it was only one piece of the puzzle after all. ‘Pass it on to Greg for me, Ben.’

‘Will do. There are some interesting connections with Lincoln. Will you be long?’

‘Another half an hour or less. I need to check out a hunch.’

For once the traffic flowed easily and even the lights on the one-way system were in her favour. Six minutes later, Sarah was smiling up at a curious Matt Cox. ‘I’m sorry to disrupt your morning Matt, but is your lodger at home?’

‘No – Warren rang yesterday evening to say there’d been a family emergency, likely to be away for a few days.’

Once again, Sarah pulled out the image from the envelope. ‘Do you recognise anyone in this picture?’

‘Is this some kind of trick, Chief Inspector? Why are you showing me a photograph of Warren?’

Finally, rock-solid proof. The engine of her Mercedes hardly had time to fire when the car phone rang. Sarah was tempted to leave it, but Amos’s name flashed at her.

‘Amos, I’m on my way back…’

‘Wiggins garage *now*, Sarah. It’s urgent.’

Chapter Twenty-One

SIREN AND BEACON FLASHING, Sarah made it to the garage in under five minutes. One of the owners might have died only hours earlier, but business appeared to be as busy as ever; cars were parked everywhere. Squeezing into a space opposite the rear entrance, Sarah spotted Amos, hands thrust deep into his pockets, pacing.

'What the hell is happening in this damned town, Sarah. It used to be such a quiet place?'

'City, Amos – and there had better be a good reason for dragging me away from my investigation.'

'Steve Thomas and his wife Joanne were at the hospital last night when Paul Wiggins died.'

'So…?'

Amos held up his hand, 'Oh, I haven't finished. So was a DI from Hepsford station.'

'What the hell? Was this Lawson playing silly buggers?'

'I doubt it by the description.' Amos flicked through a notebook. '22.10 approximately, Steve Thomas goes off to find coffee while his wife, Joanne visits the toilet. Five minutes later she arrives back on the unit to find the curtains around Paul's bed are drawn tight. She doesn't go in but stays close enough to overhear a nurse talking to a DI Asher. The inspector is explaining that he's been informed Paul is regaining consciousness. He's hoping he's awake enough to answer some questions concerning Adam Farnes. The officer leaves, and ten minutes later Paul Wiggins is dead.'

'Amos this can't be right?'

'Do you know any DI by the name of Asher, Sarah?'

'Someone must have seen a warrant card?'

'All Mrs Thomas saw was his reflection in a window as the man left. Approximately five foot ten, short fair hair. He was wearing a black scarf, which made it difficult to make out his features. It was pure luck I found out about this DI Asher at all. Joanne happened to mention she'd overheard an officer at the hospital talking about Farnes. I assumed she meant one of the 'specials', but she was adamant she'd heard him say DI. Whoever this man is, he knew a lot of detail about Paul's condition and Farnes' arrest. Carl raised the SPC who was on hospital watch and, just to pile on the bad news, the officer received a call at 21.55 telling him he could stand down. The call purportedly came directly from me.'

'Oh for goodness sake, how much more messed up can this get!'

'Carl is hunting down a list of the night staff on duty and CCTV footage as we speak, but I'd put money on it that Paul Wiggins didn't die a natural death.' Amos began to pace again. 'Over the afternoon Paul had shown clear signs of improvement. He was breathing on his own.'

'Even so, it would have been days before he was close to being fully conscious, Amos.'

'How did this bogus DI know Wiggins was on the mend, Sarah? It stinks. This has to be tied in with whatever Farnes was up to.'

'Whatever the reason Amos, we need to talk to Steve Thomas.'

The door from the office opened and Carl Moyles hurried out. 'Sir, you need to see this. It's from CCTV cameras outside the rear doors of the hospital at 22.24 hrs. This has to be our suspect.'

Whoever the man was thought they were being careful. They'd kept their face hidden from the main camera positioned directly opposite the door. What they hadn't taken into account was the subsidiary camera a few metres to the right. Sarah heard Amos's sigh of relief and breathed one of her own. It wasn't anyone they recognised.

'Sir, I've asked Aryan to try face recognition. I didn't want to go through the usual channels yet, given the concerns we had about how much the bogus DI knew.'

'I need to report this, Sarah...'

'Talk to Steve Thomas first, Amos. Try and establish a proper timeline before you report anything.' Sarah turned to the anxiously waiting Carl Moyles.

'Carl, check when Paul Wiggins' autopsy is due. If someone did help him on his way, we'll need to give Finchley the heads up as soon as possible. I'll be with Amos while he begins the interview.'

They found Steve Thomas in the snack room, head against the wall, eyes closed. The hiss of air valves and the general clatter from the workroom rolled on in the background. The man lifted his head and blinked wearily at Amos's call. 'Sorry, must've nodded off.' He yawned, stretching noisily.

Sarah clamped down the yawning response and pulled out a chair to sit next to Amos.

'I understand you're tired and it's been a difficult time, Mr Thomas,' Amos began. 'But there are some issues we need to resolve. Like the missing van and who stole it?'

'I thought you'd found it?'

'Oh, we did.' Amos kept it low-key, casual. 'The problem is where we found it. Would you like to take a stab at where that might have been?'

Thomas's eyes flickered constantly as he tried to formulate some kind of an answer. 'Some joy-rider burnt it out?'

'Nice try – let's go with the truth. Who took the van, Mr Thomas and why? Please remember, this is part of an ongoing investigation. Lying to me is a criminal offence.'

This time he didn't hesitate. 'Adam Farnes – but you'll have to ask him about it.'

'But I'm asking you. Why did Farnes have the van?'

Thomas folded his arms tightly across his chest. 'He wanted to get his own back on Paul, so he used it to grab our Lee…'

'Bullshit, Lee has been nowhere near that van. Whatever you or your wife might think, Adam Farnes had nothing to do with the lad's disappearance. So, last time of asking or if you prefer we can take this down to the station?'

'No! Please no…'

Sarah frowned at the note of panic. What the hell was going on?

'Then talk to me. Last chance…' Amos rested his large hands on the table, relaxed, two men sitting in the local pub about to drink a pint.

'Paul found out he'd been using the van to shift some things – illegal stuff and I swear, I don't know what that was. Paul is – was,' he corrected, 'many things but he'd never steal or touch drugs. The first I knew about it was two weeks ago when Adam Farnes didn't turn up for his shift. Paul tried to tell me he'd handed in his notice but I knew he was lying. That night, Paul went on a bender and the following day the truth came tumbling out, or part of it at least. He told me he'd found a few labels and bits and pieces in the back of the van. The two of them ended up having a blazing row and Paul sacked Farnes on the spot. Farnes went ape shit, told Paul the people he'd been working for were seriously heavy and, if Paul didn't keep his mouth shut, they'd come looking for him. I haven't seen Farnes or the van since.'

Sarah leaned forwards to ask about the labels but Amos got in first. 'Mr Thomas, the morning Lee went missing, did Paul believe Adam Farnes might be involved?'

'He must have. Not long after the manager of Lakeside rang on Monday morning to tell us about Lee, Paul started ranting like a mad man. He had his mobile out, so I think he must've been talking to Farnes.' Thomas buried his head in his arms. 'I should've taken the bloody phone off him, then he'd still be alive.'

Again, Sarah tried to ask the question but Amos cut her dead. 'You go Sarah, you've enough on your plate. Send Carl in for me, we'll finish off here.'

'You sure?'

'Positive, I'll finish this and telephone Finchley.'

Sarah frowned, he was doing it again, keeping something back. 'Amos, what is it you know?'

'Go find Lee and the others, Sarah. I swear, as soon as I have something to tell you, I will.'

***

In the incident room there was hardly room to move, every desk had at least two officers deep in conversation or frowning at a screen. It had been a long time since Sarah had witnessed such intense activity, six years in fact. Sarah pulled down the shutters on that thought and searched out her sergeant.

'Sorry about the delay Ben. Do you want to catch me up before you leave?'

'Do we have a problem?'

'Nothing to do with this case, thank goodness.'

'Jackie and I could go this evening if that would help?'

'No, I want you two on the ground, rested and ready to run. This could take off at a moment's notice.'

Ben pulled out his notebook. 'Aryan traced those details for Morecliffs garage, Lincolnshire. It's near a village called Spilsby.'

'Do we have a photo ID of the company director Saul James?'

With a sigh, Ben picked up the desk phone and pressed a number. After the briefest of conversations, he replaced the receiver. 'It'll be with us shortly.'

Sarah hid the smile. Her sergeant's ability to make things happen would take him a long way. 'I showed the picture of our Audi driver to Matt Cox as well as Mr Morris. Matt formally identified his lodger as the same man. Mr Morris was sure he's Emily's night time visitor.'

Ben's expression lit up. 'What are the chances our Audi driver and lodger is Saul James, the company director of Morecliffs?'

'We can hope. At least we have enough to request a warrant to search the lodger's room. Matt has given permission to run a trace on his mobile, the lodger rang him yesterday.'

'Are we putting a watch on the house?'

'It depends on what we find in the room. For now, there's a special constable cosied up with a neighbour on a watching brief. I'll send a couple of officers in to check the room out. What's happening in Lincoln?'

'Greg spoke with Lincoln police about Morecliffs garage but they told us they'd no reason to visit the place.'

'All that means is they've been careful, Ben. Were Lincoln helpful?'

'Very – DCI John Wetherton left contact details if you need him.' Ben flicked through his notepad again. 'Dan Bridges regained consciousness and I sent Jackie to do the interview as she'd seen him before. He's talking but doesn't recollect the assault.'

'Did he mention Emily – or Kelly White – as he knew her?'

'He's worked out that she must've had something to do with Lee disappearing. The nurse had to threaten to sedate him if he didn't calm down. Dan said Emily came on to him the first time she worked there. She got close and personal in a way he didn't appreciate. He told Jackie he'd felt too embarrassed to report it. On Monday morning, when he was getting ready for his work placement, he found her waiting outside his room. Emily told Dan she thought he was *special* and she'd bought him something to wear to bring him luck on his first day of work experience.'

'The beanie?'

‘Exactly, only he passed it on to Lee. I had Jake check with Lakeside and Dan reported his mobile missing at 15.17 on Sunday.’ Ben leaned back into his chair and sighed. ‘I can’t help wondering what would have happened if the kidnappers had managed to grab Dan as they’d planned.’

‘It a chilling thought. Given Dan’s history of petty theft and absconding, there’s a good chance the case would never have reached our desk…’ But Ben’s attention had wandered. He was frowning over her shoulder at something or someone? ‘Am I boring you, Sergeant?’

‘Sorry Ma’am, I need one moment.’

He was gone before Sarah could ask more. Twisting in her seat, she caught a glimpse of Mike Lawson and a figure she recognised as PC Evans from Tuesday evening, before Ben’s larger frame blocked them from view. Her curiosity warred with impatience as her fingers tapped restlessly while she waited. ‘And?’ she demanded as Ben slid back into his seat.

‘Mike Lawson was giving Evan’s a hard time.’

‘About what, or are we playing twenty questions?’

Ben’s expression was never an easy read. ‘Something to do with an evidence log.’

‘Why didn’t Mike ask the desk Sergeant for a copy himself?’

‘No idea, Ma’am. Shall I ask Aryan for an update?’

Jake Forbes lent down to hand him an information sheet. ‘The printout from DVLA just came in.’

Ben grunted in recognition. ‘Saul James – if that’s his real name, is the spitting image of the man with the Audi. It appears we’ve identified a key player.’

***

By four o’clock Ben and Jackie were already on their way to Cambridge. Their departure had left Sarah with an unexpected empty sensation in the pit of her stomach. Ben was good but it was never easy for her to let go of the reins. It didn’t help that there had been no word from Amos or Carl Moyles since she'd left Wiggins' garage. She couldn't ignore the churning worry any more.

'Aryan, I'm stretching my legs for five – shout if you need me.' He waved vaguely in her direction, far too intent on inputting the latest flood of data to ask questions.

Tracy Bates had her head buried in a book when she pushed through the double doors into reception. 'Sarah, what can I do for you?'

'Is Amos about?' Tracy was good, Sarah thought. If she hadn't known the woman for so long, she'd have missed the slight twitch, the glance to the side.

'He's not available at this moment. Would you like me to pass on a message?'

'Don't do this to me, Tracy. What's happened now?'

'Honestly Sarah, he's fine. I'll say you want a word and ask him to contact you as soon as he can. He's a bit caught up at present?'

That could have meant a million and one things but, grudgingly, Sarah nodded. 'As soon as possible would be appreciated.'

Half an hour later, Sarah glanced at her buzzing mobile to see Amos's name flashing. 'About bloody time, Brantley. I've been imagining all sorts.'

'Sorry, it's been a little hairy but Carl and I have persuaded Finchley that I haven't been party to a murder.'

'So Wiggins didn't die naturally?'

'Large dose of cocaine injected via his IV. It would have taken seconds to administer, killed him within minutes. Fortunately, Finchley's cleared it for me to carry on investigating.'

'Be careful, Amos; don't you take any undue risks.'

'That's the pot calling the kettle black, I think?'

'I'm concerned, okay. Any ideas yet what Farnes was transporting?'

‘Sorry Sarah, I have to go…’ In the background were familiar voices – the CS team were out in force. Amos covered the mouthpiece, whoever was talking to him sounded garbled. Sarah heard the crunch of a boot on something rough before he spoke again. ‘I’m on an op, difficult to explain…speak later.’

Sarah looked down at the now silent phone and frowned. What the hell was he up to?

Chapter Twenty-Two

SLICKING THE FAST-FALLING SLEET from his face, Amos pocketed his mobile. At least with Sarah caught up with *North Run* there was a decent chance she wouldn't hear about this latest incident, start asking awkward questions… He turned to find Carl, eyebrow raised, shaking his head. 'There is no way Sarah is going to settle for that, Sir.'

Behind them, a warming light spilt out from the doorway of the *Blue Beacon* to bounce off the reflective yellow tabards of the emergency workers. Spears of wood and bent metal hung at odd angles from what was left of the rear pub door. At the front of the building, the intruders had tried to lever up the plate covering the entrance to the cellar, jagged metal edges snarled back at them. An ambulance was parked, lights swirling silently, while a paramedic helped a woozy and bloodied officer inside.

'One problem at a time, Carl. Let's concentrate on what the neighbours had to say.'

'Not a lot. No one saw faces – most are denying hearing or seeing anything.'

'Are they all deaf and blind?'

'Scared more like. There are a lot of boarding houses in these streets, with a fair few immigrant families. The woman who called this in said that she saw a large vehicle pull up. Three men in dark clothing jumped out, hit the uniformed officer with something she couldn't see before attacking the rear gate and cellar door with large axes. That was at 15.49 hrs. It was less than four minutes before the emergency car turned up. The assailants heard the sirens and were gone by the time the car arrived.'

‘Has traffic come up with a trace yet?’

‘Nothing so far. What the hell is inside the pub that could be so important? All I could see when we searched was the usual bar equipment and that *still* they’d built. There was nothing else except a pile of broken boxes.’

Amos drew Carl further from the shattered doorway and the ears of the milling workmen. ‘How was Moira when you spoke to her last?’

‘Sounding better – definitely more with it. Furious that we won’t explain why we’ve dumped her in a safe house.’

‘Contact the place and set up a digital meet for tomorrow. Oh and Carl, do not mention that to anyone other than tech – understood.’

‘Understood, Sir – I’ll sort it straight away.’

Amos strode across to the ambulance and waited impatiently for the paramedic to finish patching a dressing to the side of the constable’s head. ‘I need a quick chat with my officer before you cart him off – please?’

Reluctantly, the young paramedic stepped out of the vehicle. ‘You’ve three minutes, Chief Inspector, it’s a busy evening.’

Amos waited until he was sure they were alone before he crouched down. ‘Sorry Son, I know you’ve probably got a blinder of a headache but can you tell me anything about this evening?’

‘Honestly Sir, it’s not so bad. I let them think they’d knocked me out but it was only a glancing blow. Mind, the sight of that axe handle coming towards me, I thought my time was up.’ The officer winced as he touched the side of his head. ‘Still bloody hurts though.’

‘Why were you on your own? I’d asked for a detail of two officers?’

‘Uniform are short. There’s been a spat of break-ins and what with *North Run*. A patrol car’s been driving past every thirty minutes to check in. The patrol had only just left when they turned up – sick really.'

Again Amos asked, 'So tell me what you do remember?'

'There were four of them, Sir. The driver stayed in the vehicle, a Land Rover discovery I'd guess, but I couldn't see a plate. I couldn't see any faces either.' The officer frowned as he thought. 'Weird though, I could've sworn I recognised one of the voices – older, local accent. By their builds, they were men, all wearing scarfs, hats pulled well down, dark clothing. Sorry, Sir, not much of a description. Most of what they said was muffled but they were definitely after something in the cellar. They'd come prepared; two went for the metal plate on the pavement while the other took an axe to the gate and rear door. I think they thought it'd be easy, but they hadn't reckoned on all the noise it would make.'

'And their vehicle, did you notice if it had a bull-bar attached to the front by any chance?'

The officer nodded, wincing at the effort. 'Now you mention it. A bloody great black thing, or at least that's how it looked from my view down on the floor.'

Grim-faced, Amos watched the ambulance pull away. 'Carl, you and I are going back to interview Adam Farnes. Did you sort the interview with Moira?'

'Tech said tomorrow pm, any time after two. Why are we talking to Farnes again?'

'Whoever did this knew exactly what time the patrol car was due to check in with the officer. It can't be a coincidence that they arrive only minutes after the patrol car leaves? I'm bloody positive Farnes knows exactly who told them and who leaked information on Paul Wiggins.'

'You think this is one of ours, don't you?'

'Not a whisper, Carl – we are on perilous ground.'

***

The on-duty cell officer, unlocked the last of the security doors and waved Amos in. 'Farnes is still not eating, hardly slept since he arrived and refusing all medication.'

'Does he know about Paul Wiggins' death?'

'No Sir, not a peep. The only visitors he's had are his duty solicitor and doctor.'

'Carl Moyles will be along shortly, he's bringing sandwiches from the canteen – I know,' he said quickly when the officer began to protest. 'We're not supposed to supply anything to our guests – but, I think I know what's bothering Farnes, just need him to trust me.'

Even in the twenty hours since Amos last saw him, Adam Farnes had lost weight. As soon as his cell door opened, he was on his feet, wide-eyed – terrified.

'Evening Adam, I needed a quick word and I've some news.' Amos turned to wave the panting Carl to his side. 'I'm starving, brought an early supper along. Carl, chuck all the sandwiches on the paper plate would you?'

Perched on plastic chairs, the two officers munched on sandwiches and, when Carl held up the plate to Adam Farnes, he couldn't resist. In silence, they watched him devour three sandwiches in less than a minute. 'Help yourself to more and a drink...' Carl pointed to the three sealed bottles.

'I'm still not saying anything,' Farnes said wiping his mouth on the back of his hand.

Amos sat back, relaxed – casual. 'I can understand that. In your shoes, I think I'd be the same. Sitting in a lock-up, terrified the next person who opens that cell door is one of the big men you were working for – am I right?'

The sandwich Farnes was holding fell out of his hands. 'No – no way…'

'I can only protect you if I know who from, Adam. I have to inform you that late last night, one of those men you're so afraid of, went into the local hospital and murdered Paul Wiggins – injected him full of cocaine.'

'You're lying…'

'I wish I was. Paul Wiggins was a good man, lost his brother, had a nephew, who despite all of Paul's problems, needed him – only now the man is dead?'

Adam Farnes sank back onto the low bed, head sunk onto his chest. 'The bastard – I kept telling him Paul wouldn't snitch.'

'Did you push Paul over the bridge, Adam?'

'No, I bloody did not! It must've been one of the main sellers or one of their thugs. I got this message Tuesday evening, telling me to meet my contact at the *Wheatsheaf*. He said he had a deal for me.'

'What time, Adam.'

'Four thirty I think it was, but no bugger turned up. I waited until seven, had a few pints…'

Carl interrupted, 'Is that the pub about a quarter of a mile from Canal Bridge on the Selby Road?'

'That's the one.'

'So, tell me,' Amos asked, 'What were you transporting in that van you purloined from *Hepsford Auto Repairs*?'

'Cheap booze. It started as a favour for a mate, dropping the stuff off while he was inside for six months. It was good money, a couple of hundred for a measly hour's work. Everything was going fine. I'd borrow a van overnight, pick the stuff up in a lay-by from another van or a 4x4 and take it wherever. Then one day I went to Doncaster races with a couple of mates.' The fear was back, his eyes wild. 'I went into one of the marquees to buy a drink and there was my contact. I'd seen him at a few of the drop-off points, always in the background, handing out our money, checking boxes weren't being nicked I suppose. Anyway, there he is behind the bar at Doncaster with another bloke – only they're both in suits. I couldn't make out much of what they said to the manager but I saw the badges – bloody revenue officers! I thought I'd made it out of there before he saw me but the bastard collared me. Told me exactly what he'd do if I said a word.'

'Do you have a name for either of these men?'

'My contact told me to call him Reg, but there's no way that's his real name…'

'And you're sure they worked for Customs and Revenue?'

'Their badges looked real enough to me and that bar manager at the races was crapping himself.'

Chapter Twenty-Three

Friday night the Pit

TO HIS DISGUST, LEE HAD SLEPT through the whole of the previous night.

Simon didn't look surprised. 'What did you expect, they dope the food. It wears off after a few days, just makes you groggy.'

'Well, it's not happening tonight. I'll go hungry.'

'Why, what the hell do you think is going to happen?'

'Nothing, don't want to be drugged out of my head that's all.'

Kayla's low murmur was hardly audible. 'The drug makes it bearable, sort of.'

When the evening food was lowered, Lee ignored Kayla's dark looks and only nibbled on the outer crust. He poured the already opened yoghurt down the toilet.

'If they find out they'll beat you,' Simon warned.

Lee threw the empty pot into the sack, flushed the rest of the food away. 'But they'll only find out if someone tells them, won't they.'

Kayla pointed to the ceiling 'There's probably a camera watching us.'

'Rubbish! If that was the case they'd have known that girl was sick?'

'What do you frigging know about anything. You've only just got here…'

'Sit down, Ky,' Simon hissed. 'Paula got sick that's all. They – they did the rest. Now leave it.'

Rosa was crying again, low sobs that cut through Lee like a blade. 'I'm sorry Rosa, didn't mean to upset you.'

It was a relief when the others nodded off. Opposite, the girls huddled together, dozing fitfully. Simon grunted occasionally curled up on his bench. Above their heads, the garage was silent. In the chinks of electric light filtering through the grating, the cold metal of Lee's chain glinted silver. Carefully, he ran a finger around each link. At first, the rings felt seamless, unbreakable, until near the wall, his fingertips caught the merest hint of a gap. His heartbeat quickened – would it work? The screw from the van wasn't much but it was brass and shouldn't bend. He'd watched his uncle Paul and Steve pry open jammed pieces of machinery countless times; this wasn't any different. The occasional waft of diesel and oil from above was so familiar. What he wouldn't give to be back in his uncle's garage right now –they could talk things out, make things right. His mum and dad would want that. When he got out of this hell-hole he'd sort things, properly. Lee dragged a cold hand across his eyes, daring the moisture to fall.

Icy fingers made it hard to hold onto the screw let alone apply pressure. Twice the thing slipped to the floor and Lee had to scrabble about in the gloom. He must have twisted the screw against the metal a hundred times, pulled the link against the screw a thousand times more. The sudden tinkling happened without warning – the loose chain lay curled at his feet.

'Bloody hell!' Simon's whisper carried easily.

A man's voice, guttural, annoyed, barked orders at someone above their heads. In a heartbeat, the chain was back in the metal ring; seconds later Lee was flat on his bench.

'What the hell are you planning to do?' Simon whispered.

'Get out, get help, what do you think?'

'If they find you're gone they'll kill us, no messing.'

'Then we all go.'

'And what if you can't undo all of our chains – what then?'

'I'm not sitting here waiting to be carted off to hell, Si.'

The voices became clearer. '*He's a fool and I don't care who hears me. Fancy taking a bloody chance like this.*'

'Trev, keep your voice down, he hasn't gone yet. It's only one more pick-up after all and we're dumping her straight at the launch site. The boat's lined up ready for tomorrow night, so we don't even have to babysit any more. We've got a break for three whole weeks. Sunny Jamaica here I come.'

'I've had enough, Mark. It's pure sodding greed. He'd make enough with the rest of the stuff but, oh no, he has to risk every bloody thing. He's crazy. After this run, I'm out. He can go bury his stupid head for all I care.'

'You're really on one, aren't you?'

'I want to be gone by seven-thirty Mark, so we sort their food now. Jade and I can throw it down before we set off. You take the other van tonight and pick up Dean first thing. In the morning, you two pick up these four by eight. You make sure you check the tyres and oil on both, I don't want any hold-ups.' An engine purred into life. The fumes from the exhaust stank in the still air. 'Turn the sodding thing off,' Trevor yelled. 'You'll suffocate them!'

The rim of a tyre now rested on the edge of the grating. Lee could see the outline of the man's leg as he worked.

'You're not going anywhere tonight,' Simon whispered.

'We've got to try something.'

'You heard them. The other van will be gone in the morning; it'll have to be then.'

'But what if one of them stays behind in the garage?'

'How do you plan to shift the grating with a bloody great van parked on top? Now shut it or one of them will hear us.'

'How come the girls sleep through this racket?' Lee asked as feet continued to thud above their heads.

'They don't, least Ky doesn't, she's pretending.'

Lee glanced over to where the girls slept huddled together. It was impossible to work out who was who. 'The morning then,' Lee whispered, as the men's voices drifted away.

‘You’ll kill us all,’ Kayla murmured.

‘I’ve got to try,’ Lee hissed back.

‘Did I say I cared? Anything has to be better than what they’ve got lined up for us.’

The cold night dragged endlessly. Lee kept glancing across at the girls, envying them their warmth. He may have slept a little but, when the footsteps came, he was wide awake.

Colder air filtered down as the garage doors were dragged open. Trevor’s loud shout echoed eerily. ‘It’s sodding seven-thirty already. Get a move on Jade.’

Lee felt Simon stirring beside him as the grating was pulled to the side. A loop of rope slid down, a canvas bag attached. As soon as it hit the floor, the bag fell away and the rope was hauled back up.

‘Wait!’ Simon urged. ‘It’s not safe until they close the garage doors.’

Lee felt sick as he kept his eyes on the grating, willing the van to leave. Finally, came the roar of the engine and the unmistakable clanking of the bolts on the garage doors. ‘Put the benches on top of each other Si, while I do the chain.’ Lee was free in seconds but the others hadn’t moved. ‘Oh come on, I need to do this – now!’

‘You run we die,’ Kayla declared.

‘Don’t go, please.’ Rosa sounded terrified.

Lee stared between the three – this was stupid. ‘Help me climb up and I swear I’ll look around and come straight back. There has to be something useful up there?’

‘There’s a phone,’ Rosa admitted.

‘No there bloody isn’t!’

‘You know there is, Kayla. We’ve all heard it?’

‘Do you think I’m stupid, Rosa? If he goes up, there’s no way he’ll be coming back!’

‘I promise; I’ll just use the phone. A few minutes that’s all but, if I don’t go now we’ve lost our only chance. Please,’ Lee begged, aware the seconds were ticking on.

‘He’s right, let’s do it.’ Simon began to drag a bench directly under the grating. ‘Come on Ky, give us a hand!’

Even with the others helping, trying to slide the grating from underneath was difficult. With the gap barely wide enough to push his head through, Lee used his shoulder to shove it the last few centimetres.

‘Watch out for alarms,’ Simon called as he gave him a final boost up.

Wrapping the long chain around his wrist, Lee scanned around. Even had he wanted to run, it wasn’t an option. Heavy-duty security bars criss-crossed all the windows and the double doors were locked tight. On the far side of the garage, metal cabinets lined the back wall, tools stacked on wooden benches. Then Lee saw it, the desk with a telephone. Heart thundering in his chest, he raced across the concrete floor.

‘Hurry up!’ Simon urged.

Lee’s fingers were already pressing buttons before he realised it wasn’t the police he was calling. Too late now…

‘*Lakeside, Matt Cox speaking. How can I help?*’

Chapter Twenty-Four

THE CALL HAD COME INTO HER PHONE at 08.14 hrs, as Sarah was pouring a fresh coffee. Blue light flashing, it took less than eight minutes to drive from the station to the doors of Lakeside. Amos's car was already there and Matt Cox was pacing outside the main entrance.

'It was definitely Lee,' Matt said, as soon as Sarah had one foot out of the car.

'Come and talk to me, Matt. We'll use the kitchen.'

'The phone, he didn't slot it back…' Matt was gabbling, words tumbling over each other.

'Sarah,' Amos's head appeared around the office door. 'We had a live feed for a while – not that we could hear much. I'm sending the info straight through to Aryan at Hepsford.'

'I'll take Matt into the kitchen Amos, shout if you need me.'

'I'm only in for a couple of hours, covering for Mr De-Silva – he's gone to the temple...' Matt's words were almost incoherent.

'Sit Matt, I'll make us a drink and you can tell me what happened.' Sarah doled a generous serving of sugar into both mugs before pouring on the steaming water. Hand trembling, his coffee slopped over the rim.

'Shit! – sorry,' groaning, Matt dropped his head into his hands, breath deep and ragged. I thought it was a joke at first, Chief Inspector, maybe one of our youngsters – Lee sounded so scared. He told me the other three were still trapped in a pit, chained up…'

'Matt, he's alive and still in the country – that is such good news – but you're positive Lee said three others?'

'Absolutely; he did mention something about they were getting another? Does that make any sense?'

Too much, Sarah thought and skipped over the question. Once she'd extracted as much as Matt could remember she asked, 'Have you heard anything else from your lodger?'

'Nothing since yesterday.' Hand steadier, he gulped a mouthful of coffee. 'You think Warren's involved in this don't you?'

Sarah didn't comment. 'Have you had any more thoughts about where Megan might have gone?'

Matt's shoulders drooped. 'No idea. Megan rarely talked about herself. She mentioned her grandmother a few times. I've worked with her for almost nine months and it was by accident that I found out her gran came from Scotland. Given the work I do, it's easy enough to know when someone isn't giving a straight answer.'

'And that doesn't bother you?'

'Not really, I still fancy her like mad.' The grin was genuine. 'Makes her more intriguing I suppose. Whatever she's running from – if she's running – it isn't of her doing. I want her to trust me enough to let me help her.'

'Why do you say it isn't of her doing?'

'Gut I suppose – Lisa, all of us really like her. There is no way she'd be caught up in kidnapping kids.'

'But I haven't suggested that.'

'Please Chief Inspector, given what's happened, she has to be on your list. I'm no fool.'

He had it bad, Sarah realised. Love wasn't just blind – sometimes it was dumb stupid.

The kitchen door swung open and Gail, the other social worker on duty, walked in.

'Oh, I'm sorry,' she said immediately, turning to go.

'No, it's fine, we're all done.' Sarah rose to her feet. 'Could I ask you to make sure no one goes into the office until you receive the all-clear?'

Gail laughed. 'That won't be a problem. It's the weekend and our lot won't be up for at least another hour.'

Amos raised a hand when Sarah slipped into the office. 'A minute,' he mouthed holding onto an earpiece. A young officer was writing frantically beside him. 'The good news,' he finally said, ‘Is that the lad couldn’t have slipped the phone back properly – the line was live for over five minutes. Matt kept the record button on, which helped.’ Groaning, he straightened up, rubbing at the small of his back. ‘The techies have traced the number to a garage called Morecliffs near Lincoln.’

‘And the bad news, Amos?’

‘They’ve moved the kids…’

Dizzy, Sarah clutched at the edge of the desk. ‘Oh God – Lee – did they discover him phoning out?’

‘Hey – it’s okay,’ Amos caught Sarah’s arm and pushed her down onto a chair. ‘Hell Sarah, you’re as grey as a ghost. Lee was back with the others long before the men arrived – breathe for god sake.’

‘I’m fine – you caught me unawares.’ The room was still spinning.

‘Let me guess – little sleep, a gallon of coffee, no food?’

She offered a weak smile. ‘You know me too well, Brantley. I’ve some energy bars in the car. I’ll snack on those before I drive back.’

‘Make sure you do. I’ve sent the info about the garage straight to Lincoln police. Don’t worry, Greg’s given the them the heads up about our operation. They’ve promised to wait for your update before taking any action.’

‘Have we any idea where they’ve taken the youngsters?’

‘Not so far. Maybe there’s something on the tape or the traffic teams spot something. We’ll keep an ear on the line but I won’t hold my breath. Finchley wasn’t best pleased by our request for the phone tap by the way.’

Sarah rubbed a hand over her weary eyes. She’d managed all of four hours of broken sleep. ‘He’ll have to live with it, Amos. I’m going back to the station; I need to check in with Cambridge.’

Amos began packing away equipment. ‘I’ll stay and finish off here, shouldn’t be long. How’s Matt Cox bearing up?’

'It might be an idea to have someone drive him back to his place. He's pretty shaken up.'

'All part of the service, Sarah. As long as he doesn't mind a short wait.'

Her colleague was studiously avoiding eye contact. 'Amos, about yesterday and Paul Wiggins' death. What's the position with you continuing to work?'

'I'm here aren't I?' he flashed the briefest of smiles that was all show and little substance. 'At least Finchley is earning his money for a change.'

'And did you find out what Farnes was using the van for?'

'Seriously, you want to do this now? I'll fill you in if and when I have something substantial. Right now it's hearsay.'

Reluctantly, Sarah gave in. Amos could be a stubborn bastard when he wanted to be and she needed to be back at the station. While the engine ticked over, she munched on a couple of energy bars and telephoned ahead. Outside, rain slammed against the roof.

'Chief Inspector,' Aryan's youthful enthusiasm only added to her sense of weariness. 'Ben said there's nothing to report so far from Cambridge. The same in Leicester.'

'I'm on my way back, Aryan. The weather's atrocious, but I shouldn't be long.'

Chris Hollings and Tracy Bates were deep in conversation when she hurried into reception. 'I'd have thought you'd have been tucked up in bed ages ago, Chris?'

'It was my last night for a while Sarah, and I never sleep until the evening. I thought I'd help out.' It wasn't a request.

'If you're sure Chris?' She wasn't going to refuse the help of an experienced officer.

'I take it the techies didn't turn up to fix the reader again, Tracy?'

'I had a phone call saying there was a problem at the council offices. We're obviously not a priority.'

'Nothing new then. Is Mike in for any particular reason?' His name was near the top of that day's page.

'Not that I'm aware of and he wasn't in a good mood.'

Sarah picked up her bag. 'How surprising. I'll be in the incident room if anyone needs me.'

Most eyes were fixed on the wall of monitors waiting for updates.

'Anything happening yet, Greg?'

'Nothing so far, Sarah. Ben is still outside the children's home in Cambridge.' Greg typed in a command and two clear images appeared on the larger screen. 'On the left is Hatters Court, Cambridge. Ben is in his car just behind the camera angle. Jackie Simmons and a local DC are in the building. The other is Loft House, in Leicester. The door directly opposite the camera is the main entrance. Leicester kindly put in a new camera overnight. It switches between there and each end of the road. They have two undercover in the building as well. Given Lee's phone call, I've alerted everyone that we're likely to have action soon.'

'But everyone's secure at the moment?'

'Still in their beds, Sarah. They're teenagers, what do we expect.'

'And it's raining in Cambridge I see, which should help. What's the forecast?'

'Like this all day.' Greg eyed her curiously. 'Why is that good?'

'Would you go to a music festival or a protest rally if it was raining? It should give us more bodies on the ground if we need them. Have we had any feedback from Lincolnshire police about Morecliffs garage?'

'They've done an initial reconnoitre of the area and the garage appears deserted.' Greg handed her yet another sheet. 'I was clear about keeping it low key for now. I've spoken personally with DCI John Wetherton. He's leading the Lincoln team.'

'Thanks Greg, a great job…'

Problem? Is it all too much for that pretty head to handle?'

Mike Lawson's gruff tone wasn't welcome. With an effort, Sarah pushed down the bubble of irritation and turned. 'Mike, was there something you needed?'

'A couple of officers – Neil Harper is nowhere to be found and my constables are busy doing something for damned Finchley. I'm bloody pissed off. Now Amos has all the other spares doing something or other. I suppose you'll tell me you'll need the rest?'

'There are three 'specials' allocated for general duties Mike if you need them?' It was an effort but she kept her voice even. If Lawson couldn't organise his own team that was his problem.

'I'll have to make do with the grunts I suppose, unless you want to lend me the native boy-wonder...'

Behind her, Sarah heard Greg rise to his feet. The last thing she needed was a slanging match. 'You're out of order Inspector! I suggest you take your racist comments to CS Finchley…' Sarah prayed Greg would hold his tongue.

Lawson leaned in close, venom oozing from every syllable as he muttered. 'You'd better watch your sodding back. Don't think I don't know your little secret…'

The urge to floor the man was hard to resist. 'Are you bloody threatening me? You'd better start walking, Mike – now!'

Most heads had turned to watch the muted confrontation; apart from the beep of a radio, there wasn't a sound. Whatever Mike Lawson growled in response was lost in the thud of his retreating boots. Sarah pushed down the waves of anger. There was no way he knew about Freya and even if he did…

'He's a miserable ignorant sod, Sarah. Are you okay?'

Greg's concerned murmur snapped her back to the room. 'Fine.' Sarah drew in a ragged breath and tried again. 'Really, nothing a stiff gin and a long holiday wouldn't cure Greg, but I'll make do with a hot drink and Danish for now.'

Chapter Twenty-Five

Cambridge 10.15.

ONLY AN IDIOT WOULD ENJOY SITTING in a car for four hours watching a door, Ben Peterson thought, not that he'd volunteered, but when the boss said go – you went, willingly or not. Ben stifled a yawn and took a swig from a tinned coffee drink. Elena Williams had been on duty for over two-and-half hours and no one had set foot outside the building. According to regular updates from Jackie Simmons, the teenagers were in their beds. It was beginning to look as if they had it wrong – the action going off in Leicester or worse, somewhere else entirely.

Abruptly, his earpiece crackled into life. 'Serg, bad news!' Jackie sounded furious.

'Don't tell me you've lost her.'

'No, I've had to do the arrest. Williams was about to leave work; told the manager she was feeling sick. I searched her bag and found a mobile belonging to a Jemma Fields. The manager only *forgot* to mention Jemma was on leave, staying with an aunt for a couple of days...'

'What?' Ben couldn't believe what he was hearing. 'He told us they were all accounted for!'

'He thought we were only concerned with those in house.'

'Crap!' Ben ground his teeth; this was not going to go down well with the boss. 'Is the aunt nearby?'

Jackie read out an address. 'The local boys will take Williams to the station, we'll meet you at the aunt's house. I'm checking Williams' mobile for any contact with Jemma. I'll let you know when I've got more...' In the background, a woman was swearing loudly – Elena Williams, Ben guessed.

Pulling out onto the back street, Ben sped towards the busier 'A' road. How the hell had they messed up so badly? He took a deep breath and pressed Sarah's number. Fortunately, the call was short – just long enough to leave his ear ringing and his stomach a queasy mess. 'Incoming call' was already buzzing when the Chief Inspector rang off.

'Ben,' Jackie sounded breathless. 'I've downloaded the info from Elena Williams' mobile and sent it to Hepsford, they'll sort it quicker than Cambridge, but the news isn't good. Williams rang the aunt's home number twenty-six minutes ago and spoke to Jemma.'

'What's your ETA, Jackie?' Ben checked the sat nav – it would be another two minutes before he was anywhere close.

'The local officer reckons we'll be there in under five.'

'Do you know when Jemma left the house?'

'Ten minutes ago, told her aunt that the home's minibus was picking her up from the usual bus stop to go ice skating. The aunt didn't think it was strange, Jemma often goes off places.'

He could hear the desperation in Jackie's voice. 'This isn't your fault, Jackie. Give me the coordinates for the bus stop.' Ben pushed in the information. The stop was a good mile from the aunt's house – there was still hope.

Jackie spoke again. 'We've had an update from Cambridge traffic.' In the background, he could hear bursts of static as a radio buzzed. 'A suspect van has been spotted on street cameras driving past the bus stop. It appears to be doing a recon. What do you want to do?'

Ben checked the time. 'Does it look like it's about to do the pick-up?'

'It's doing another circuit. Taking into account traffic lights, it should be at the bus stop in approximately two minutes.'

'Who's closest?'

'You are, Ben. We're not far behind. The locals are moving in fast but they're still a couple of minutes behind us.'

'Tell the locals to let me know when they're in position and keep me updated of any changes, Jackie – tell everyone, no sirens.'

'Understood – what did the boss say?'

'Do you really want to know?'

'Probably not. I take it Hepsford is listening in?'

'Every move we make, Jackie.'

Jackie's driver, interrupted. 'Sir, you should head down St Stephens Lane, toward Maynard Road. Park at the end of St Stephens. The bus stop is almost directly opposite – you'll be twenty metres away at most.'

'Understood, see you in two and stay sharp.'

***

It was cold standing at the bus stop. Jemma pulled out a hand from the warm pocket to check the time – ten twenty, they were late. The shelter wasn't up to much either. Rain dripped through the gaps and large foot-sized holes in the Perspex allowed the wind to whistle through. Jemma pulled up her scarf before thrusting her hand deep into her pocket. Maybe she'd got the time wrong? At the sound of an engine she put her head out into the drizzle but it was only a van, no one she knew. Jay would be going skating plus Abby of course. If she hadn't lost her mobile she'd have rung them, found out for definite. Jemma glanced down at the jeans she was wearing and sighed. They weren't the best and nowhere near as cool as the black skinny's she'd bought last weekend but those were back at Hatter's court.

'Hey love, can you tell us where this is? I've been travelling for hours and I haven't a clue where I am.'

Startled, Jemma looked out into the road. Parked a few metres away was the dark green van she'd seen earlier. A man in a bobble hat leaned against the bonnet, a map in one hand. He smiled at her. 'I'm not good with maps. Why not use your phone?'

'My mate's forgotten his and my charger's not working. Just tell me if this is anywhere near Envers Avenue?'

Warily, Jemma nodded. 'Sort of, it's right down the end of the road and to the left.'

'Can you show us?' He walked the few paces to draw alongside, the map held out.

'I told you, it's down there.' Afraid, Jemma backed off only to find the side of the shelter stopping her dead. 'Piss off or I'll scream…'

'Like there's anyone around to hear. Let's get this done, kid, I'm running late.' His hand shot out reaching for her.

Jemma ducked trying to dodge past his legs, yelping as he dragged her back by her ponytail. 'GET OFF ME...!'

Cold fingers muffled her scream as a sharp pain jabbed into her neck, liquid fire raced through her veins. Terrified, she kicked out squirming and wriggling. She couldn't breathe. She tried scratching, then punching. All the time a heaviness was creeping through her arms and her legs until she couldn't move. She was in the air – floating. Hands were reaching out of a deep, dark hole – she was falling…

***

Ben slid out of the car talking rapidly into his throat mic. 'Jackie, where the hell are you?'

'Three hundred metres down the road to your right.'

'The snatch is happening. Get your vehicle here now and block them. Any other vehicles close?'

'One patrol thirty seconds away, coming in from your left.'

'No sirens and hurry it up. I'm moving in now.'

Across the road the small green van was still parked, its rear doors ajar – no sign of the girl. To Ben's right, a panting woman half-ran towards him, a walking stick raised high. If that was the aunt, it was poor timing. In the distance, he caught the roar of an engine, tyres slick on the wet tarmac – his backup, hopefully.

From the rear of the van, a man slid out, slammed the doors closed – reached for the passenger door. This was going to turn into the car chase from hell if he didn't do something and soon. Ben called out, 'Hey mate, did you know you've a flat tyre?' Automatically, the man glanced down to check where Ben pointed as the car with Jackie Simmons sped past. The handbrake-turn spun the car sharply, blocking the van's escape.

Ben was fast but his assailant was already clenching a glinting blade. Ben's knee drove in. Dodging the flash of metal, he slammed the furious man hard against the rear doors. Stinking fumes spat into the air as the engine roared into life, the reek of hot rubber catching in his throat as tyres fought for traction. He could hear Jackie yelling even as the thud of batons crashed against the glass. The kidnapper jabbed – and Ben winced as the blade nicked his hip. Half blinded by rain, he grabbed the man's wrist, smashing it hard against the side of the van until the blade slipped from his attacker's fingers. With a heave, he dragged the man to the pavement away from the threat of reversing rubber.

'*You stinking cowardly bastards! Thought you'd take my girl, did you? Let me get at the bitch. I'll rip her sodding head off!*'

From the floor, Ben saw the furious Mrs Fields leaning over the bonnet, trying her best to kill the driver.

The local officer raced towards Ben. 'Sir, are you all right?'

'Help Jackie…' He held on to the struggling man, grateful to hear sirens in the distance.

'Where is she?' Mrs Fields' screams were worse than nails on glass.

The aunt strode towards him. Ben saw her foot draw back, heard the kidnapper's grunt as her boot found his shoulder. 'Mrs Fields, back off…'

'I'll sit on his sodding head. See how he likes that!'

The man squealed as the next kick caught him squarely on the knee. 'Get the mad bitch off me!'

Jackie pulled the swearing woman away, shielding Ben while he rolled the man over to cuff him. Siren's blaring, two patrol cars screeched to a halt. Undaunted, the aunt ran at the confused officers. 'Where the bloody hell were you lot? They almost killed us all. You find my girl, you hear!'

Hysteria edged Jackie's laugh as she tried to calm the furious woman. Panting, Ben rolled onto his back to blink up at the glowering sky. Rain had never felt so damned good.

Chapter Twenty-Six

Hepsford 10.28 hrs

THE CHEER ROLLED AROUND the incident room like a warm breeze.

'Nicely saved Chief Inspector.'

Sarah turned to find Finchley standing to one side. She, along with the rest of the room had been caught up listening to the rescue, courtesy of Ben and Jackie's mics and Cambridge central traffic. 'Apologies Sir, I didn't see you arrive.'

'In time for the main feature,' he nodded at the monitors where the doors to Hatters Court had opened and a sullen Elena Williams was being escorted out. 'And what's your next move?'

'It's going to depend on what we find on their phones and what the suspects can tell us. We know the four teenagers were being held at a garage near Spilsby in Lincolnshire. We believe they've been moved close to a beach, somewhere they can be transported out to a vessel of some kind. We have a little time on our side – there's no reasonable tide on that part of the coast until 16.30. Right now, I'm preparing to set up a cover story to buy us some breathing space.'

Finchley eyed her shrewdly. 'What sort of a cover story?'

'One of the suspects we apprehended will be phoning their contact to explain that Jemma didn't turn up. It doesn't matter why.'

'You seriously think you can get one of them to agree to do this?' He didn't hide his cynicism.

'No, Sir, we're going to use...'

'Don't,' he held up a hand. 'Put it in your report and make sure you aren't breaking any privacy laws, understood.'

'Wouldn't dream of it, Sir,' but she was talking to his retreating back.

A deep voice intruded. 'Lincolnshire team are set up and waiting on us for the go-ahead to enter the garage.'

'Tell them that's a negative. Nobody does anything until we have those mobiles sorted.' She turned to the desk opposite. Greg Roberts had a phone wedged between his ear and shoulder, fingers tapping rapidly on a keyboard.

'Greg, talk to me. Where are we with the other regions and suspects?' Her stomach churned with worry – a dozen balls were floating in the air at once. If she got one thing wrong, they wouldn't simply fall they'd disappear in a puff of smoke.

'Five of the eight players have been eyeballed, Sarah. They're at their places of work until 15.00 hrs. The other three are being traced to home addresses. I'm awaiting updates.'

'The same applies Greg, no one makes a move until we say so. Make sure everyone understands.

'Sorry Chief Inspector, but I've Amos Brantley for you,' Aryan was holding out a phone.'

'At last! Amos, where the hell...'

'Hospital,' he said cutting her off. 'Things have taken an interesting turn...'

Sarah could do nothing but listen as Amos relayed the latest disaster.

'That lodger, Warren or Saul – whatever his name is – we found him in the house clearing out his room. As soon as Matt Cox saw the man he sent him flying. I have to say Matt's got a decent right hook. It took everything I had to pull him off...'

Sarah rarely swore, but she let loose a string of expletives.

'Feel better for that?' Amos asked when she fell silent.

'Some – any identification on him?'

'Nothing – but I did find his laptop, the problem being – it's encrypted. The lodger smirked when I attempted to open up a file.' There was a hiatus before Amos continued. 'Sarah, he has to be tied up with the trafficking. What if this has compromised the operation?'

'No chance. They went for their last snatch in Cambridge ten minutes ago. The traffickers wouldn't have gone ahead if he'd alerted them.'

'I'm loving your optimism, Sarah. Not sure we'll get much out of him though, he isn't saying a word.'

'Maybe he won't have to if we can crack his passwords. But why are you at the hospital? Please tell me you haven't been stabbed or shot?'

'Matt briefly knocked the lodger out, I needed him checked over. I've arranged an escort to take him to a holding cell. I should be back shortly.'

'And Matt – how's he doing?'

'Furious, shaken, compounded by a broken little finger but he'll be fine. I've told him to report to the station when he's been fixed up in casualty. I thought you might want a word.'

When Sarah finally hung up, the room had slipped into an expectant silence. She squared her shoulders. There was no point putting it off, every officer in the room would've guessed something had happened.

'I've got the latest update. A suspected trafficker – quite possibly a key organiser, was apprehended trying to remove evidence from Matt Cox's house. Unfortunately, that evidence is currently locked up tight behind a wall of encryption…'

Murmurs rose in waves. 'Listen up.' She waited until every eye was on her – she needed them to believe she knew what she was doing and hated moments like this, expecting their confidence when deep down she had no way of knowing if she could deliver. She pulled on her best fight face as Freya called it. 'As far as I'm concerned, nothing has changed. The suspect was cleaning up – preparing to move to another area. The traffickers wouldn't have gone ahead with the snatch in Cambridge if they thought for one moment we were on to them. There are at least four teenagers and potentially two young women whose lives depend on *us*. By the end of today we *are* going to find them, and we *will* be bringing them home. Now – anyone – give me some good news?'

It was Aryan who tentatively raised a hand. 'Ben's uploaded the call lists from the mobiles taken at Cambridge and a techie from *Sound Lab* is being signed in. Where do you want us to work?'

Sarah glanced around the busy room – it wasn't conducive to listening to voice patterns. 'Here's the key to Bill Porter's office and don't get caught up in the science, Aryan.' He was already scraping back his chair, eager to go. 'We need to know who of the two in the van is the lead operative. If you can, cobble together voice messages from each of them and fast?'

'Do you want a voice copy for Elena Williams as well?'

'Definitely – she needs to make her boss believe that the pickup will go ahead this afternoon.' She watched him stride away, wishing she had half his energy. 'Greg, where are we with the other potential *players*?'

'All pinned down Sarah, awaiting your instruction.'

Sarah glanced up. Finchley stood near the door watching proceedings closely. Deliberately, she turned back to Greg. 'You've explained to the arresting officers what we need?'

'I insisted on plain-clothed officers, all mobiles to be confiscated immediately and no sirens or alarms.'

'Then call it. Make sure Ben is sent mug shots of all suspects once they're in custody. He's going to need something to work with when he starts the interrogations.'

Finchley walked through the crowded room to join her. 'You're questioning the suspects in Cambridge?'

'We're running out of time. If that message from Lee was correct and they're being moved out by boat, they could leave as early as 16.30 hrs, which gives us less than...'

'Yes, I can do the maths.'

'Sorry Sir, but our best hope is that one of them is prepared to talk. If they think they're first in line...'

'Queens evidence? I'm not sure that's within our remit.'

‘No promises,’ she added quickly. ‘The courts are bound to look more favourably on someone who cooperates.’

He picked up the file, eyes scanning the front page. ‘Watch your step. Using voice copies could be seen as entrapment. Even a hint of impropriety and the whole thing gets thrown out.’

‘I’m only planning to use them as a delaying tactic Sir, not to trap anyone.’

‘Make sure that’s exactly what it is Chief Inspector. Keep me updated.’

Amos Brantley walked in twenty minutes later carrying two large mugs. ‘Greg filled me in,’ he said briskly. ‘I know it was a close call in Cambridge Sarah, but this might work in our favour.’

‘Not sure the aunt is going to be thinking that way Amos. Is the lodger any more cooperative?’

‘Refusing to say a word. There are three uniformed looking for his car. He must have arrived there somehow. Local taxis are coming back negative.’

‘And you told them the car is likely to be dark red?’

Amos nodded. ‘Aryan suggested I deliver the computer straight to the tech department. He reckoned it was likely to have malware programming built in so will need to go through the department’s firewalls before anyone attempts to decrypt anything. I dropped it off on the way here and they promised to take a look immediately. I’ll give them a ring now, see what they think.’

While he waited to be connected, Sarah mulled over the implications. ‘He was damned clever Amos, finding lodgings with a social worker, build up Matt’s trust, gently prod him for information, check no one had sussed what was going on.’

‘Matt was telling me he’d put the ad for a lodger on the council’s social care site. He couldn’t believe his luck when he had a response so quickly. I’ll wager that Warren, or whatever he's called, has similar lodgings set up all around the country.'

'And Hepsford has major road links to the coast, an airport close by. The man could've been anywhere in the UK within an hour or so…'

Amos held up a hand as his call was answered. The conversation was brief but Amos looked grimly satisfied when he replaced the receiver. 'Aryan was right about the malware but they've done whatever techies do and they should be able to retrieve the information within the hour.'

'Finally, some good news…'

'Ma'am,' Jake Forbes handed down a note. 'Uniform have found a red BMW parked up two streets away from Matt Cox's. It's registered to *Euro Collect and Hire* and leased to one Saul James – and there's more good news. We've found a match for the man's fingerprints in juvenile records, Scotland. Warren the lodger, alias Saul James, his real name is Laurence Alastair Jamieson. He was done for dangerous driving sixteen years ago, aged 17.'

'The same Jamieson clan you think Megan is connected to?' Amos asked.

'Well he's the son of Callum, grandfather Alastair, Sir.'

There was satisfaction watching pieces of the puzzle slide into place. Sarah handed Amos a copy of the research into the Jamieson family. 'This makes a short but fascinating read. Did I tell you the sites are still blocked either by us or our Scottish friends?' she sipped the strong coffee as he scanned the briefing note.

'Don't underestimate the power of old family ties. Some of the Scottish roots go back centuries.' Amos read on, soaking up the implications as Sarah studied the activity on the monitors. He finally looked up. 'Laurence Jamieson is the only son of Callum Jamieson?'

‘There are two daughters, much younger. Megan would be Laurence’s cousin I believe. Other than the family, I have no idea what her connection is to all this.’

‘Do we think the trafficking is a family enterprise or a side-line for our young entrepreneur Laurence?’

‘Oh, I doubt he’d have the connections Amos. It would take someone with clout and a lot of money to set this up. It’s more likely to be Callum or possibly the old man, Alastair. He’s the one with a track record in trafficking, mostly in India and South America. He’s slipped through homeland security and Interpol’s fingers several times over the decades.’

‘But Alastair must be in his early eighties by now Sarah, he’d have to employ others to do the snatching and keep watch on the youngsters until they’re shipped off. That’s going to involve a lot of organisation with a huge potential for someone to rat them out.’

‘Which is why it’s stayed in the family I’d think. Alastair uses his son Callum, who in turn brings in Laurence. Even so, I wonder how they’ve managed to evade the security agencies for so long. Backhanders do you think?’

‘Have you taken out a subscription to conspiracy united, Sarah?’

‘We make basic enquiries and not only Interpol but the cyber buffs jump all over it? During the past two years Alastair and Callum have moved their activities into England and done pretty much what the hell they like, all under homeland security’s nose?’

‘All we have so far on Laurence is forged documentation. Until he or one of the other *players* talk, or that computer gives up its secrets, there’s nothing to connect him or the rest of the family to those youngsters, or Megan Shaw’s disappearance for that matter.’

‘Don’t forget the grandmother, Amos. Catherine Jamieson went to a lot of trouble to stay hidden from that family and, if they thought Megan could identify Emily Cotton and start to unravel the trafficking ring...'

'A great theory, but that is not going to cut it with the CPS is it? Please Sarah, don't get pulled into a grand conspiracy.'

'Like hell, I will,' she looked up into his dark serious eyes and smiled. 'This is one of those times when I wouldn't mind being hands-on, Amos. It irritates me having to stand by and watch.'

'But you're damned good at this organisational stuff and Ben will handle it on the ground. Although thinking about it, Sarah, you being closer to the action, wouldn't be such a bad idea…'

Chapter Twenty-Seven

Cambridge 11.45hrs

PETERSON HAD HARDLY SET FOOT in the Cambridgeshire police station when DI Quentin handed him a pile of printouts and an order to telephone Allerton immediately. The call had been brief but left him in no doubt of what was expected. As the call ended, Quentin pushed over a steaming drink and a plate of biscuits. 'I guessed you could do with this. Did you pick up any injuries?'

The adrenaline rush from earlier had left behind the usual woozy head and aching legs. 'A scratch on my hip but mostly I'm just damp, Sir. It's nothing the coffee and sugar won't fix. I'm ready to start the interviews whenever you are?'

'Fair enough, I understand time is important here. We've a Brief lined up for the Williams woman, so we could start with her.'

'She'd be the easiest, I'd think. I'll show her the mug-shots and see who she recognises, hint they're prepared to talk.'

Quentin didn't look confident. 'That might be naive Sergeant, but you never know.'

Sullen and pale-faced, Elena Williams sat in the interview room refusing to make eye contact. Her legal representative, Ms Davey, listened closely as Ben made the introductions, explaining that shortly Elena would be taken to Hepsford East Yorkshire for further questioning. 'Dragging my client halfway around the country is unnecessary, Sergeant.'

'Ms Williams is facing multiple charges, including the use of a false identity, that of Rebecca Short, to create fraudulent documentation to obtain police clearance for work with vulnerable clients as well as the trafficking of minors for profit. Several of these charges relate to incidents within the Yorkshire region.'

Elena Williams showed little emotion. 'I changed my name, is all. You've no proof I've done anything else.'

Sliding a file onto the table, Ben pulled out a photograph. 'I'm showing Ms Williams an image extracted from a video recording from this morning at Hatters Court. Please confirm for the tape that it's you in the picture.'

'Yeah and...'

'Why did you telephone Jemma Fields at her aunt's house this morning?'

'Who said I did?'

Ben placed an evidence bag beside the picture. Inside was a mobile phone. The phone's plastic cover bore the same distinct tree pattern as the one she'd been holding in the photograph. 'Do you deny that the mobile phone I'm showing you is yours?'

Elena shrugged. 'Looks the same, so what?'

Another photograph joined the line-up. 'This photograph was taken this morning after Jemma Fields was rescued following a failed kidnapping attempt. I'm asking you again, why did you telephone Jemma Fields this morning?'

Elena's bored expression abruptly changed to one of shock. 'I – I – you can't prove anything.'

'Jemma was still woozy from the drugs they'd pumped into her but let me read what she managed to tell me, Ms Williams?' Fear held Elena rigid. She couldn't drag her eyes up from the image of Jemma held in the arms of a paramedic.

'I quote – *I had this phone call at my auntie's, asking if I wanted to go ice-skating. I had to meet them at the bus stop...*'

'NO, she got it wrong, she...'

'The number for Jemma Fields aunt is on your mobile. There's a call registered at 09.47 hrs this morning. The same as the time-stamp on the image of you using your mobile. You should think carefully about what I'm about to say. The trafficking of minors carries a heavy penalty; life I believe?'

Ms Davey tutted disapprovingly. 'Stop trying to intimidate my client.'

'Your client is up to her neck, Ms Davey. We can prove she contacted Jemma. We have proof she had contact with two others who are also in custody and were involved in the abduction.' Ben pulled out the photographs of the man and woman from the van. The flicker of recognition was unmistakable. 'It's up to you Elena, but I'm quite sure they'll be happy to let you take the blame for as much as they can.'

'All I did was make the bloody phone call. You can't pin anything else on me!'

'I don't believe you! You knew exactly what was going on. You know where they take the teenagers and what happens to them. When we've finished going through your bank accounts, and believe me we'll find every one of your aliases, I'm going to make sure the judge knows exactly how many kidnappings you are responsible for. The interview ended at...'

'You can't – you can't,' she was on her feet screaming at him. 'I only did what I was told.'

'Sit down, do yourself a favour, Ms Williams. We know about the holding pit. Tell me where they are taken from there. Is it a boatyard, another garage?'

'I don't know, never went. You have to believe me...'

'You never went where Ms Williams? You might not have visited the place but you talked about it with the others, gossiped about the clever plan and how easy it all was?' Elena Williams' jaw moved soundlessly. He could see the hesitation, doubt building. 'This interview ended at...'

'Graveyard, that's all I know.' She was visibly shaken. 'The place they take them to – from the garage – is on the coast, call it the graveyard. I swear, I don't have any idea where it is!'

***

14.45 hrs

Cambridge traffic was diabolical. It was a Saturday but could have been rush hour in the middle of London. Again, Ben checked the time. His passenger, Jackie Simmons was busy adding more tape to the top of one hand.

'Are you sure that doesn't need A&E?'

'It's a cut, Ben. I've enough plasters on there to keep the Humber Bridge up. It'll be fine and before you ask, I had a tetanus shot less than a year ago.'

He clamped his lips shut – that had been the next question. 'Fair enough – what did you put on the accident form?' he was doing his best not to smirk.

'Caught on broken glass. I didn't think Mrs Fields would appreciate the truth.'

'Battery by walking stick? No, it doesn't have quite the same ring, does it?' This time he didn't bother to hide the snort of laughter.

'It still hurts,' she muttered shooting him a dirty look.

'I'm sure that hunk of yours will kiss it better. Did I tell you I found out the reason the boss hasn't ordered our immediate execution?'

'I thought you told me she was fuming?'

'Well, it's helped that we got Jemma out relatively unscathed – but Carl rang to say they'd finally identified the lodger as a Laurence Jamieson. Amos caught him in the act of removing a laptop from Matt Cox's place.'

'Bloody hell; is *North Run* a bust then?'

'Not as far as they can work out. They picked up the lodger as we were taking out the van. We are still good to go.'

'Is Amos off to Lincoln with Sarah?'

'Apparently not, although Carl clammed up when I started digging. Amos is definitely up to something.'

'Come off it Ben, Amos and Sarah go way back.'

‘Oh, it’s nothing to do with this case, or Sarah, not directly.’ He was frowning again.

‘So?’ she asked when he fell silent.

‘Don’t you think it’s strange that we haven’t been asked to do anything with the *Blue Beacon*?’

‘Well, we have been a bit tied up. I just thought he was doing our team a favour.’

‘Maybe – oh, sod this for a lark. Pull out the lights Jackie, or we’ll still be stuck here until midnight’

Chapter Twenty-Eight

Hepsford Station

AMOS BRANTLEY GLANCED AT THE TIME, 14.40. Impatiently he tapped a broad finger on the edge of the keyboard. Moira Robins should be coming online any time now. Outside in the corridor heavy footsteps hurried past; Tracy Bates was under strict orders to tell everyone he was out and unavailable. In reality, he was huddled over a laptop in one of the tiny admin offices. As much as he wanted to, he couldn't drag anyone else into this. There was too much riding on *North Run* to involve Sarah's team. Beside him, his mobile vibrated. 'Carl?

He's left the building. Do you want me to follow?' 'Damn… No, he'll spot you in a heartbeat. The icon on Amos's screen began to flash. 'Moira's made contact, stay on the line, Carl.'

Moira's image was sharp and crisp, the frown of impatience impossible to misread. 'Sir?'

'I swear, you won't have to stay there much longer Moira, but I need to know if you've remembered any more about your mobile?'

'Didn't the landlord or the bastard who knocked me out take it?'

'Moira, please…'

'Okay – let me think.'

Amos tried to hold on to his patience but the seconds were ticking on.

'I remember running to the cellar because I couldn't get out through the pub door; they'd barred it to stop punters coming in. I legged it down the stairs and…' Silence.

‘And?’

‘Bloody hell, I’d forgotten I’d done that!’

***

Amos was on his feet when Carl Moyles pushed into the small office. ‘I’m going ahead to the *Beacon*. He held up a hand to stop the protest. ‘Explain to Tracy what’s happening, then follow me – but quietly!’ He didn’t wait for an argument – just hurried out to his car.

The roads were slick with fresh fallen sleet but the darkening sky was clearing. Amos pulled into the road parallel to the *Blue Beacon,* and parked behind a small Citroen. Moody grey clouds cloaked the last of the daylight, making it difficult to differentiate details. He checked the time again – almost 15.20 hrs, another half an hour before darkness descended. Cutting through a narrow alley, he glanced left and right up the empty street before rushing to the corner of the public house. The new padlock on the gate unlocked easily and the temporary rear door of the *Beacon* opened without a sound. Stepping inside the indigo space, Amos held his breath, ears straining for signs of movement. Something scuttled across the floorboards – normal – mice or rats, he could deal with them.

Torch on dim, he shuffled through to the bar, navigating his way past fallen stools and upturned tables left from Tuesday night. To his right, the door of the cellar hung on broken hinges. The *Beacon’s* landlord had been a wily man who’d purchased the terraced properties either side of the pub and excavated through into their cellars. One side held the *still* and equipment while the other stored crates of illegal spirits and bottling equipment. The pub’s own cellar held nothing more than a pulley system to hoist barrels of beer into the bar, along with the usual clutter associated with a pub. The false walls he’d built to hide the entrance into the other cellars were a work of genius.

Halfway down the cellar stairs Amos stopped, every sense alert. Above his head a door creaked – hardly more than a whisper but enough to send him jumping the last few steps. Striding across to the false wall to his right, his fingers fumbled for the hidden latch; he needed somewhere – anywhere – to hide.

The spotlight of a torch was blinding. Blinking rapidly, Amos turned, trying to remain calm. 'This is a crime scene. You shouldn't be in here!' In his pocket, his mobile vibrated. Deftly, his finger found '*answer*' all he could hope was, Carl would hear something through the layer of material.

'Didn't I tell you he'd be back for it, Mike?' One of the shadowy figures was pointing a gun in his direction. 'You've got two minutes to find that sodding mobile phone before I put a bullet in your chest – start hunting, Brantley!'

***

Minutes later, Amos stood flat against the far wall, surrounded by a mass of disgorged boxes and crates, desperately hoping Carl would put in an appearance and soon! In front of him, Mike Lawson and one of the Leeds revenue officers, Eddy Driscole, eyed him impatiently. 'And I'm telling you it isn't here! Look for yourselves if you don't believe me?'

Eddy scowled his disbelief. The gun hadn't moved. Amos had no doubt the man would use it. 'Then why come back? Do you think we're bloody stupid?' Eddy raised the weapon, the barrel aimed at his head.

From above Amos's straining ears caught the creak of a floorboard. He kicked out at a box, said the first thing that came into his head. 'Killing me isn't going to solve anything. Do you seriously believe I didn't report my suspicions, Mike? I've been tracking you for days.'

'Like hell you have! You couldn't tie your own f*ing shoelaces without one of your precious lackeys to help.'

'You're too damned cocky, Lawson. I had you sussed Tuesday night. And whose mad idea was it to alert Ingles? Trying to distract Sarah while you lot off-loaded your precious booze I suppose?'

Lawson's fist swung hard; Amos dipped to the left – the blow missing by a fraction. 'Shut it or I'll pull the damned trigger myself!'

Where the hell was Moyles? Amos kept on talking – 'Sarah caught you out though didn't she? Wrapped up Ingles – Carson, right under your bloody nose. A bit of a nasty shock that Mike, finding out those two were best buddies…'

Eddy pushed Lawson to the side 'We are not listening to this crap. Dig out a couple of hessian sacks, Mike. We'll dump him in those and bury him later.' The gun was now pointing unwaveringly at Amos's heart.

'For Christ sake Eddy, we don't need to shoot the man, tie him up – knock the sod out if you must. Tomorrow, we'll be with Dean and well out of harm's way. New ID, the works.'

'There is no way the bastard will let this go and you know it; now shut the crap and do what I said…' Again the gun lifted a fraction. Amos felt the cold clammy sweat of fear grip his gut even as he made ready to lunge.

Eddy's yelp of pain was masked by the sharp retort of the gunshot as it flew wide – smashing into the small window. A spinning bottle had ploughed into the gunman's shoulder – splinters of glass flew in all directions, pricking Amos's cheeks. Eddy was already pivoting, firing again, the shot splattering into the wall centimetres from where Carl had been standing. Amos's elbow landed hard in Lawson's ribs, sending him flying into the gunman.

Eddy's face creased into a smirk even as the shot rang out. Soundlessly, Mike Lawson staggered back gaping down at his blood soaked shirt.

‘You bastard!’ Amos’s left fist swung, catching Eddy’s chin a massive blow. With a clatter, the weapon slipped from the stunned man’s fingers as he crashed to the floor.

‘Carl, get rid of that sodding gun and help Mike!’ Wedged against a box, Mike’s eyes were wide with shock, staring, bewildered at his blood-soaked hands.

Kicking the weapon out of reach, Carl knelt, pressing firm hands against the bloody wound. Outside on the street came the scream of sirens. Mike Lawson’s lips were barely moving. Carl bent close, trying to make out the man’s words but it was too late – he was gone. Carl sat back on his heels, holding out his bloodied hands like some errant child. ‘What the hell just happened?’

‘This bastard pulled the trigger on his mate is what happened. Mike was helpless.’ Eddy grunted in discomfort as Amos tightened the wrist ties a little more.

A shout of disbelief echoed from behind them. ‘Bloody hell?!’ Neil Harper took the steps in two jumps, uniformed officers close behind. ‘Is that Mike Lawson?’

‘Neil,’ Amos stumbled to his feet. ‘Contact Finchley and the CS unit. Tell them this is a priority, we have an officer down and Neil – find Carl something so he can clean up.’

***

Hustling the unhappy Eddy up the wooden stairs took two officers several minutes. In the silence that followed, Amos stood with Carl and Neil, watching the Region’s senior forensic officer solemnly examine Mike Lawson’s body. ‘Who’s taking lead on the case?’

‘That would be me,’ Amos said. ‘Although the IPC might possibly have something to say about that.’

The doctor shrugged, turned back to the body. ‘Mike Lawson was killed by a single bullet, which appears to have penetrated his right ventricle. Death would have occurred within a minute or less. The weapon was held close to the body

– touching the clothing I'd guess, but I will be able to say more after the full examination. Anything you want to tell me, Chief Inspector Brantley?'

'Mike may have gunshot residue on his fingers. He was touching the assailant's hands at the time of the shot.'

'Useful, thank you… And I'm sorry. Whatever the circumstances, losing a colleague is never easy. I've had word from CS Finchley, he should be arriving shortly.'

Amos waited until the doctor had moved away to make a phone call. 'You two help me search. I know it's a lot to ask, but I need to find that sodding mobile phone before I go mad.' He was already at the top of the staircase, a torch in his hand. 'Use your torches. Between the wall and stairs, there should be a gap. Moira remembers pushing her mobile down into the space between.'

Halfway up Neil called, 'Sir, found the damned thing!'

They sat, huddled under the arc-lighting that the forensic team had installed and switched on the mobile.

'At least no one is going to dispute that.' Amos held up the screen so they could all see. Eddy the gunman was easily recognisable; beside him, a younger blonde-haired man was laughing. Mike Lawson stood between them holding a pint. There were five pictures, all sharp and clear; all contained the three men and the landlord. 'The blonde man is a junior revenue officer, Dean Wilson. You might recognise him; he came to the station with Eddy to assess the case for raiding the *Blue Beacon*?'

Neil squinted, making the image larger. 'So it damn well is. How did I not know what Lawson was doing? I should've bloody seen it!'

Amos sighed, shook his head. 'You were too close and Mike was clever…'

Carl touched the screen. 'He looks a lot like our bogus DI from the hospital. Do you know where this Wilson is, Sir?'

‘No and from what Eddy and Lawson were saying, I fear he may have already skipped the country.’

‘At least Sarah is well out of it by now, boss.’

Amos grimaced. ‘She might be a couple of hundred miles away, Carl but we still need to keep a lid on this. I do not want her distracted…’

‘I hope the Chief Super understands, Sir.’ Above their heads, Finchley’s deep tones could clearly be heard, growling his impatience – asking where they were.

Amos’s groan was deep and heartfelt. ‘Here we go again. And by the way, Carl – thanks, I owe you one. That was a cracking throw.’

Carl grinned and shook the outstretched hand. ‘Anytime, Sir, I’ve always been a decent bowler…’

Chapter 29

AMOS BRANTLEY'S SUGGESTION that Sarah should move closer to the centre of the action had made a sort of sense at the time – or at least that was what Sarah kept telling herself as the car she was in sped away from Hepsford Station towards the Lincolnshire coast. Not that she had considered for one second that Amos had been serious or that CS Finchley would *okay* the idea. Yet, far from squashing the notion, he'd not only agreed but as good as pushed her into the car and waved her off. It was hard to shake off the impression that Finchley and Amos wanted her out of the way – but that was ridiculous. It was like Amos kept telling her, she was overtired, jumping at shadows.

In the back, Aryan Khan studied his laptop, listening to the messages on the numerous gadgets splayed across the seat. Occasionally, Sarah caught a muted, '*Will do,*' or '*Selecting now.*' She hoped the voice patterns they'd pulled together would fool the traffickers, at least for long enough to allow her team to track down the youngsters – they were so close.

'Are you surviving back there, Aryan?'

He peered up from the screen he was studying. 'Pretty well considering. We're having a problem with the encryption on Laurence's machine, so we're still relying on the mobiles we cloned.'

'Have there been any more messages?'

'There was an attempt to contact Elena Williams. It was the same number that tried to contact the driver of that van in Cambridge. We've sent a response saying – *On for two forty*. A follow-up text instructs Elena Williams to message as soon as the pick-up is confirmed. We can identify the telephone number but it's another burn-phone and only transmitting for short periods. It's making it impossible to pin down an exact location.'

'Thinking to cross-reference the sat nav devices in the van and Laurence's car was a stroke of genius. It's narrowed down the dozens of possible sites to a handful.'

'Just luck, Ma'am.'

'Rubbish Aryan, luck had little to do with it. Can you give me an idea about our ETA Sergeant?'

The young driver checked the digital display. 'We should arrive around 16.00 hrs or thereabouts, but I'm going to use the lights for the next part, we've miles of roadworks to negotiate. I've also been told to ask what you'd all like to eat so I can pass it on.'

They stopped briefly at the pull-in where an officer was waiting, food bag in hand. 'Chief Inspector, the traffic's lightened up a little but the weather's closing in. The Coastguard rang the office to say they've two vessels keeping an eye out for suspicious craft and a helicopter ready to go on your word. There's nothing to report so far.'

The smell of food was intoxicating. Feeling only slightly guilty about the driver, Sarah bit into the huge roll, savouring the chilli chicken kick. The sweet pastry and banana disappeared equally as fast.

'I needed that,' Aryan admitted. 'I didn't have any breakfast.'

His laptop pinged; Sarah heard tapping and waited for the update. The long silence was ominous. She twisted in her seat; Aryan was looking slightly panicked. 'Spit it out, man?'

'Not sure I believe this, Ma'am. The call's been patched through from Hepsford Station.' He swivelled the screen to show her a very familiar name.

Chapter Thirty

SARAH PUSHED IN THE EARPIECE Aryan gave her. 'Megan, I'm Chief Inspector Allerton. Did the officer tell you we're on the way? Are you somewhere safe?'

The reply was muted, whispered, the young woman's terror obvious. 'Sort of, but I don't know for how long. I swear, I didn't have anything to do with that jewellery going missing – or Lee…'

'Megan, slow down. Take a breath, tell me where you are if you can.'

'Callum, he murdered her... Shauna, only she's Emily. He killed her right in front of me…' Heart-wrenching sobs echoed in Sarah's ear. 'There was nothing I could do, nothing! There was so much blood – and it's my fault! None of this would have happened if I'd said something on Monday...'

Sarah cut in. 'You need to breathe, stay in control. You've been amazingly clever to find a mobile. Concentrate on that.'

'It's hers – Emily's – she's called Emily, I thought she was Shauna… I took it off her when she was…' the sentence ended on another muted sob.

'Megan I'm going to ask you to talk to my officer, Aryan Khan. He'll record what you say. You explain what's happened. I'll be listening as well but I need to take some other calls?'

She let them talk, grateful the woman couldn't overhear the update from John Wetherton.

'Sarah, we've discovered the pit inside Morecliff garage where the youngsters had been kept. It's as the lad Lee described, essentially an inspection pit with a reinforced roof and grille, large enough to hoist them in and out. No one would know it was there unless they were looking for it. Worse though, our cadaver dog found a recent burial at the back of the property, a young girl, probably twelve, thirteen. She's been dead no more than a few days by what the CSO is saying and she's not the only one. There are at least four other sites the dog is interested in.

'Thanks for the update, John. It's bleak work for you.' The description he'd given was harrowing enough.

His voice vibrated with fury as he spoke. 'Those bastards chained them up, Sarah. The conditions they had to endure must have been sheer hell…'

'John, was there anything at all in the garage that might tell us where they've gone?'

'I've had the tech guys check the sat nav on a couple of vans parked up here. We have a match from each vehicle for the same coordinates – *Wright's Breakers,* a metal salvage yard right on the coast, about twenty miles away. It's full of old shipping containers, cars etc. Perfect I'd think.'

'Hold one second, John – Aryan, is *Wright's Breakers* on the list of potential sites?'

It took seconds for him to check. 'Yes Ma'am, near the top of the list.'

'That has to be the place, John.'

'I'm leaving the forensic unit to sort through this end. My team and I will meet you there. You'll need men on the ground for this.'

Sarah wasn't taken in by his quiet tone – the man was seething with anger. 'You wait until we arrive, no pre-emptive moves. You don't twitch a finger until I say so.'

John Wetherton laughed deep and low. 'I love an assertive woman, see you shortly.'

Chapter Thirty-One

15.55 hrs

THE CONSTANT DRUMMING OF RAIN on the car's roof had slowed. Ben handed Jackie the small binoculars and carefully opened his door. The chief Inspector and the teams might be on the way but they were running out of time. Mobile to his ear, he waited impatiently for Sarah to pick up.

'Ma'am, the rain's easing. If Aryan could give me a fix on Megan's mobile, I can at least try and pinpoint her location.'

Ben heard the hesitation, convinced she'd refuse. 'Aryan is texting the coordinates now but you are to stay well out of the traffickers' way Ben, do you understand. We'll be with you in less than ten.'

'Seriously, she agreed?' Jackie sounded as surprised as he felt. 'How do you want to do this, Ben?'

'Bloody carefully. Keep your phone on mute Jackie and your eyes peeled.'

The late afternoon light was fading, low grey clouds threatening to drop another deluge at any moment. Ben pushed his way under the metal fence and held it up for Jackie to follow. Crouched beside the first of the huge rusting containers, Jackie murmured, 'Graveyard – it's well named. The place gives me the creeps.'

'You and me both.' Ben glanced down at the flashing arrows on his mobile. 'It's straight on, stay low.'

Row upon row of shipping containers were interspersed with the wrecks of cars and lorries. The metal carnage stretched away in every direction. Without Aryan's flashing map, finding their way would have been impossible. Ben peered around yet another corner only to pull back his head sharply. 'Ten metres to our left – two vehicles parked near a wooden cabin.' He held up his mobile to show Jackie the flashing arrows. 'We need to cross the path and keep straight on.'

The rain had started again and with it ominous rumbles of thunder. Ben ran across the rutted road, aware of Jackie close on his heels. Megan's container was less than fifty metres in front. The urgent tug on his arm had him twisting around.

'Voices – close!'

Claps of thunder covered their footsteps as they raced to the far end of the container and slid around the corner. 'Up!' Ben pushed Jackie into the rusting cab of an ancient lorry. With seconds to spare he followed, dipping away from the hurrying figures below. Pelting rain drummed against the metal roof, drowning out everything else.

Mobile to his ear, he shoved a finger into the other trying to block out the storm. 'Ma'am, we've visual on six suspects including Callum Jamieson, but we're caught in the middle of a thunderstorm.'

'Lincoln team five minutes away. We're close and the storm is due to blow through shortly.'

***

Megan heard Callum's shout over the drumming of the rain and felt every ounce of courage drain from her body. The rescue would be too late!

'You three, sort them out. I want them down and inside those pods in ten minutes. Put the girl on the launch once they're stowed – and if I find any of you have been messing with her...'

'What about Trev and the new one?' Mark sounded grumpy, agitated.

'She'll keep for a week or so. Jade can babysit for a change. Dump Emily in the usual place once the kids are secured. Now, get them down to the beach – the other two are already down there, preparing. I need to phone that useless son of mine, tell him to inform Georges that the drop is ready– move!'

Huddled in the corner of the container, Megan pressed the mobile close to her mouth. 'They're coming for us. Please – can you hear me?'

Sarah heard the desperation in the young woman's voice. 'Megan, officers are within metres of your position. Hang on in there.'

***

From inside the rusting cab, Ben relayed the action. 'Ma'am, we've got eyeballs on four teenagers. They're being taken out of a shipping container…' The piercing scream knocked every other thought out of Ben's head.

'*I don't want to – let me go!*'

'*Leave her alone*!' Lee's curling red hair was unmistakable as he tried to protect the youngest girl. Vicious slaps followed, knocking each of them into submission.

'Sergeant Peterson, focus!' The inspector's sharp words penetrated his anger. 'Lincoln crew at the gates, with you in under three minutes. Do you hear me?'

'Understood, Ma'am. Megan's signal is close. We'll do what we can.'

'Ben, we can't stand by and watch this bloody happen?!' The four terrified youngsters were being dragged away kicking and yelling.

'Lincoln officers are at the gate, Jackie. We'll release Megan then follow… I know,' he urged, catching her arm to stop her bolting after the fast disappearing teenagers. 'Those men will be armed – I want you and those kids alive, not half-dead hostages!'

The rain made finding purchase on the thick, heavy bolt of the container difficult. Ben winced at the grinding clang, praying the rumbling thunder would cover the worst of the noise. The stench as the door swung free made him gag. A mixture of decay, mould and who knew what else stung his eyes, caught at his throat. 'Watch our backs Jackie, I won't be long.'

Stepping inside, he tried not to breathe in too deeply. 'Megan?' His voice echoed off the metal walls, impossible to see anything clearly. Moving forwards, his foot caught on something soft. In the flickering torchlight, the pool of congealing blood shimmered like rubies. Ben swung the torch in an arc. Emily Cotton's body rested awkwardly against the cold wall, sightless eyes staring down at her own blood-soaked hands. Deliberately, Ben dropped his gaze away from the gaping slash in her neck and called again. 'Megan, it's Sergeant Peterson…'

He thought she'd faint. Clothes torn, lips bloodied and swollen, Megan staggered towards him, bruises on her cheeks and neck were black in the gloom. 'Get me out of here,'

Outside, the rain was easing. Jackie hurried the distressed woman away to shelter under the roof of an overhanging cab. Mobile to his ear, Ben kept it short. 'Chief Inspector, we've retrieved Megan Shaw. How close are Lincoln crew to our position?'

The answer seemed to take hours. 'Two officers have you in sight. Where are Lee and the others?'

'I'll find out and report back. Jackie will stay with Megan until the Lincoln crew arrive…' Ben didn't wait for an answer. He was already metres away when he caught Jackie's hiss of disapproval.

'Don't go alone, Ben…'

Running low between the metal giants, his eyes were everywhere. Dragging four uncooperative teenagers would take time – working out how much time was the problem. He caught the rasp of waves breaking on a pebbled shore – the teenagers had to be close. The last shipping container stood some twenty metres from a line of rocks and beyond that, only straggling clumps of the tall waving grass gave the barest cover. Bent double, Ben darted between jagged lumps of shale, the pebbled beach a few metres away.

The scene in front of him seemed like a sci-fi film. Four large metal cylinders gleamed silver, slick with the rain. Below three of them a metal fin protruded, raising one end so the container was balanced at a jaunty angle. Long ropes snaked from each nose-cone to run through the lapping water into rings on the stern of a large motor launch. Two men were leaning over one of the cylinders, forcing something down inside. Ben heard the clang as the curving lid slammed shut. Hoisting the container up onto its nose, one of the traffickers flicked the lower fin into place. It took him seconds to work out the purpose of the cylinders.

'Ma'am, this is bloody insane! The kids are smuggled out to sea in sodding metal cylinders – like the Colombian drug cartels use!'

'Ben, keep it calm. We need to know details…'

'Five traffickers on the beach, one at least has a gun. No sign of Callum. Four cylinders, a youngster trapped inside each. A rope attaches the cylinder to a motor launch…' A hurrying figure came scuttling down the short path to the beach forcing Ben to drop lower. 'Callum Jamieson has arrived and he doesn't look happy!'

Feet crunching on the shale behind him had Ben swinging around, fist raised. 'Jackie – get down!'

She threw herself onto the wet sand. 'What the hell are those things?'

'Floating bloody prisons…'

'Ben, can you hear me?' The chief inspector sounded as if she was running. 'Callum knows we have Megan. He's going to make a run for it…'

They were out of time.

Yelling orders to his men as he went, Callum strode through the shallow waters ready to haul himself on board. The other traffickers circled near the path. It was impossible to hear what they said over the rain and swell of the sea.

'Jackie, on your belly and start cutting those ropes.' Ben handed her his knife. 'Watch yourself – those bastards won't go quietly. I'm going for the boat.'

Plunging through the icy waters, Ben grasped the cold metal of the safety rail. He was less than halfway up when Callum's shadow loomed. Quickly Ben dropped, bullets spraying harmlessly into the ocean above his head. Surging up, he heaved against the side of the launch sending it into a crazy dance. One-handed, he clung to the rail, desperate to avoid being dragged under by the plunging boat. Above him the Scotsman staggered, swearing furiously as he crashed to the deck. Ben dared a glance to the shore. Jackie was on her stomach attempting to slice through ropes. Around her, a bloody war had erupted as officers fought off desperate traffickers.

Water surging from his clothing, Ben dragged himself on board, kicking the gun into the surging waves. Callum was back on his feet and stretching for the controls. With a guttering roar, the motor purred into life. The deck juddered as the launch slowly edged forwards. Behind him the ropes tightened, dragging cylinders with their terrified cargo out into the freezing waters.

Desperately, Ben made a grab for the controls only to dodge away from Callum's fist, the powerful punch sliding past his chin. With a snarl, the Scotsman thrust the throttle forwards, plunging the launch into the oncoming waves. Ben dived at the man's legs, bringing him crashing to the heaving deck. Callum's hot breath raked his face – rough fingers clawed at his throat as Ben fought to keep the man down. Without a hand on the controls, the launch began to slow, wave after wave exploding against the prow, drenching them both.

The pain didn't register for some seconds. Callum's cold sneer began to make sense when Ben tried to raise his arm to punch – the bastard had stabbed him! Blood dripped from his belly onto the deck, mixing with the pools of saltwater. Callous hands pushed him away towards the heaving swell of the sea. Drowning, Ben thought, was not how he'd planned to die.

Chapter Thirty-Two

HE WAS DREAMING – hallucinating, had to be. Some mythical being surged up through the waves, water streaming from their sleek body as it thrust itself on board. The creature towered above them, fury in black. Through a haze of rain and mist, Ben saw the blow that sent the startled Callum hurtling off the side.

A strange voice echoed inside his skull, pulling him back into a cold, pain-filled world.

'Sergeant Peterson, hang on in there, mate, help's coming.' Cold hands pushed against his stomach. 'I've got strict instructions not to let you die. You stay with me, you hear…'

***

Breathing hard, Sarah reached the path leading to the beach and groaned. Around her lay chaos and death. In the water, John Wetherton with two teenagers and a uniformed officer were attempting to drag a submerged cylinder out, while three blood-streaked armed officers kept the other traffickers at bay. On the pebbles were three metal cylinders, their grey bellies ripped open. On the rocks to her left, a bloodied body lay, face down, unmoving. The hum of a motor was abruptly silenced as the keel rose onto the pebbles. On board, two paramedics knelt beside a too still figure. Sarah's heart almost stopped. 'Ben!'

Aryan and the driver ran, throwing off shoes and jackets to wade out waist-deep, helping to drag the last waterlogged cylinder to safety. It was only then Sarah saw the small figure of Jackie Simmons bent over one of the opened cylinders comforting a young girl. Hurrying to the water's edge, Sarah grabbed the end of the coarse rope and heaved with the rest. The freezing waves rose to her knees.

'We need to get this thing open!' John Wetherton roared, as willing hands fought to pull away the metal clasps. Water ran out through a small hole on each side of the cylinder to trickle back towards the oncoming tide. Sarah wasn't sure she could bear to watch as the lid finally gave up the fight.

Kayla lay so still, hands and feet firmly secured – there would have been no escape. 'We need her out on her belly,' ordered a paramedic. Methodically the medic began to massage the girl's back. A trickle of water oozed from the side of Kayla's mouth. 'There's a pulse but it's faint,' the officer said not breaking her rhythm. 'Hypothermia and shock won't be helping.'

Lee and Simon stood to one side, teeth chattering. 'I need blankets, now,' Sarah called. She ripped off her bullet-proof vest for Lee, wrapping her coat around Simon's thin shoulders. 'Lee, I'm a police officer...' She pulled the boys closer, trying to share her warmth.

'They killed Paula,' Simon whispered. 'She had a cough – they killed her for it.'

'You won't let Kyla die, will you,' Lee pleaded.

'I've got a twitch.' The officer began massaging more vigorously, 'Come on little lady, cough.'

Lee broke away. Huge in the vest, he knelt beside the girl. 'You heard him Ky, cough it up. Come on, I want to go have some real food.' He kept talking as the twitch turned into a spasm. Abruptly, Kayla retched throwing up a spew of saltwater.

'Ma'am, take one of these, you're soaking.' An officer was holding out silver thermal blankets for her and the boys.

At her side, Simon shivered uncontrollably, despite the blanket. 'She's got to be all right! Ky kept me sane, you know…'

'You must have been terrified, Simon.'

'Rosa was screaming so loud…' The boy gulped finding it hard to speak.

'Is that Rosa with my officer?' Sarah pointed to the girl nestled at Jackie Simmons' side.

'Yeah – she was all alone for the first week and she's only eleven…'

'Lee – Oh God Lee! I can't believe you're all safe…' Megan Shaw pushed away from the officer she was with to hobble towards them. 'I could hear you all, but I couldn't get out of that stinking hole.'

'Megan?' Lee flung his arms around her, held on tight. 'Please – just take me home. I want to go home!'

Chapter Thirty-Three

PERCHED ON A ROCK, Sarah heard the whir of the helicopter as it whisked Ben Peterson away to the nearest trauma centre and she breathed a little easier. He was still alive but, if the Coastguard hadn't turned up when they did... She forced her thoughts back to the beach and the eerie shapes of the foil-wrapped figures. Lee, Megan and the other two youngsters were following the stretcher carrying Kayla towards the waiting ambulances. Rescued or not, Sarah doubted any of them would sleep peacefully for a long time. It had been months after Freya's rescue before the nightmares receded enough to allow her to rest for more than a few hours. Memories of those difficult days had her reaching for her mobile.

'Just a quick one – I'm fine. Likely to be away overnight. The worst is over. Love U xx.' Sarah pressed *send* before she could change her mind. Sentimentality wasn't her thing, but today was different. Images of Kayla's still cold face as they'd opened her metal prison rose unbidden.

'Sarah, I've something hot and sweet that might be coffee, if you're interested?' The large frame of John Wetherton stooped down. He was holding out a thermos and a cup.

'As long as it's hot, John.' She waited until he'd poured and squeezed onto the rock beside her before she asked. 'How are *you* doing?'

'Better, now I've changed into something dry. The coastguard folk are well organised.'

'Comes of living and working so close to the water I suppose. Are any of your officers hurt?'

'A couple of scratches and one has a bruised jaw, nothing serious. I hear your sergeant had it rough?'

'Knife in the spleen…' Sarah swigged coffee trying not to think of Ben fighting for his life in the copter.'

'It's only minutes to the trauma unit Sarah and they're excellent. They'll have him sorted before you know it.'

'Thanks John. Ben's a really nice young man and a bloody good Sergeant.'

'He saved the kids' lives. One of the divers was telling me, Callum had fitted each of those cylinders with adapted seacocks. If that maniac had managed to drag the things out to sea, he'd have pulled the seals and we'd never have got to them in time. We were lucky we managed to rescue Kayla.'

'Hell, it doesn't bear thinking about.'

'I wish they'd let the bastard drown, I really do.'

Sarah grimaced into her rapidly cooling drink 'That makes two of us, but at least now we might get some answers.'

'From Callum?' John picked up the thermos. 'Not a chance. Hell will freeze over first.'

Off to their right, stretcher-bearers were carrying away the body of one of the traffickers. Sarah held out her cup for a refill. 'They managed to put a name to our dead man. He's a Mark Todd, car mechanic by trade. Lives in Skegness.'

'That's one down although there's a few more to go. Forensics have found eight sets of fingerprints in the garage so far, another few in the adjoining house. The follow-up work will keep us going for months. Anything more from the coastguards about Callum Jamieson's contact at sea?'

'Not yet, John. There are dozens of places he could have arranged to make the drop. It would help if we knew where to look or the name of the boat. It's hopeless.'

John's sigh was heavy – heartfelt. 'How the hell did everyone miss this, Sarah?'

It was a phrase she feared they'd be repeating for months if not years to come. 'Do you want the truth?'

‘Always…’

‘Between you and me, it was pure bloody luck we discovered the trafficking ring at all. If they hadn’t taken the wrong teenager on Monday, none of this would have happened. The snatches were well planned and too spread out to be immediately obvious. They only took teenagers who were the most likely to abscond but on Monday, they made a simple mistake and it all started to unravel.’

‘It’s beyond belief you broke this up in under a week.’

‘Don’t – I go cold thinking about the *what if’s*. I’m dreading the fallout from all this. The press is going to have a field day.’

‘Aye well, you hang on to the fact that you and your team tore this racket to shreds. Tell the lot of them they can go to hell.’

Chapter Thirty-Four

SHOWERING AND CHANGING CLOTHES at Lincoln police station helped, even if it was into uniform trousers and a jumper. There was still so much to do. They'd never find the vital link to the transport ship and buyers if they lost the momentum now.

The hospital was a maze of corridors and it took a while to navigate her way to the private wing. The two armed officers at the entrance were a sure sign she'd found the right place. Greg Roberts came out to greet her. He'd been flown in as soon as news of the teenagers' release reached him. He looked haggard, Sarah thought, cheeks drawn, a world of pain flashing behind his serious expression.

'Kayla is doing great,' he assured her before Sarah could ask. 'The others are in adjoining rooms to hers. It's not a good idea to separate them yet, the girls are especially close. Did you know Matt Cox flew in with me?'

Sarah nodded; it had been her idea. 'Is he coping okay?'

'He's good to have around and Megan was relieved to see him, as was Lee.'

'Are they saying much yet?'

'In fits and starts. There's more euphoria than anything but I don't think we'll have a particularly good night. Lee's the least affected but he was only there a few days so it's not surprising.' He lowered his voice, checking over his shoulder before he carried on. 'There is one thing I should mention, Sarah, although maybe you already know? Paula Hancock was suffocated early on Wednesday morning. Simon and the two girls heard Callum issuing the orders, had to listen while it happened. The man was worried a customer would hear the girl coughing, apparently.'

'This isn't going to be easy for you, Greg.'

‘I’m okay – or I will be. This is the worst time, just listening, assimilating the information. Sorry, I’m teaching my grandmother to suck eggs aren’t I.’

‘Hey, do you mind? I’m not that old.’ That at least raised a flicker of a smile. ‘Was there anything else I need to know immediately?’

‘Aryan is worried about Jackie Simmons. She appears to have gone missing from A&E. Can I suggest you interview Megan Shaw fairly soon? I think she may have overheard a great deal of information over the past four days.’

‘The hospital is giving us a suite of rooms. Lincoln has already set up the equipment so I’ll do a preliminary interview shortly. Do you want in on this?’

Sarah watched his hesitation. ‘Better not. I’ll listen to the tapes when I can. I’d rather stay focused on the younger ones if that’s okay.’

‘You always did make good choices, Greg. Anything you need, ask.’

‘Understood, – and you did a great job…’

‘*We* did an amazing job. I’m only ever as good as the team I’m with. And, Greg, make sure you find time to eat. That’s an order!’

Walking away, Sarah heard a wry chuckle and sighed. Police work and icebergs had a great deal in common. The public rarely saw more than the tip, the clamour for results, the short bursts of publicity when the puzzle was finally unravelled. Frequently overlooked were the hours, days or months of painstaking listening to horrendous facts from the mouths of the victims. Her team had taken the brunt of a nightmarish week and it was far from over.

Opening the door of the small waiting room near the ICU, Sarah’s hunch proved correct. A miserable looking Jackie sat on a grey plastic chair, arms hanging down between her legs. ‘I thought I might find you here. Are you okay?’

‘Ben is still in theatre. Did they say anything to you?’

‘He’s been in there less than an hour, Jackie. Ben’s a strong young man, he’s going to come through this.’

‘I keep hearing her screaming in my head…’ Jackie’s words were rushed, her eyes full of anguish. ‘I kept trying, but I couldn’t cut the fourth rope in time. The blade was blunt and the boat dragged it out of my hands… I tried so hard to hang on to it. Kayla kept screaming and screaming...’

Gently, Sarah turned Jackie’s hands over. Where the skin had been torn away, the palms were scarlet with swelling blisters oozing from what was left. They were a mess. From her pocket, Sarah pulled out her mobile. ‘Why don’t you tell me what happened. Take as long as you need. Then we’ll go and fix up those hands of yours. Sarah pressed record, quoted date, time and location. ‘When you’re ready Detective Constable Simmons.’

By the end of the short interview, Jackie’s anguished expression had given way to one of exhaustion. ‘The worst of it was, I felt so useless. If…’ she gulped back the tears as she fought for the words. ‘If the others hadn’t arrived when they did…’

‘By your own account, you cut three of the four ropes. Your efforts gave the other officers time to focus on the last cylinder. You were under fire from the traffickers whilst attempting to release those youngsters and all in driving rain…’

‘I know-but…’

‘No buts. If you want to take anything away from this Jackie, next time you’re on an op make sure you carry a knife with you. Having your own as a spare would have helped.’

Sarah caught the flicker of doubt and reached for her own belt. ‘I carry mine right here. Saves me having to explain when I go through security checks in buildings.’ With the ease of practice, Sarah flicked up the belt buckle and pulled out a long flat blade. Another flick had the knife folding into the soft leather handle. ‘Perfectly legal, just don’t like to have it on display.’

‘Wow, that’s so neat – may I?’

Sarah smiled as she held out the small knife. Little distractions, she thought.

Chapter Thirty-Five

THE CALL FROM THE THEATRE came as Megan Shaw arrived at the make-shift interview room.

Sarah stepped out into the creamy light of the corridor. 'DCI Allerton speaking…' The silence that followed was worrying. Steeling herself for the worst, Sarah clenched her jaw – and waited.

'Chief Inspector, sorry – I'm the senior registrar. I need to inform you that Sergeant Ben Peterson is now in recovery… hello, are you still there?'

Pushing a shaking hand through her still damp hair, Sarah managed to reply. 'Thank you, did everything go well?'

'I'm pleased to say your sergeant's spleen was only nicked and the damage repairable. There is no reason he shouldn't make an excellent recovery.'

Finishing the call, Sarah pressed her back against the cold wall and breathed out an emotional sigh of relief. Pressing the number for Finchley, Sarah heard the click of the exchange telling her the call had been transferred.

'DCI Allerton, I'm with the Chief Constable. I'm putting you on speaker.'

'Ma'am, Sir…' as she relayed the news of Ben, there was no doubting the relief in their voices.

'Great news and congratulations on a job well done, Sarah. I understand you have the majority of the key traffickers in custody?'

'Yes, Ma'am. We intend to carry out the formal interviews in Hepsford once we've established the full stories of the victims. I'm about to interview Megan Shaw, the young social work student who was taken. The youngsters will be interviewed over the next few days by Greg Roberts and his specialist team.'

'Are there any issues with the press at your end, Sarah?'

'Not currently, Ma'am…'

'Keep your CS advised and pass on my thanks to your team and Lincoln's, Sarah. And once again, very well done.'

The call ended and Sarah took a moment to gather her thoughts before sending a text to Hepsford HQ about Ben. Hell, she needed a sugar fix but a mint would have to do.

Inside the examination room Megan was seated at a small table, slim fingers of one hand rubbing restlessly on its edge. The swelling on her face had reduced a little but her left eye remained half-closed. Beside her was Matt Cox and, from the angle of their arms, Sarah guessed they were holding hands.

'I'm sorry to keep you waiting, Megan – Matt. That was news about my Sergeant, good news I'm pleased to say. He's in recovery, doing fine.'

'I'm so sorry about everything. If I'd said something when I saw her on Monday, only I couldn't believe it…' With the damage to Megan's face, trying to read the young woman's expression wasn't easy.

Gently, John Wetherton stopped her. 'Megan, let me start the tape and then we'll take this from the beginning. Mr Cox, I'll ask you to give your name but if I could ask you not to participate unless it's particularly relevant.'

The first part of Megan's story was decades old, as Sarah had guessed it would be. Megan's grandmother had discovered she was married to a brute of a man. Falling in love with his older kinder half-brother Lewis, grandma had ended up pregnant with his child. It wasn't until years later that Alastair, her husband, discovered the truth.

'Grandma didn't have a choice, she had to run,' Megan explained. 'It was Alastair who ordered his oldest son Anthony to kill me, my mother and his brother, Lewis. Callum was crowing about it when he told me – except my mum managed to stab Anthony with a kitchen knife before he shot her. Gran walked into the flat – found them both dead and fled with me.'

'From what we've discovered, Alastair Jamieson has a long reach. How on earth did your grandmother manage to keep you hidden for all these years?' Sarah asked.

For the first time in the interview, Megan's swollen lips twisted into a smile. 'Gran didn't leave Scotland empty-handed. She helped herself to a few of Alastair's precious Picasso sketches from the safe. He was livid but couldn't report the theft because he'd bought them all with dirty money from illegal deals and the fraud squad were sniffing around. I know this now because Gran told me everything in the months before she died. She was amazing…'

'So, she sold the sketches to pay for housing, food?' John asked.

'Each time she did, we had to change our names and move, out of the country usually. I've lived in so many different places.'

'Which explains why you don't have any addresses we could trace before Hull.' Sarah drummed her fingers. 'Wouldn't it have been better for your grandmother to have returned Alastair's property?'

'That's exactly what I told her Chief Inspector, but she was adamant it wouldn't have made any difference. It wasn't only the stolen Picassos he was angry about – it was the fact that grandma had fallen in love with the half-brother he hated.'

'So, your grandmother tells you the story and then she dies? What happened next, Megan.'

'I didn't take her warnings seriously, Chief Inspector. Gran had asked me to scatter her ashes where Lewis was buried in Liverpool. Once that was done, she wanted me to change my name and move. Only, I couldn't face being alone again, starting over.' Megan dropped her head into her hands.

Matt leaned across to put a comforting arm on her shoulder. 'You're doing great. I know this is hard.'

Megan drew in a shuddering breath. 'I went to Liverpool but the cemetery is huge. It was a nightmare trying to find the right plot so I went to the office and used their digital list. You tap in the name you want and the plot number is highlighted. That was a big mistake. The software must have been rigged to alert Callum when someone searched for my grandfather. There were cameras dotted all over the place – it wouldn't have taken Callum long to discover what I looked like. All those years of hiding – wasted…'

Sarah spoke quietly. 'You were grief-stricken, miles from home – why would you suspect something so devious?'

'Gran never trusted anyone – but I wanted things to be different, you know? She always said I was naïve and she was bloody well right! In Hull, when Shauna – I mean Emily – accused me of stealing, I didn't have a clue she was connected to the Jamieson's. I put it down to a mistake.'

'But you know differently now?'

The haunted look was back. Megan's eyes were black mirrors 'On Monday, when I heard her voice in the office, I convinced myself I was wrong. There had to be loads of people who would sound the same. Then the jewellery and Lee went missing and suddenly, I was back in the same old nightmare. When I tried to find her, she'd already left. All day I kept thinking I should tell someone – but tell them what? That I'd overheard a woman who sounded like someone I'd once known in Hull?'

'So it was Emily who told Callum where you were?'

'No, that was my fault, Chief Inspector…' Matt cleared his throat, sat a little straighter. 'On Sunday, the lodger Warren or Laurence – whatever he's called – was in the kitchen. I was looking at a picture of Megan I'd taken in the garden at Lakeside, one of those silly selfies. I'd no idea who *he* was, what it would mean. I am so sorry.'

Megan shivered, wrapping her arms tightly around her thin body. 'Not your fault, Matt. Had I been honest with you, told you about recognising her voice…'

Sarah cut in. 'Megan, how did they snatch you?'

'I was driving home on the Chantry Road after shopping and this woman flagged me down, told me she'd run out of petrol, asked if I could give her a lift to the nearest petrol station. I'd opened my window to talk and she jabbed me with a needle. Next thing, I'm in this crappy room chained to a wall. It must have been a couple of days later when *he* came. Sorry, I need a drink Chief Inspector – this is hard.'

Sarah spoke briefly into her mobile to ask an officer to bring through refreshments. 'Megan, you said, *he* came. Who was that?'

'Callum!' she spat the name as if it was poison. 'Everything Grandma told me about that family is true and worse. He – he beat me, made me do things – I can't, I'm sorry.'

There was no easy way of asking. 'Did he rape you, Megan?'

Tear-filled eyes stared back at her. 'No – but he might as well have. He was disgusting. He kept going on and on about the Picassos, telling me if I didn't hand over the rest, he'd give me as a present to Georges. Last night, Callum came back with his son, Laurence.' She touched her lip wincing at the memory. 'Two of them held me down while Callum beat the soles of my feet. I kept telling him that Gran had sold the sketches but he wouldn't listen.'

They took a ten-minute break to give Megan time to recover a little. Sipping drinks, they talked of nothing in particular until Sarah asked. 'Megan, shall we finish this?'

'I suppose…'

'You mentioned that Callum's son Laurence arrived on Friday. Do you recall any of the conversations between them?'

Shifting a little closer to Matt, Megan thought for a few moments. 'I know Callum was angry. Laurence had left a computer behind and Callum wanted it to make contact with this Georges. Laurence didn't want to drive back to Hepsford, didn't see the point when he had most of the info on his phone.'

John asked. 'Did they mention this Georges again? Give you any idea who he might be?'

Megan shook her head. 'No, that happened before they started in on me. I don't remember much after that, just pain.'

'Which brings us to today,' Sarah said. 'This morning seems like a lifetime away, doesn't it?'

Megan's eyes drifted off into the middle distance, her voice dropping to a monotone. 'Two men drove me to the place where your sergeant found me. They called it the graveyard – I could hear them laughing about it. They kept on and on about what they wanted to do to me…' Megan gulped down her water, fighting back the fear Sarah could see so clearly in her eyes. 'When they first opened the door of that stinking hole and threw me in, I thought, this is it, I'm going to die right here. Then out of the darkness, there was Emily – only she was laughing Chief Inspector. I've never heard anything so weird? When she saw it was me she began to swear, kept telling me to piss off – or I'd messed things up! She really thought one of the men had tricked her in there, part of some sort of sex game.' Megan's tone deepened, her hand rubbing at the collar of her jumper as she spoke. 'All of a sudden the doors opened and Callum was there – Emily didn't stand a chance. He grabbed her by the neck, kept calling her a liar – a cheat… he's choking her and she's gasping, trying to pull his hands away. He pulls out a knife and… I've never seen so much blood!'

'Who cut Emily Cotton's throat, Megan?'

Megan trembled as she forced the words out. 'Callum Jamieson – the bastard slashed at her and threw her away as if she was nothing. He'd been paying her extra money to find me. She should have reported that she'd found me when we met in Hull but she liked the money too much...'

'Megan, I know this is hard, but did the Callum or one of the others say anything else at all, anything that might help?'

Leaning into Matt's shoulder, Megan drew in a slow, juddering breath. 'Just before your sergeant arrived, I heard Callum outside shouting at his men. I'm not sure, but something about useless Laurence contacting Georges to say the drop was ready… It didn't make much sense.'

As soon as they were alone, Sarah pointed to the name scrawled in large letters on her pad. 'Georges – the captain's name do we think John?'

'Or the name of the ship? I'll contact the coastguard but you might want to try your DC Khan. – he might be faster if he's as good as you say.'

Sarah grimaced. 'Oh, he is.' She checked the time again, 20.12. 'Even with a following wind, we're late.'

'Never say never, Sarah. We do this, then we eat.'

Aryan Khan's yawning response to her call had her guessing he'd been asleep – and who could blame him. 'I'll start now, Chief Inspector. I think it might be wise to start with the ships registered to the Jamieson's first. I'll be in touch as soon as I have something.'

Sarah glanced down at her silent mobile and sighed. Freya's messaged response was there, warm and encouraging as usual – nothing from Amos, which was strange given the circumstances. Pressing his personal number, she waited, trying to push away the nagging worry.

'Sarah, are you okay?' Amos sounded fraught – impatient even.

'I'm fine. Just checking in. It's latish which is why I rang.'

'I hear you caught the whole damned lot of the bastards – great job.'

'We're still trying to pin down the ship, foreign contacts. We're not home and dry yet.'

'Five youngsters saved from who knows what – don't downplay this, Sarah.'

‘And your end?’ She heard the hesitation, could imagine his shifty expression as he tried to think up something to explain the silence.

‘Nothing much, just more of the usual.’

‘Bollocks, Amos, what the hell is going on?’

‘Nothing you can do anything about – so don’t ask. I swear if you needed to know I’d be telling you, trust me.’

Reluctantly, she let it go. ‘You’d better have a bloody good reason for being so closed-mouthed, Amos Brantley.’

‘The best – now, I need to do some actual work. I’ll ring tomorrow. Try and sleep, Sarah.’

Chapter Thirty-Six

Sunday

BEN PETERSON WAS PROPPED UP IN BED when Sarah looked in on him the following morning.

'Morning Ma'am, would you mind doing the ticking off now, it might be easier?' His drug-induced euphoria shone out.

Sarah covered the swell of relieved emotion with a laugh. 'Oh, I wouldn't want to spoil it for you, Ben. How are you feeling?'

'Like I could run a marathon – or walk to the bathroom at least.'

'Excellent, so you should be able to enjoy that holiday after all.'

'I'm coming back to work first,' he said adamantly. 'Can't let you sort it all out on your own.' He yawned, his jaw cracking with the effort. 'Sorry, can't seem to stay awake.'

'Rest and take care, Ben. You did amazing work.'

'Did I tell you that I thought the coastguard was Poseidon? He's got a great right hook.'

Sarah left him to his dreams, reminding herself to have a word with the diver who'd saved Ben's life.

John was waiting outside the main hospital doors, his back against a stone pillar. When Sarah called his name he turned with a smile. 'I'm enjoying the brief respite,' he admitted. 'I've had word that the press is all over the story, so be warned.'

'I'm surprised it took them so long. Did you see the response from the coastguards, John?'

The message the previous evening had been a welcome relief. 'V*essel St Georges boarded at 22.52 hrs in UK waters.*

The vessel is now in the harbour under supervision. The crew is in custody and awaiting further questioning. Retrieved the mobile phone you identified – full forensic search commenced as per your instructions.'

'I did and I've received a request for help with the interviews if you're interested. They've been moved to a satellite station so we should be out of the limelight for a while.'

'Then lead the way. Anything to stay two steps ahead of the press for a few hours.'

Moving through the roads of Lincolnshire was easy early on a Sunday morning. The storm of the previous day had disappeared as if it had never existed; soggy fields were now crisp and white under a dense layer of frost. Happy to be driven, Sarah relaxed into her seat enjoying the peaceful, pristine landscape. It was hard to push her brain back into work mode when all around her was silent and sleepy.

'There's nothing of note to report from overnight,' John began. 'Callum and the other suspects from the beach have been transferred to Hepsford. Callum was doing his best Scottish laird impression when he left – which didn't go down so well.'

'I can imagine.'

'What news on the youngsters?'

'All as good as you could expect, John. Kayla has a bit of a cough but the doctor said she should make a full recovery. They'll keep her in for a few days, just to make sure. Megan and Matt Cox are staying put for a day or so. Megan needs surgery on one of her feet.'

'That callous bastard…' John's words rippled with emotion.

'We make sure every detail of that scene on the beach is in the report, John. I want the jury to hear exactly what those youngsters had to endure.'

‘My officers were wearing video cams Sarah, so no problem there.’

Sarah caught his grim smile and answered with one of her own. ‘For once I’m grateful for the tech.’

A lone reporter’s camera flashed briefly as the car swept past to drive through the guarded entrance. It wouldn’t be long before the media circus descended. Inside, a flurry of uniformed officers stood quickly to attention, nodding in recognition. Sarah caught a few low mutterings and a ‘Nice job, Ma’am, Sir…’ before they were ushered into the interview suite and away from the general clamour.

‘I don’t know about your lot, Sarah, but officers here are reeling from the import of what you’ve uncovered. They’re finding it difficult to assimilate.’

‘I’m not surprised; it took Hepsford a while to absorb the implications.’ Sarah took the mug a junior officer handed her, enjoying the aroma of freshly made coffee.

At first the interviews were like wading through treacle as crew members shrugged shoulders, protesting their innocence or feigned lack of English. Things finally picked up a quarter of an hour into the interview with the captain, Senor Miguel Perez. A constable slipped a file onto the table and bent to whisper in Sarah’s ear. ‘Initial forensic report from the boat, Ma’am. Makes interesting reading.’

It took Sarah less than a minute to scan the basic information and another to push it across to John and wait while he assimilated the news. Across from them, Miguel Perez slouched nonchalantly in his chair, apparently unconcerned. Next to Perez, his counsel impatiently twiddled a silver pen, frequently glancing between the two officers.

‘We have been in this box of a room for long enough, officers. Unless you intend to charge my client then I must insist that Senor Perez be released immediately.’

Smoothly, John passed back the file. Turning to Perez, his words were clipped – icy. 'I believe Detective Chief Inspector Allerton should have the honour of laying out the charges.'

Resting her hands on top of the file, Sarah met Perez's disdainful gaze with a steely one of her own. 'Following an intensive search of the vessel registered as St Georges, fingerprints belonging to three missing minors were discovered in a small hidden compartment below deck. The names of those missing children are – Tanya Daley, Ainsley Babcock and a Lyla Web.' From the file Sarah slid out the images – Perez's cheeks grew ashen. 'Traces of blood, hair and partial prints were also found in other parts of the vessel and have been sent away for further analysis.'

'You planted this. It is a fix, none of it is true…'

'And now you can speak English, Senor Perez?' Sarah shuffled the pages into order. 'Furthermore, once St Georges was taken into dry dock, investigators discovered below the waterline, two hidden compartments and retrieved a total of sixty kilos of cocaine which I'm informed has a street value of over a million and a half pounds sterling. Senor Perez, do you have anything to say before you are formally charged with the trafficking and exploitation of minors and the illegal transportation and importing of a banned class A substance?'

Fear drained the last of the colour from the Spaniard's cheeks as reality hit. 'No! I will not sit here and take the blame for this. Talk to the man who owns St Georges – the one who holds a gun to the heads of my children. Talk to Jamieson!'

***

Walking out into the late morning sunshine, Sarah lifted her head to the light, grateful to breathe in fresh clean air untainted by lies and the atrocities she'd had to listen to for the past two hours. Despite his counsel's pleadings to wait and make a deal, Perez had crumbled – his confession had become a torrent of words, impossible to stop. He'd named Callum and Laurence

Jamieson plus Alastair. The trafficking ring had been going on for years – ten at least – mostly in India but more recently in the UK. The scale of the crime was overwhelming, impossible to believe that no one in authority knew it was happening. As the rest of the crew discovered their captain was spilling his guts, they'd become desperate to talk, adding more and more sickening facts to an already horrific story.

Behind her, the door clicked open. John Wetherton, appearing as shell-shocked as she felt, stepped out to stand beside her. 'I feel physically sick, Sarah. I had to get out before I killed one of the bastards. How the hell could this have been going on for so bloody long?'

She didn't try to answer but instead leant into his side, grateful for the strength of the man. 'Somehow, we need to hold it together for the press. How's your fight face doing?' She heard the grim laugh and relaxed a little.

'Our Chief Constable is heading up the press call Sarah, and for once I'm pleased. He'll fend off the worst of it, keep it short. At least I only have to do it once. You'll have a repeat scenario back in Hepsford I'd imagine?'

'Thanks for that reminder John, although my lot have been unusually quiet.'

John's alert beeped, warning them of the impending press conference. With a last glance at the lowering sun, Sarah followed her colleague inside to the waiting cameras and the inevitable stream of unanswerable questions.

Chapter Thirty-Seven

HEPSFORD CITY STREETS were strangely tranquil as the car Sarah occupied drove up to the familiar building. She hadn't been given a choice. The message from Finchley had been short and direct. *Be here by 15.00 hrs.* Every window in the station was ablaze with light but outside, nothing stirred. The driver stopped close to the rear exit and opened her door before Sarah had a chance to rearrange her thoughts. She'd half expected Amos to be waiting for her but it was the driver who solemnly escorted her inside.

'The Chief Constable and CS Finchley are in the main conference room,' the driver informed her.

'I take it there's a room full of press waiting for me?'

'I'm afraid so, Chief Inspector.' The few colleagues they passed in the corridors all astutely avoided her gaze, barely saying '*hello*'. What the hell was going on?

Finchley was pacing outside the conference room, his dour expression lightening as she drew close. He held out a hand. 'Welcome home Sarah and a job very well done.'

'Thank you, Sir.'

'I've made a start and given the press a summary of events. You are to let the Chief Constable and I take the majority of the questions. This will take no longer than fifteen – twenty minutes at most.'

The flashing cameras were blinding as they walked onto the low podium – impossible to see individual faces under the lights. Sarah kept her eyes on Finchley's back, wishing she'd thought to run a brush through her hair. In her head, Freya's voice mocked her for being so vain – it helped a little.

The questions started immediately. 'Chief Inspector is it true the boy Lee Wiggins has been rescued…' At least that was one question she could answer openly – the rest was a general tussle of words, back and forth.

***

The last of the journalists had gone, leaving a litter of cartons and paper in their wake. Sarah turned to her senior officers. 'Thank you Ma'am, Sir, at least that was bearable. It's been a long day and if you don't mind, I'd like to drop my notes into my desk drawer and sign off.'

Finchley touched her arm, something he never did. 'Sarah, I have some urgent information that I need to pass on. My office would be best I think. I'll make it as swift as I can…'

It took some effort to maintain the calm exterior as she walked the cool corridor. *Soon, she'd be at home* she reminded herself – *hot bath, large red – Freya*. It was a surprise to see Amos sitting to the side of the CS's large desk. A brown folder in front of him, he looked grim.

Rising to his feet, Amos wrapped his long arms around her. 'Well done – an amazing achievement Sarah. You must be exhausted.'

'And some – Amos, what the hell is going on? No one is talking. Everyone I've seen since I got back appears to be afraid to look at me. This isn't about Freya…'

Finchley cut in. 'This is nothing personal, Sarah. Please sit and I'll outline the bare facts.' Whatever initial relief she'd felt disappeared as she took in the solemn expressions.

'Yesterday, late afternoon in the cellar of the *Blue Beacon,* Detective Inspector Mike Lawson was killed, shot by one of his accomplices. Lawson along with two customs and excise officers are believed to be the ringleaders of *Lamplight* – the illegal distilling of alcohol. They'd gone to the *Blue Beacon* to search for the mobile phone left behind by DC Moira Robins. Amos was already at the cellar when he was accosted by two of the men. Thankfully, Carl Moyles arrived in time and saved the day.'

Sarah could hardly breathe. 'Dear god, Amos! Are you and Carl okay? She scanned him up and down searching for signs of a wound.'

'A few scratches that's all. We're fine…'

'How is this possible? Please tell me Neil wasn't involved?'

Finchley sighed. 'Obviously there will be an in-depth investigation, Sarah, but Neil Harper is not under suspicion and is as shocked as the rest of us.'

'Is that why you've been so closed-mouthed this last week, Amos? Did you know Mike was caught up in *Lamplight*?'

'I knew something was up as soon as I came back to work. Being away for three months, it was obvious to me at least that you were under massive pressure. An enormous caseload, plus all the added extras, then Lawson dumps a missing minor case on you? He wanted you out of the way as much as possible Sarah, worried you were getting too close to the *Blue Beacon* and his dirty secret. Did you know the station received an anonymous tip-off Tuesday evening at 20.52 hrs, saying Ingles was back in town?'

'No bloody way?'

'Mike Lawson gave Ingles the nod, told him you were about to close in and to move his gear, pronto. Mike and his buddies were hoping that you'd be so busy nicking Ingles it would give them time to move the *still* and the booze. Ingles admitted on tape he'd received a call, though he couldn't say who it was from. You weren't notified about the tip-off Sarah because Lawson got the timing wrong. Ingles had already been spotted. You and Ben were on the Quigley estate and Ingles was being picked up. Lawson didn't have a clue Ingles and Carson were best buddies by the way… funny that.'

'Oh hilarious, Amos!'

‘Then, discovering our Moira snapping away, it must have given the three of them a near heart attack, especially Lawson. I have no doubt they would have killed her, Sarah.’

Sarah slumped back against the hard chair, numb. ‘What a fiasco. Every damned day for the last six years, Mike Lawson has made my life a bloody misery. He might be dead, but it’s hard to find any compassion. God – this job.’

Finchley sounded bleak. ‘He sold us all out, Sarah. It’s his wife and family I feel for.’

Stretching over Amos gripped Sarah’s hand. ‘All we can do is hang on to the positives. You and the teams did an amazing job. Five teenagers will live to grow old – countless others will never know what they’ve been saved from – and I get to live to annoy Jen, you and the Chief Super for another few days, thanks to Carl.’

Finchley cleared his throat. ‘Quite – and I’m always thankful for those small mercies Amos, however, if you two don’t mind – some of us have reports to write?’

Chapter Thirty-Eight

December 18th

THE FOUR WEEKS FOLLOWING the discovery of the trafficking ring and Mike's death had been difficult – to say the least. By the Monday, news of the bizarre rescue of four teenagers from the beach had exploded across the front pages of national and international newspapers. Every media, radio and television channel carried a version of the story. There was one particularly harrowing aerial image that had captured the public's imagination – of the four metal cylinders, lids discarded, the soft belly of packing ripped out to trail across the pebbles. '*Rescued from the guts of hell,*' had been one of many disturbing headlines. The reports made it seem as if the investigation was over – bar the shouting – but the case was far from complete. The search for the final few bogus care workers was painstakingly slow and, as for the network of buyers/sellers worldwide, the task of finding the perpetrators was immense.

At least with the media frenzy associated with the child trafficking, Mike Lawson's criminal activities and subsequent death barely made it to the second page. At the police station, the *Blue Beacon* case had left an unpleasant taste in everyone's mouth. No one had particularly liked Mike but knowing the man they'd worked alongside for almost a decade had been corrupt was a bitter pill to swallow. It didn't help that everyone was hauled in for an interview with the IPC, never a pleasant experience. For Sarah, the seven hours she was grilled for details were a nightmare and she'd walked away from the encounter feeling as if she had been responsible for the whole damned mess.

Christmas was fast approaching but around her the incident room was as busy as ever. Ben was recuperating well but it would weeks before he was back at work.

Sarah signed off yet another file and with a sigh picked up the next from the pile. Methodically, the hours of patient slog were paying off. Most of the alleged traffickers had pleaded guilty, the older Jamieson men were the two exceptions. The initial paperwork for Callum Jamieson's pre-trial hearing was finally ready and his case was to be heard later that afternoon. The trial date wouldn't be for months but the initial hearing represented the beginning of the end.

Sarah glanced up at Jackie Simmons' urgent call. 'Chief Inspector – sorry to interrupt but you'll want to see this, It's the old man, Alastair, he's dead!'

It took a long moment for the information to register. Jackie handed down the briefing sheet. 'This came through from Edinburgh. He died in the prison hospital from a massive heart attack less than an hour ago.'

'Do we know if Callum's been informed, Jackie?'

'I'll check with his brief, Ma'am. Do you think it will change Callum's mind about how he pleads?'

'We can hope but I doubt it. He'll want his day in court I'd think.'

Three hours later and Sarah was hurrying in from the cold into the cathedral-like entrance hall of the Crown Court to begin the winding climb to the first floor. She'd been expecting a phone call announcing a deferral due to the death of Callum's father – no such luck.

'Detective Inspector Allerton – a moment of your time?' On the first landing, the bewigged figure of Callum Jamieson's counsel, Stuart Hartnell, waved a hand in her direction. 'My apologies for doing this here, Chief Inspector but you'd already left the office. My client, Callum Jamieson, has decided to change his plea to guilty.'

'And he isn't playing games, Mr Hartnell?'

'Not this time. His father's death earlier today followed the discovery of a substantial amount of evidence, which, unambiguously linked Callum and Alastair to the child trafficking trade in India. There have been powerful rumblings from the Indian government to have the men extradited. Far better to serve his time here I should think…'

'I'm not sure the young people he condemned to a life of hell would agree, Mr Hartnell?'

'Quite, Chief Inspector. I'll see you inside.'

The black cape swirled away leaving Sarah alone with her thoughts. A part of her had wanted to watch Callum react as the evidence had been presented – hoped he'd finally show something resembling remorse. Pulling out her mobile she dialled the number for Lakeside children's home. Rahul De-Silva at least would be pleased. He, along with the rest of the staff, had been dreading the trial. 'Rahul it's Sarah Allerton – I've some good news to pass on...'

Two hours later, Sarah walked out of the Crown Court building to catch a blast of a bitter, easterly wind – one that had done little to deter the throng of reporters and onlookers. Two security guards stayed close as she walked down a few steps to the hastily erected microphone. Hepsford Crown Court hadn't ever experienced such a level of attention and this was only a Pre Trial hearing.

'When you're ready Chief Inspector, the mic's up and running.'

Nodding her thanks to the court assistant, Sarah cleared her throat. Standing in front of a judge was a cinch compared to this.

Questions were yelled at her from all directions. *'Chief Inspector, will there be a trial – did he plead guilty – is it true the trafficking has been going on for over ten years?'*

'I can formally announce that a plea of guilty has been entered and a date will be set for sentencing. Once sentencing is complete, a formal press conference will be held when further information will be available.'

'And what about the bent copper – have you discovered any more rotten eggs, Chief Inspector?'

It was impossible to identify the speaker but Sarah cut in sharply. 'I cannot comment on an ongoing investigation. What I do have is positive news on the search and recovery of some of the trafficked teenagers. During the last week, a further six young people have been recovered from several international sites. Our own Inspector Greg Roberts, lead officer of the search team, will release a statement within the next twenty-four hours. Thank you for your time ladies and gentlemen…' There were surprisingly few derisive shouts as Sarah walked back into the building.

'Nicely done, Sarah. I knew you'd handle it better than I could.' Amos held out a bottle of water and smiled as she gulped it down.

Her stomach was still a queasy mess. 'I'd rather run up a mountain any day than stand in front of the press.'

'Carl's just rung – he's tracked down a little more of Lawson's ill-gotten gains. There's a pleasant villa in Portugal. Mike's wife told Carl that he'd won a packet on the horses, which is why they could afford the place. I'm still bloody positive she knew what was going on, Sarah.'

'She'll lose everything, Amos – pension, property…'

Amos looked doubtful. 'Depends – Lawson put the villa and a racehorse he'd bought in her name. Unless we can prove she was complicit, she'll keep them. Let's hope the press doesn't get wind of *that* little gem. And there's still no sign of the third man – Wilson. He's done a good job of disappearing. Just to give you the heads up, Greg arrived in the office before I left. His team picked up another couple of youngsters on top of the six but God Sarah, the man's looking grim.'

'I'm not surprised. With those two that makes fourteen they've rescued in total and that's only because they were taken recently. I have no idea how he's going to start tracing the other hundred or so.'

'Stay with the positives Sarah, as hard as that is.'

'And is that what you told Greg?'

Amos thrust hands deep into his pockets, his chuckle warm and melodious. 'I thought for a moment that Greg was going to floor me – then we had the chat about priorities – not being much use with a brain mushed up by lack of sleep etc. etc. You know, our usual spiel.'

'You're an old softie Amos. And did it work?'

'He's promised to book some leave, so who knows – talking of which?' Amos raised his wrist to tap his watch. 17.30 hrs, aren't you officially off duty Chief Inspector Allerton?'

Just the thought pushed the last dregs of tensions away. 'Be nice to Martha while I'm away Amos. I'm hoping she'll want the serious crime post permanently… and don't forget to push Finchley to fill the other vacancy. And before I forget…'

'Out, now!' Taking her by the shoulders, Amos spun Sarah around. 'Go, relax in the sunshine with your woman.'

Walking out of the rear exit into the car park, Sarah stood, drinking in the silence. At last, three whole weeks of sun, sea and Freya. Hepsford and the rest of the world could damn well take a hike.

The End

BOOK TWO OF THE SARAH ALLERTON CRIME SERIES

The Splintered Web – Out 2023

ACKNOWLEDGEMENTS

Writing for adults in a completely new genre was both terrifying and an exhilarating experience. Impossible without the help of my extraordinary editor, Paul Smith and a small army of patient and generous Beta Readers who gave up their time so freely.

This novel deals with an emotive subject, missing children. The book is dedicated to the amazing voluntary organisations, the officers, social workers, teachers, volunteers, foster carers who, day after day, work with young people to safeguard their future...

If you require further information you can contact The Children's Society via their website.

https://www.childrenssociety.org.uk/

Printed in Great Britain
by Amazon

16529521R00153